A MARQUESS TOO RAKISH TO WED

Liz Tyner

KT-164-719

MILLS & BOON

First published in Great Britain 2022
by Mills & Boon, an imprint of HarperCollins*Publishers* Ltd,
1 London Bridge Street, London, SE1 9GF

www.harpercollins.co.uk

HarperCollins*Publishers*
1st Floor, Watermarque Building,
Ringsend Road, Dublin 4, Ireland

A Marquess Too Rakish to Wed © 2022 Elizabeth Tyner

ISBN: 978-0-263-30181-6

07/22

MIX
Paper from
responsible sources
FSC™ C007454

Dedicated to Sue White

Chapter One

All the dimly lit chamber needed was a howling wind to pass through, fanning the fireplace and adding the scent of brimstone, but instead a rather pleasant aroma of shaving soap lingered in the air.

Guinevere and her father stepped nearer the physician who stood at the bedside, holding Reid's wrist. He lowered the arm to the covers.

'He has passed from this life.'

'The accident took him.' Her father spoke softly.

'Sadly, no. The apothecary put the wrong powders in the bottle when he sent the pain mixture.'

A stab of regret hit her. She put her closed knuckles over her lips. That moment, she wished she had danced just once with him.

Perhaps, if she'd known this was how she'd see him last, she might have been more forgiving.

'Has his mother been informed?' Guinevere's father asked.

'I was waiting until you and your wife arrived. Hours ago, I told the servants to expect the demise, and they have been preparing for it.' The physician spoke to her father. 'But now that you're here, Your Grace, I'll inform the Marchioness.' He shuffled from the room.

'The old Marquess was a decent man all his long life. Not…' Her father nodded towards the bed. 'Well, can't speak ill of the dead, no matter how much it's deserved. His father, my dearest friend, was so disappointed in him.'

Now that she stood so close to Reid, she could study his features, amazed at the strength which appeared in the simple planes and contours of his face.

In the past, she'd only seen him through a haze of dislike, but now she saw the true artistry.

Even in his final sleep, his jawline impressed her. Strong lips perfectly formed. Thick lashes complementing the hearty stubble. She'd never before been aware of so much masculinity in one person.

'He needs a shave,' she added, surprised.

'That stubble will get scorched off where he's going.'

She glanced at her father, the truth of her words taking her by surprise. 'Then he will likely be the handsomest man there.'

She turned back to Reid, wanting to lock his face in her memory.

Reid appeared so peaceful. Nothing like she would have expected. All his rakishness had faded, replaced with a bittersweet upturn of the lips she hadn't noticed before.

She'd not known a man could smile in death, but leave it to Reid to do such a thing.

'Soon after you were born—' Her father stood at her side. 'His father, may he rest in peace, thought you might make a bride for his son when the two of you reached an age to wed. But I knew—even then he was growing too strong-willed. Ignoring everyone who tried to correct him. I laughed off the Marquess's words. It was obvious to me how he'd turn out, and his father was my best friend. I couldn't be honest.'

Her father bowed his head. 'The Marquess was such an upstanding man that after his son matured, he never mentioned it again.'

He moved to the drapes and pulled them closed. 'I suppose this is for the best. Reid was too much like his…grandfather.' He said the last word as an oath, which surprised her. 'I didn't know if your brother's arm would heal after his tussle with Reid, but it did.'

'I was happy their friendship ended. Reid was always up to some prank.'

Without realising what she was doing, she reached out to brush her fingers across his jaw, but halted, then rested a hand on his shoulder, giving a squeeze, impressed with the suggestion of strength emanating from the immobile form.

But it no longer mattered.

Even with all his boisterous friends, he was alone now. Grief saddened her. Someone must tell him goodbye. She bent to kiss his cheek.

His lashes fluttered.

She shrieked and was two steps away before she stopped.

'I must have…jostled him,' she whispered, turning to her father.

'Oh, Guinevere, I shouldn't have brought you.' He strode to her. 'This is too much for your delicate spirit.'

She put her hand up to touch her father's arm, and collected herself. 'It's only the tiredness of travel, and the shadows. And my imagination.'

Her father took her elbow. 'Well, we've done our duty for tonight. Come along—'

'Wait,' she said, turning back. 'It's— I—'

She stepped over Reid again.

'He looks so alive, I imagined…' she whispered, shaking her head. 'It is so regretful that he…'

'Come along, Guinevere.'

'Wait. I know we weren't friends, but I—' She struggled for the proper thing to say. 'I wish we had been. That he would have been someone I might have liked.'

'He would *never* be friends with a decent person like you. The heathen isn't even worth a glance in death. His father was like a brother to me. Your mother and the Marchioness are closer than sisters. But Reid, the only son, was…disreputable. The world is a better place without him.'

'I know he wasn't perfect. In fact, I warned my friends from him. But he was a person, deserving of our sympathy.'

'Sympathy. A person. The cleric is going to have to embellish on those words at the funeral, but likely he'll ramble on a bit, and I'll look sad, and his cousin and I can get on about our day. Reid leaves behind exemplary cattle, though.'

Guinevere touched her chin, imagining the potential that had been inside Reid. 'Please let the cleric know about the horses so he will have something pleasant to say at the service.'

'That pretty well sums up his life.'

She stared at Reid. 'When we were children, he did help me across a stream once.'

'That was gallant of him.'

'He lifted me, his arm around my waist, and purposefully let my plaits drag the water. When he released me, I told him he would have made an excellent second son.'

'I'm surprised you said such a thing.'

'And then I told him I was giving him more praise than due. The third or fourth son would have been more suitable.'

She looked down again, but felt no guilt for the statement she'd made. She'd been irritated and he'd not appeared at all offended. Reid had laughed and said he would remember her words.

She looked at Reid. 'An appealing form, and exemplary livestock. I suppose that was the total of his years.'

'Gifts from his father.' The Duke moved to the door. 'He accomplished nothing on his own but revelry, and overbearing ways… Material things. Can't think of anything else.'

Guinevere felt pulled to Reid, hating to leave him for the last time. Hating to see him so alone. 'Well, I have to say something considerate before I leave. To wish him well.'

'Have a go at it,' her father said. 'Just don't lie.'

Guinevere brushed a hand across his knuckles. 'Goodbye, Reid, Marquess of Hartcroft. May you use all the skills you gained in this life to give the devil a difficult time.'

Then his chest heaved in a breath. And a second one.

Her brain tried to catch up to her vision, and her mouth couldn't remember how to speak.

'Eh?' her father said, brows furrowed. 'What's wrong, Guinevere?'

'Alive.' She pointed at him, fingers shaking. 'Alive.'

Her father squinted.

She stepped closer, scrutinising Reid. 'Can you hear me?' she whispered.

Her father stopped so near, his side brushed hers. He gazed down, shaking his head. 'Scoundrel to the very end.' Examining Reid, he grumbled before saying, 'Just a death twitch. Happens all the time. I've seen it before. Just one of the things we don't understand about the dying.' He shook his head. 'This will just be one more story about how he's a bother even in death. Lucifer is trying to return him.' He took her shoulders. 'Come along. We'll leave the servants to their duties.'

Her voice came out in a whisper. 'You must believe me.'

'You're overwrought. I am sincerely sorry to

have allowed you here. I should have left you to give solace to his mother. It was unthinkable to bring you into this room.'

'He might be alive.'

Her father paused, then peered at the visage again. 'Guinevere. Look at him. He's dead. The arrogant Marquess is dead. Long live the new Marquess.'

'If you're certain.' She put a hand to her temples. 'I suppose I need spectacles. And the light is so dim.'

'It's for the best that he's gone and his cousin will inherit the title. Reid was such a disgrace,' the Duke continued. 'I know his father would be upset to see this, but he was sad to see his son in life as well. The heir flew into a rage over something as simple as a spilled drink at breakfast.'

Her attention remained locked on the still form. She reached out, touching his cheek. He did feel a bit warm. Perhaps Lucifer *was* trying to expel him.

Then she called out, 'Reid. Reid. I spilled your chocolate.'

'That is not what he drank for breakfast, I assure you,' her father asserted.

She pulled her hand to her chest, fingers curled. 'I don't know what happened to me. You're right. He has passed on.'

She glanced at his face, peaceful in repose. Her imagination had flourished again.

Perhaps it would make her feel better if he had something sentimental of hers with him in the afterlife.

She clasped the brooch on her dress. The pearl jewellery her mother had given her. The one she'd sworn never to part with. She unpinned it from her garment and gave one lingering glance at it.

Her hand didn't seem to want to release it. No, she would not part with it.

Then she reached down and jabbed the pin against his shoulder.

His eyes opened, flashing a blue squint at her as he muttered an audible curse.

Her father's jaw dropped.

Fingers trembling, she tried to affix the pin to her dress, but it wouldn't attach. She dropped it into the reticule hanging from her wrist. 'Everyone's going to be so…' She looked into the eyes again. 'Er…happy, to have him with us.'

He groaned, and his eyes closed.

'Reid,' she called.

His eyes didn't open.

She slipped her hand to his jawline, against the stubble, and felt a slight heartbeat. She pressed her lips together, and clasped Reid's hand. 'You're going to be fine.'

His fingers squeezed hers.

He was alive.

She whispered to her father, 'Perhaps we should summon the staff to postpone the funeral. At least another day.'

They stood, staring down onto the now still form, two servants at the side of the bed.

'Someone should inform the Marchioness,' her father stated.

The staff members shared a glance. The butler, Winchell, instructed the footman. 'Get a maid. Tell her she must alert the Marchioness… that events are undecided.'

'And put the coffin away,' her father said. 'But not too far. And then get that physician and tell him the patient has survived for the moment.'

Guinevere took out a folded handkerchief from her reticule. She mopped Reid's brow.

When she finished, she held his hand again, but he didn't respond. No finger clasp. Nothing. No awareness.

'It would be just like him to pass on now that we've sent someone to reassure his mother,' her father said.

'Father,' Guinevere hushed him. 'He might be listening.'

Her father moved closer to the bed and spoke to Reid. 'Make up your mind. One way or the other. Don't keep the servants moving about, draping mirrors and uncovering them.'

'Father.' Guinevere gasped.

'I'm only speaking to him as his own father should have done.'

Then the door burst open, banging against the wall, the movement causing the fireplace to flare and all the lights in the room to flicker.

Lady Hartcroft dashed inside, saw the bed and became immobile. 'Reid's alive?'

'We're not sure,' her father said. 'But he did swear.'

Lady Hartcroft clasped her chest and stumbled. A servant caught her as she slipped to the floor.

Guinevere's mother moved to Lady Hartcroft's side and knelt. 'Marjorie. Marjorie. It's good news.' She fanned the Marchioness's face.

The Marchioness woke quickly and the servant helped her to her feet. 'Is it true?'

'I'm not sure,' the Duke said. 'But Guinevere spoke to Reid, and he responded.'

The Marchioness hurried to the bedside.

'Reid? Can you hear me?' She took his hand in both of hers. 'Reid?'

He didn't move.

'Reid?'

The room remained still.

'Is this a cruel jest?' She swallowed and stared at the Duke's family.

'No.' Guinevere made her way to the other side of the bed.

'Reid. Reid,' she called.

His eyes opened, and flicked in her direction before closing.

Again, the Marchioness slumped forward, and Guinevere's mother rushed to revive her friend.

'He's likely killed his mother, now,' her father said. 'Just like him to respond to a young woman's voice and ignore his family.'

Her mother helped the Marchioness stand and got a chair for her.

'Send for the physician,' her father instructed, and took his wife's elbow. 'We're not needed here.' He turned to address Reid's mother. 'Marjorie, if you need anything, send Guinevere to let us know.' Her parents then exited the room, her father muttering, 'We're too old for this.'

'What happened?' his mother asked Guinevere. 'What revived him?'

'I saw a twitch of his face,' Guinevere said.

'And then I… And perhaps I jostled him, and he spoke.'

His mother's eyes glistened. 'I'm so pleased you were here. He might never have— Without you…'

Guinevere glanced at the bed. 'I would do it again.'

Reid's lashes moved.

'I could now, if you'd like.' She leaned over him, waiting. 'I think I might.'

For one brief heartbeat, he gave her the same stare that he'd given when she told his friends what she thought of his new phaeton.

The Marchioness gasped. 'I saw that. He looked at you. Guinevere, his eyes opened.' His mother patted his hand. Nothing. 'Please. Please. Jostle him again.'

Guinevere pointed one finger and slowly moved it towards the same area she'd put the pin, and then she tapped him.

Blue flashed at her.

The Marchioness stood, hugged Guinevere and said, 'Oh, you must stay until he's completely recovered. I will insist you must remain.'

'I don't know what Father will think of it.'

'He will be thrilled,' the Marchioness said. 'After all, we all want Reid to be back to his old self.'

Guinevere made sure her lips turned up, but the Marchioness had already changed her attention to her son, smoothing the covers on the bed.

'If you do not mind, Guinevere, I will take the first turn of staying with him, and you can take the next.'

Guinevere stared at Reid. He'd not moved again, and she'd been sitting with him for hours. His mother had been fraught when she left, saying he'd not stirred.

After speaking to him several times, Guinevere had received no response.

She took his wrist. Tapped his shoulder where she'd poked with the pin. Nothing.

To touch his face again was too personal, but she gathered her courage. She moved aside the white clothing at his neck, but paused before placing her hand at his throat. A pulse throbbed beneath her touch.

'Not dead.' The words bounced into the room, their parched sound adding force, and echoing inside her.

She jumped away, clasping the fingers she'd held at his neck as if trying to hide them.

'I…' She'd planned to say she was just adjusting the nightshirt, but didn't think it would appease him.

His eyes were barely open, a scowl in them. Relief soared through her body.

'I'm pleased,' she said, struggling to get the words past the lump in her throat.

His eyes closed. He appeared completely immobile again.

'Are you sleeping?' she asked.

She waited. 'Can you hear me?' She touched his knuckles for a second.

'No. Yes.'

'Would you like me to be silent?'

'Yes.'

'I don't feel like I can right now,' she said, 'if I stay here.' Her dress rustled as she stood. She hesitated. 'I'll send someone else to sit with you.'

'No.'

She rested her hand over his. 'I've observed you to be demanding, though of course I could have been in error. I suspect not. But you can correct me if I'm wrong.'

She squeezed his hand, his knuckles firm under hers. No movement.

She waited for as long as she could handle his silence.

'I've also heard you're a rake, and not terribly concerned about women's reputations—no more than your own. And I feel I must believe it. If someone comes into the room, I am pulling my hand out of yours when I hear footsteps. I would not want my name ruined by you, and even in your state, I'm sure that tongues would wag about me. Even on your…um, sickbed.' She stumbled on, wishing for a response, but suddenly feeling alone in the room, and the world.

She gripped his hand, almost trying to pinch his fingers, surprised by how much larger his clasp was than her own. 'You *are* hurt, aren't you, not merely tired from a night of carousing?'

One side of his lips turned up a minute amount. A reaction. 'Carousing.'

She wasn't sure if he jested, or his senses had waned.

'Well, then I must be exceedingly careful. I'm sure my standing would be upended by proximity to the arrogant Marquess. That's the proper version of what you're called. I believe the word for a posterior is substituted, but that's just a supposition.'

Nothing. 'Or I made it up. Just now. Which is rude of me. Almost the same as a person who would lie abed when a guest is in his house.' She waited, scrutinising his face for the slightest movement.

'Reid?' She hesitated, but believed he listened, although she wasn't sure why she thought so.

'May I be honest?' she continued, rushing her

words. 'Oh, please, you may stop me at any moment. I would not want to offend your tender sensibilities, though I don't know how it would be possible for me to do that. It's said you can tell the most ribald jests and think them Shakespearean.'

She moved closer, watching, and whispered so close that her breath touched his cheek. 'Is that true? Surely not?'

Moving away, she shook her head in frustration.

'And no one told me what an adept listener you are. No one. You are simply the best listener I have ever seen.'

She waited. 'Yes, you are. Please don't interrupt. I thought I saw your eyelash move.'

'Shh…' He spoke.

Her heart pounded.

'Well, I will be silent then, and let you sleep, but don't be surprised if I wake you in a few hours while I leave for some rest myself and I'll have the footman bring you breakfast. You must eat. Because I insist, as reparation for my time.'

He didn't respond, but then his eyes opened for another second, before shutting again. He'd rather looked as if he'd like her to be ejected from the room.

'Sometimes I think you're listening and you don't answer out of spite. Could that be true?'

His lips tightened. 'No. Thinking.'

'You've kept me stirring the whole of the day, due to being awoken last evening with the first message telling us news of your accident but saying all was expected to be well. Then another rider in the morning saying you'd taken a bad turn and we should leave immediately because the Marchioness needed us.'

Readying to leave for Reid's country estate had taken some time as her father hadn't been home and they'd had to wait for him.

'And your vile language when you greeted me. Which is not the way I'm usually greeted, I assure you. I prefer something along the lines of… *How can so much intelligence be contained in one so beautiful?* Not that I'm conceited, mind you, or a fan of empty flattery, but I will accept it on occasion if it is delivered with sincere respect.'

'Quiet…is…good…'

Three words. Three words were even better than quiet.

'Well, I really will be silent now, and will try to sleep in this chair. No one told me I would have to attend to you when I arrived. That is asking a bit much as I had been in the carriage some time and the events afterwards have been most unsettling. I have not lolled in bed as you are doing.'

She moved to take her hand from his. She wanted to tell his mother he was speaking. But his grasp tensed and he would not let her hand go. His grip was firm.

'Very well, but you must remember, if someone walks into this room, propriety has to be observed. Always. With me,' she muttered, continuing, 'And if I were in charge of your life, I would suggest that you do the same with everyone, but that's asking a bit much.'

He sighed deep from within his chest.

'And you need a shave. Very badly. I didn't want to say anything earlier, but it was one of the things I noted about you. I will see that someone takes care of that first thing in the morning.'

'I will.'

She returned his tight clasp. If imagined birds could sing, she heard them, and invented flowers could bloom, they did in the room. Blue flowers, with startling petals and dark feathery lashes above them.

'A servant can do that for you.' Oh, she was certain that he understood her fully and dared her with that azure gaze. Then his eyes drifted shut.

'I will.'

Her heart thudded. Goodness, no wonder he was such a rake.

'Egg,' he said.

She stared at him but his lids closed again. She would have assumed him asleep if not for the clasp.

'Breakfast. Egg.' His hand moved within hers, and he made the signal to match his words. 'Two.'

'I will see that you have them.'

For the first time in her life, she knew what it felt like to be part of a couple. Intertwined in a sense, and yet, it was all in her imagination. Only it wasn't. She'd noticed his movement, and they'd shared his reawakening.

She'd never forget it.

He'd be recovered soon, and she and her family would be returning to London, and he would be going to his town house, but she might never again feel so close to anyone as the nearness she experienced at his bedside.

Yet this wasn't the true Reid she was with. She'd never hold *that* dissolute Marquess's hand.

'Do you know what happened?' she asked.

'Riding. Hermes. Stumbled.'

One eye opened before shutting again. 'Eggs. Hungry.'

'I think you will have a full recovery.'

'Not. Without. Food.'

Chapter Two

Guinevere and her parents sat in the main sitting room, her mother relaxing on the sofa, sketching peacefully as she never travelled without her drawing kit, and the Duke was pacing, or, as her mother claimed, going to great lengths and getting nowhere except on a worn path to his bootmaker.

Guinevere sat by the door, sipping chocolate, as she'd missed breakfast, and wasn't hungry. Several hours of sleep had revived her.

Reid's mother rushed in, her crumpled handkerchief waving, causing the frazzled curls at her forehead to flutter. 'The physician noted Reid will recover completely within a few days.' With her left hand, she touched the pearls surrounding her neck. 'Reid is so much better. After breakfast, he told the physician to leave and never return.'

'Your son is indeed fortunate,' the Duke said, stopping at his wife's chair.

'Yes. He will not talk about it, and I don't know if it is because he doesn't wish to, or doesn't remember,' his mother said. 'Or can't.'

'He can,' Guinevere reassured her. 'He told me he had a riding accident.'

'All things in time, Marjorie,' her mother said, putting aside her sketchpad. 'The important thing is that he is with us.' She reached out, patting her friend's hand.

'Yes. And I told him how Guinevere woke him.' The Marchioness sniffed, and buried her face in her handkerchief.

Boot-heels sounded in the hallway. A golden-haired man stepped in, a forced smile on his lips. Instantly she recognised his cousin. Stephen. The next in line for the peerage if Reid died without a son.

He strode to the Marchioness and gave a small bow. 'My condolences. I came as soon as I received your message. I hope I did not miss the… services.'

Guinevere heard the grief in his voice.

The Marchioness burst into tears anew.

'Reid is still alive,' her father said.

Stephen whirled to her father, and the Duke repeated his words. Guinevere watched Stephen, waiting for his happiness when he discovered Reid was still alive.

Reid's cousin looked at each face in turn. 'Truly?'

'Yes.' The Marchioness's voice trembled. 'We are all so happy.'

'No funeral?'

Guinevere studied Stephen. He appeared to have had the breath knocked from him.

'No,' her father said. 'Your cousin is still with us. And seems to be recovering nicely.'

The man's eyes narrowed, and his chin lowered. 'So…it was just one of his jests?'

The Duke answered. 'No. Not even he could have managed this one.'

'He did tell the physician to get out, so we expect a complete recovery,' the Marchioness said.

Stephen spoke softly. 'Reid is always planning something. It would be just like him to orchestrate this.' He glanced down, then his chin rose, and he scowled. 'Where is he? I'll make sure there's a funeral.'

The Marchioness wailed and grabbed her handkerchief.

'Now, son, he's not well yet,' her father said. 'Wait until he's himself and then you can settle this.'

The cousin charged from the room, and her

father hesitated before dashing after him. Guinevere followed.

She stepped behind the two men when they
stopped in Reid's sitting room, and gasped when
she saw Reid in an easy chair, dressed in black.

He pushed himself to his feet.

'Here to bury me?' Reid, glare glittering,
spoke to his cousin.

'I'd hoped to.'

'No inheritance today.'

The cousin made a fist, and her father caught
his arm, the forward momentum causing her
father to quickstep. 'You need to think this
through,' the Duke muttered. 'This isn't the time
to be rash.'

Stephen cursed. Reid had just escaped death,
and Stephen's disappointment was palatable.

The cousin jerked his arm free, and stalked
out of the door, the Duke behind him.

'I'm sorry your cousin was so rude. I'm sure
he cares for you deeply,' Guinevere said.

A man could express a lot with one upward
sweep of his eyes.

She didn't know if talking was difficult for
him, or if he was just irritated, but there was no
question his mind was functioning properly. 'He
thought you were playing a trick on everyone.'

'Only myself.'

'Are you feeling better?' she asked, tilting her head to the side.

'Mostly.'

'If I don't see you again before we leave, I wish you well.' She truly meant it.

'Stay.'

It wasn't so much a request as a command that a military officer would give. He only needed a uniform and a sabre, but she wasn't one of the troops. Yet he had just seen a ghastly display of familial unconcern.

He moved sideways. 'Too soon to leave.'

'You give the impression of a complete recovery, and I'm sure everything will be fine.'

His jaw tensed. He stood, backbone straight, jaw firm and contemplation direct.

She doubted he was used to being refused.

'You seem well. Not exactly the Reid I remember but it's been years since we've spoken. If you continue improving, then I would say you'll be revisiting your old habits within a few days. You will be laughing with friends and having one jest after another.'

That stung a bit, mentioning his pranks, but nothing on his countenance changed.

'Old habits.' Only his head moved, and he glanced to the window. 'Old habits.'

'It is of no consequence to me,' she said,

wanting to be certain he understood that. 'I'm sure you have many places to visit and friends to see.'

He surely had a lot of acquaintances to speak with about his mishap. She could imagine them all laughing together. She'd seen their rudeness, but she preferred not to think about it.

Something tugged at her, and she wasn't sure what.

His gaze left the window and commanded her attention.

'Lady—'

'Lady Guinevere.'

'I know.'

'I thought you might have forgotten.'

'No.'

She gave a slight dip of her head in goodbye, and her arm flexed to pull the door closed, but instead she paused.

'Don't leave,' he commanded, but she didn't think it was truly an order, but more of a request only he didn't know how to ask for things.

She held the cool wood of the jamb. She could see into his eyes, and perhaps his soul, and beyond.

'I can't think you'd want me to stay. We've never been friends.'

'Cousin Stephen is my friend.' A smile, lacking any humour. He seemed to be mocking himself.

She met the gaze, and all the pretence fell away. 'I really don't have anything to say to you.' Tiredness lay beneath her words. 'Not anything you'd find interesting. Or like to hear. I'm not—'

'Not a friend. I know.'

She moved to the fireplace with the now empty grate. She picked up one of the andirons, tapping it against stone. 'You caused my brother to break his arm.'

'We were being foolish.'

'Both of you were drunken.'

'Both of us.'

'Just because he did wrong, it's not an excuse for you not to take responsibility as well.'

'Can't change it.'

'Would you?'

'Yes.'

'If we weren't having this conversation, would you have wished to change it?'

Silence answered her question.

She rapped the andiron, letting the clank vibrate her hand. 'I have known you my entire life,' she said. 'You've been—'

He smiled. 'I'm sorry. The stream.'

'Oh, you should be. I was terrified. You kept

putting my hair closer and closer to the water while you walked across, squeezing me like a puppy, and then when we got to the other side, you took my dripping plait and swished it across my nose.'

'You kicked me for that.'

'No. No. No.' She tapped the andiron with each word, the sound ringing. 'I did not. I tried. Even though I knew it was wrong. But you put your palm on my forehead, holding me away, and then you told me that if I had only looked round the bend, there was a footbridge.'

'Lady Kickevere.'

'Yes. And every single time I raised my voice the slightest bit after that, my sister called me that name.' She pursed her lips and looked down. 'Until I tapped her with my foot. Lightly.'

He pointed to his leg. 'You can kick me now.'

'I could not do that. I am not a child.'

'Then why be angry now?'

'You are twisting what I said.' She paused, ir-ritation fading, and relief flowering inside. 'Your mother is going to be so happy that the injury didn't change you.'

'I know.' His words slowed, and she would have thought speech too difficult for him, except she didn't believe it was that, but what he said.

'I'm thinking,' he said. 'Maybe it should.'

She put the iron in place. 'Today you say that. Tomorrow is a lifetime away.'

She pulled the door closed, and felt as if she'd torn out a tiny piece of herself and left it behind. She touched the surface as if to knock, but shook away the impulse. He would be his old self after a few days, and probably regret talking to her.

Reid's cousin had stayed for dinner, and he had apologised to them all, explaining that he'd misinterpreted the events, and assumed his cousin up to another of his…adventures.

Reid hadn't attended, and no one had commented on it.

They'd retired to the main sitting room, and Guinevere doubted the atmosphere would have been any different than if a funeral had been held earlier.

'Do you mind if I play the piano?' Reid's mother asked. 'I would be so thrilled to have soothing music tonight.'

'I would enjoy it,' the Duchess answered.

After a few songs, Lady Hartcroft paused and spoke to the Duchess. 'I do hope you are staying longer as we'd planned.' She put a hand to her chest. 'The events have unsettled me, and I don't wish to be alone. And Guinevere is such a help.'

'Of course, Marjorie. We understand completely.' Her mother rose, moving to the piano. 'We'll visit a bit longer.'

'It would be more…festive, with everyone here,' Lady Hartcroft said.

No one felt any festivity. Guinevere could sense the unsettled air.

'Yes, I would so much like it if you could remain.' The cousin rose. 'I'd not planned to return home immediately, wishing to visit my aunt a few days as well. And Lady Guinevere adds such a brightness to the house.'

Her mother studied Stephen, and then her, and looked at the Duke. 'Yes. We should delay a few more days, and then Guinevere and I can accompany you home.'

'I'm so pleased this became a joyous occasion, instead of a dreadful one,' Stephen continued. 'It would be delightful for us if you remained.' He flashed a smile at them all, but his gaze found her last, and rested.

As the next in line to the title, he could have been inviting them to his estate if things had progressed ever so slightly in another direction. But Guinevere was so relieved it hadn't.

Her father's brow rose, and he hesitated, then seemed to shrug.

'Just for a few days,' her father said, and she

wasn't as surprised as she could have been. Her father would have considered Stephen a suitable match for her. And he was. The thoughtful one. The one always in the shadows, seeming ever so solicitous. The perfect smile. Except he'd not been happy when his cousin had survived.

She could understand that he didn't love Reid, but still, he'd not had to appear so disappointed.

Reid was the opposite of his cousin, but she'd seen Reid at a few soirees when he'd decided to charm someone. His laughter had been infectious to the people surrounding him, but she'd watched it dispassionately.

It wasn't that Reid appeared to be acting, but that she'd been able to study him with her knowledge casting a fog over his appearance.

Even so, after watching him charm the others, she could almost feel herself being pulled into his orbit. She'd not wanted to turn away, but she had. Because one didn't overindulge on sweetness or treats, and one definitely didn't get too close to flames just to observe what the results would be.

'Well, I believe we should retire to our rooms.' Her father interrupted her musings and held out a hand to her mother. 'We all need a good night's sleep, and a chance to start tomorrow anew.'

'I look forward to seeing you in the morning,'

Stephen said, taking his aunt's arm, but his attention was on Guinevere. 'It is so pleasant to have family friends here.'

The next day, Guinevere expected Reid at every corner, but he'd not appeared. His mother had reassured them all he'd recovered beyond her dreams.

They'd all sat around the piano and listened to the music, but Reid hadn't joined them. What if he'd had a relapse?

Guinevere retired to her quarters, but once there, she couldn't rest.

She paced, but then pushed away her foolishness. If she was concerned for him, it would be easy enough to make certain he was fine. It would only take putting one foot in front of the other.

Leaving, she made her way down the hallway, and rapped softly on Reid's sitting room door.

It opened, and she stared into a face of darkness.

He stepped aside so she could enter. She didn't.

'I just wished to make sure you were well,' she said.

He held the door wider.

She appraised him. 'I have satisfied myself

that you are fine. So, have a pleasant night.' She caught up her skirt in her hand, and rotated away, the swirl of the hem not slowing her.

'Guinevere.' The word drifted into the air like a snowflake, floating in a breeze. 'If you can forgive me of everything I said to you before I was twenty, then you would have little to be angry with me for.'

She paused, catching his eyes in the dimness, but her mind saw his expression plainly. 'Only because we've avoided each other when we had the choice.'

'You should get over the past,' he said, tapping lightly on the door.

She took in a breath, then stopped, waiting. 'A woman never has to get over anything she doesn't want to.'

'I go forward. Not backwards.'

'Says the man with the past.'

'I can live with it.'

'You rejected the other choice.'

'Which I couldn't live with.' He shrugged, eyes glinting warm, but with a challenge. 'Besides, I woke up to you.'

She wondered if he had a double entendre in there. Her chin went up. 'How am I supposed to react to that?'

'Better than you did to having your plaits dunked, I hope.'

'I've just outgrown kicking things. Now, I smile instead.' She blinked, and her lips turned up.

He studied her. 'Well, I wouldn't call that a smile. More of a wrong-side-up grimace.'

'I don't want to overdo it.'

'Because I might get the impression that you've forgiven me?'

'Oh, no,' she said. 'You're a much better assessor of people than that.'

Judging by his reaction, her words could have been silent.

He held the door with one hand and pulled it wide again. 'I would wager that you will not be entering my room even if the invitation is more than innocent. But it is. Please come in. As a friend.'

She shook her head, but her smile faded.

Guinevere Chenowith. Head erect. Rather haughty. Not his first choice of companionship, but he had too many minutes of the night facing him. Too much darkness.

He'd recovered, but he still remembered the blackness. The moments of people talking in the room as if he weren't there. But the sound of Guinevere's voice had rolled over him like music, forcing him to listen.

Even if she'd said that his accomplishments were negligible. Less than. He could show her that he'd not been such a wastrel as she claimed. He had done lots of good deeds and he needed to prove it to her.

'Lady Guinevere. Might we stroll in the gardens?'

She considered his suggestion. 'I doubt there's enough moonlight to see well. And it would be unfair to get a servant to secure a lantern for us so late. A lamp might be unwieldy. It might be best to stay inside.'

'What is best has not always been my course of action. I would be honoured if you would step outside with me and help me rid myself of the stench of the reminder of the last few days of my life.' He released the wood and brushed a hand over his knuckles. 'This room—I've been in here too much the last few days.'

She watched him. As unmoving as the marble seraphs his father had had carved into the fireplace mantels, and just as cold as when there were no fires lit from within.

'I could hear. The plans. The discussion,' he said. 'As I lay there. Having trouble understanding what was going on around me. But I heard enough, and I seemed unable to move because I didn't want to spend the extra strength on opening my eyes.'

'I hope it didn't unsettle you?'

He chuckled. 'How could something so innocent as sincere conversation of my actions unsettle me?'

She bit her bottom lip.

He'd known her his whole life, practically. She'd matured from a little girl looking disdainfully at his antics with her brother, to a woman who'd perfected her disinterested but polite— with a hint of criticism—awareness of him.

He could see her trying to form another wellbred refusal.

'I don't want to go out and talk with my horses. They're rather irritable if awoken this time of night for conversation. It would be rather one-sided. Much the same as the recent ones I heard.'

'I can't think your horses wouldn't be happy to see you.'

'But I don't want to speak with them. They tend not to give much reason on why they think as they do. Perhaps a kick or a whinny, or a misstep, but that's about it. You're more apt to state your opinions.'

'I've not found that people want to hear a

point of view differing from their own. They tend to get along best with people who see things as they do.'

'Then we will try to avoid those topics and stick to what we can agree on, even if it is only the beauty of silence—which now that I think of it, I'm not sure it is so beautiful.'

'Are you disagreeing with yourself?' she asked.

'Could be.' He couldn't resist adding, 'Might save you some time because we've not found much common ground in the past.'

He had never seen such a lovely brow quirk up so delicately.

'But I wanted to speak with you—about what happened. I don't want solitude tonight because it feels like I've been alone for several days. And even though we've not found much reason to converse in the past, I would rather talk with you right now than anyone else in the world who might happily agree with me.'

He offered her his arm. No one would understand better than her. No one. And he felt she comprehended more about him than he grasped. She had no gauze wrapped around her perception of him. No illusions.

'I should get a wrap.'

He didn't think she'd return if she left.

He held out his arm. 'Just a brief stroll.'

'It might be extremely short.'

'If it is, it is.' He was only in his shirtsleeves and waistcoat, and he grabbed a frock coat.

'My pardon,' he said, and held the garment to wrap around her shoulders.

'I can't wear your coat.' She raised a palm. 'If anyone—'

'If anyone happens upon us, which would be unlikely, they will form assumptions based on their own behaviour and beliefs.'

'That could still be a problem. My father can sometimes be stubborn.'

'I wanted you to enlighten me on a few things. I've had some time to think recently.'

He waited to make sure she agreed, but if he knew her at all, she would not be able to refuse. A woman who believed it her duty to help someone who'd been in an accident.

'I will take care.' He placed the cloth around her shoulders, hoping she stayed comfortable. 'And if I am a little cool tonight, it is much better than being a little too warm.'

She held the coat tightly at the neck and took his arm with her free hand. He guided her to the stairs, and followed her, the gentle waft of her perfume and her womanly scent pulling him through a doorway he couldn't see, and one he would have barged through. She was the angel who called him to life.

'I have a bruise on my arm,' he said. 'And I think you are the reason. I was aware of your speaking, telling me goodbye, and then a searing pain.'

'The pin is bent,' she said. 'Perhaps I jabbed too strongly. I wanted to see…to make sure… It was as if I knew you were listening and wouldn't answer.'

'I thought you liked me to ignore you.'

'Not then.'

They stepped outside, and the cold air hit him in the face, and he filled his lungs with the simple scents of leaves, grass and the night.

He led her to the garden bench and waited as she settled. 'I give you my solemn oath that tonight I only wish to stay warm, and feel the vibrancy of the night air, and your presence.'

He lowered himself beside her.

'Guinevere, we have never truly been friends and if we never are again, I understand. But tonight, I will speak directly.'

She looked at him. 'Of course. Always speak squarely with me. Always. And I thought you had.'

'True.'

She paused, continuing, 'I suppose you have.

Even as you dunked my hair in the water. And irritated me. And we avoided each other. Actions speak loudly.'

'But they don't always tell the whole truth.'

'I would disagree.'

'But how much truth do words contain? Particularly when people don't know anyone is listening?'

She didn't answer.

'The servants chattered away,' he said. 'I woke with everyone speaking in quiet tones, but I didn't want to open my eyes. Or move.'

'You're used to having your staff at your side. You knew all of them.'

'Yes, but they're not usually planning a celebration. I was happy to disappoint them.'

'Were they truly festive, or are you jesting?'

'I'm serious.'

He felt her shift slightly on the bench beside him, the awareness of her banishing the harshest memories of his previous hours. 'It means a lot. My station. I change people's lives. I do a lot for them. And the servants were anticipating emptying my wine cabinet.'

She didn't respond at first. 'Does it hurt?'

'Just a few minor aches. The pain medicine took care of that more roundly than I ever expected apparently.'

'That's not what I meant. Did it upset you to hear your servants discussing you, and be unable to command them about?'

'The butler will be sacked in the morning. He's fortunate to be able to leave under his own power.'

'For the truth?'

'I'm not paying him for truth.'

'Are you sacking the entire household?'

'Probably.'

'The arrogant Marquess strikes again.'

'They're servants.'

'Perhaps you should treat them better.'

'They make decent wages and toil in a respected household.'

'Why don't you act pleasantly towards them— or am I making a mistaken assumption that you don't?'

He moved to his feet. 'Your view of pleasantness to servants and mine may be entirely different.'

'I don't think it should be, however.' She stood. She moved closer. His coat brushed against him, and it was the first time in his life he'd noticed the actual feel of the garment. As if he wasn't wearing a shirt and could only feel the clothing she wore.

'Imagine how it must be for the staff. They

have to do their job. But it would be better if they have fond memories of you. You don't ever want anyone decent pleased with your downfall.'

He moved, grasping her elbow so lightly he wasn't sure she could feel it. 'I have done right by everyone in my staff.' He stepped away, releasing her because her nearness disrupted his thoughts. 'Everyone here lives a better life than they would be living without me. Everyone.'

'Are you certain?' Her voice reminded him of morning birdsong, bringing the world to life.

'They just don't see it,' he said. 'And I will continue to be certain that their lives are better whether they notice or not.'

'I should go inside,' she said.

He opened the door, and she preceded him. She was leaving his life. He'd won the argument—one he should have purposely lost. But it wasn't in him to do such a thing.

He followed her up the stairway.

When she reached the top, he couldn't bear the thought of her exit.

'I may let the butler stay.'

'Perhaps you should ask him if he would prefer to stay or leave,' she said. 'He might be thinking of finding another position anyway.'

She took the coat from her shoulders and half folded it, but she didn't give it to him.

'I'm surprised you stuck me with the pin,' he said.

'I'd really meant to give you the brooch, something of mine to have with you into eternity. But then I thought how foolish that was.'

She'd wanted him to have something of hers? The thought connected him to her in a way he'd not expected.

A silence grew between them, and he knew he was the one who needed to end it, and what he must say. 'I'm sorry for what I said. When we were younger. And I'm sorry if I've inadvertently done anything else to offend you.'

She chuckled. 'It's forgotten. I got you back with the pin stick. And you broke the jewellery. It will have to be repaired if I'm ever to wear it again.'

'Send me the bill. It would be an honour to pay it.' He touched her shoulder in the approximate area where his own had been pierced. 'Any time you need to test a pin's strength, I will be available for you. A small price to pay for my life.'

She lingered, the night air shielding them in a moment of togetherness. 'Oh, I will remember that.' Her voice resonated with a throatiness he'd never heard from her before.

But then she moved away, breaking the connection, and destroying the bond he'd felt between them.

He couldn't see her face, but he didn't need to. The Duke's daughter, who'd inherited her father's air of command. Nothing like the women he preferred in his life. His mind flashed to the laughter of being surrounded by agreeable, beautiful women vying for his attention.

A perfect way to live, and a life awaiting him in London. His friends would celebrate his return with him and drink the night away—not listening to simple little night owls but their own revelry.

His wine would be in his own belly, not his ungrateful servants'.

Then Guinevere was leaving. A woman who imparted something different from inside her.

She still clutched his coat. He would have let her take it, but it wouldn't be good for a servant to find it in her room.

'Pardon me,' he said, and held out his hand. 'My coat?'

'Oh.'

Their fingers brushed and made him feel more alive than ever.

'Thank you for coming when you heard I was ill. I would have thought you would have stayed home.'

'Oh, no.' He heard the shock in her voice. 'Your mother. I could not.'

'On behalf of my mother, but more importantly myself, I'm pleased you were here.'

'I wouldn't have missed it for anything,' she said, then stumbling over her words when she heard how that could have been taken. 'Your awakening. I am so pleased I was there. I never thought I'd be so happy to have someone swear at me.'

'I wasn't swearing at you. But the pain in my arm. And my sincerest apologies.'

'Accepted. And may you have a pleasant night, Reid.'

He gave a slight bow as she left.

And he would have a good night, but only because he knew she would be there in the morning. She made the house feel different, but that didn't seem possible. And he felt—almost drunken, which had to be the effects of his accident.

Inside the sitting room, after noticing a tantalising aroma in the air, he held his coat closer, and a floral scent that hadn't been on it before wafted to him.

In fact, everything around him seemed more vibrant than before. He tossed the coat onto a chair.

In his dressing room, he sat by the bootjack, and toed off his boots. Then he recalled that he'd meant to tell her of the accomplishments he'd made in his life.

He removed his stockings and wadded them. He searched his mind. Perhaps it was best he hadn't. He slung the bundle across the room.

Chapter Three

Reid took his chair at the head of the dining table, alone in the room except for a servant.

His mother arrived next, on his cousin Stephen's arm, and gasped when she saw him. 'Are you well?'

'Perfectly.'

'Then why are you here?'

'Breakfast.'

'W—wonderful,' she said.

'Of course,' Stephen added, and Reid had to admire him for putting a brave face on his grief.

Then the Duke and Duchess arrived, and Reid greeted them, giving no extra attention to Guinevere.

'I do believe this is the first time I've had breakfast with Reid,' the Duke said. 'Pleased to see you are up and about.'

'Pleased to be here,' Reid said, taking a sip

from his cup. Of chocolate. Which he briefly held up, and tilted the rim a hair in her direction.

He had Guinevere's full awareness based on her expression. Everyone else accepted his statement without question.

'The butler needs a respite. I've sent him on his way.'

Guinevere didn't move, and Reid faced his mother, but Reid's attention was solely on the guest. He was at the table only because he wanted to see her. He would have eaten in his rooms otherwise, because he preferred solitude in the morning—almost the only time he craved silence.

He let the pause linger, and then said, 'The butler has an uncle to visit. We will manage with a footman for now.' He brushed a hand across his clean-shaven jaw, but his eyes were on Guinevere. 'He's returning next week.'

'I do think the episode may have damaged you,' his mother said. 'Breakfast. Sending the butler away for a family visit.'

'I am my old self.' But now he had at least one considerate thing for Guinevere to be aware of. Not sacking the butler, who'd planned the celebration.

'That's wonderful,' the Duchess said. 'Your mother was so concerned.'

'I also want to thank you, Your Grace, for bringing Guinevere. She awoke me. She put her entire being into it.' He lightly brushed fingertips over the bruised area.

'She is a treasure.' Guinevere's father's scowl didn't change. The man and Reid's father were more alike than brothers.

Stephen practically drooled on his egg. 'She truly is remarkable. I'm hoping to go with her on a trek around the estate today. I thought we might walk to north of the meadows. It's so pastoral there.'

Reid didn't comment on the word *pastoral*.

'I know the trail you're speaking of.' The Duke smiled at his wife and daughter, and then Stephen. 'I would like to see it again. So nice of you to take us.'

'That would be lovely,' the Marchioness said. 'And perhaps we could all visit the Pakenhams.'

'Oh, it's been an age since I've seen them. Wonderful idea,' Lady Glouston agreed. 'The Duke will likely stay there all day once he and Pakenham start talking.'

'I can hardly wait to get started,' Stephen said, sending a besotted gaze in Guinevere's direction, the same one Reid knew he used on every barmaid he wanted to impress. 'A stroll in the countryside will be grand.'

His cousin would very much like a ducal father-in-law, particularly one with a large estate he could live in. Stephen had complained to Reid that the old Marquess should have allowed Stephen's family a more impressive home but Reid had refused to enlarge it; it was more than large enough already.

He allowed Stephen to stay at that home, the country estate, the London town house or send the bill for bachelor's lodgings to him, and his cousin alternated between all four.

'Idyllic. I will abstain, however.' Reid grimaced at the chocolate. 'This needs more spice. Or a splash of wine. Brandy. Whisky. Something.'

'You are your old self,' his mother said.

He rose, moved to her side and took her hand, kissing above it. 'Yes, I am.'

'I don't see you ever changing,' Stephen said. 'How could you improve?'

'It would be difficult,' Reid said, giving an overall nod in the direction of the table as he bid them farewell.

And he couldn't help himself when he left. His gaze travelled to hers, and he touched his shoulder and gave an infinitesimal bow.

Her father saw. Reid had to be thankful that

duelling was not favoured by dukes, or he might need to select a second.

He knew when everyone arrived at the house. Muffled laughter. A thump of a boot. Perhaps a creaking welcome from the walls as they adjusted to weight on the stairway.

He'd taken a paper and made a whirligig while they were gone. It fluttered to the ground as expected, and it was a diversion, but he needed to be concentrating on important matters. He suspected he'd not fully recovered.

After he gave the others an appropriate amount of time to settle, he visited the main sitting room.

They were embroidering. Stephen was sitting at Guinevere's side, and while he didn't hold a needle, he was definitely embroidering some story.

Reid hid his smile. Perhaps he should give Stephen the whirligig to explain to Guinevere. He could likely talk hours about it.

But he understood the fascination of the stitchery. The needle. Thread. A delicate hand. Slender wrist. Slim arm. A spirited woman.

The two mothers sat across, both sewing and talking. The window open. Oak leaves swirling by. It was so…pastoral, as Stephen would say.

He propped his shoulder against the frame, and he could still feel the bruise, although he wasn't sure if it was real, or imagined, but he would miss it.

Guinevere's gaze darted to him, and in that instant, they were alone in the room. Unfortunately, Stephen moved, a sniffle that diverted her attention.

If Reid showed any interest in Guinevere whatsoever, Stephen would likely propose to her on the spot.

His mother and the Duchess were talking about the enchanting walk.

'Sounds bucolic,' he said.

'Yes,' his mother said, and everyone agreed but Stephen.

'We are all so thankful to have you well,' the Marchioness said.

'I'm sure,' he said to Stephen, and dared him to contradict.

Reid excused himself and left, needing to get outside to some of that pastoral nonsense, Guinevere's face engraved in his mind.

He didn't understand how she'd missed being proposed to but he was certain she'd been partnered every dance when he'd seen her at a soiree.

She might have been the most assured woman he'd ever encountered, yet she didn't seem to have those criticisms of other people that she had for him. Perhaps he'd deserved it, though. But she had a certain poise, grace and a way of bristling at just the smallest thing he said.

Her voice altered when she was angered. A slight lilt. Perhaps a bit of a northern accent from her father's side of the family. Actually, her voice was the most melodious one he'd ever heard, except when she was angry.

Ah, well, it was intriguing then, too. Had been even when they were youngsters and he'd carried her across the river. He'd never been so soundly thrashed without a single swear word. She'd called him fish innards, slug slime, and he'd had to bite the inside of his lip to keep from laughing when she'd called him runny bird droppings.

Actually, he'd used the same term on one of his friends later, but changed it a bit to make it appropriate to the situation.

He'd found her intriguing to irritate then, even though he'd left her alone because he knew she'd thoroughly disliked him. And it wouldn't have been good to bring down the wrath of the world on his head, which was what her ducal father would have responded with.

A marquess's son had a lot of power, except where an older duke was concerned who'd been navigating society his whole life.

Then Reid paused. But Guinevere wouldn't have told her father. Oh, no. The girl who'd spoken with a sideways sling of her plaits, splashing water on him, and told him off and mentioned that he should have been a fourth son, preferred to handle things herself. He'd been amused, and she'd kicked at him.

Everything around him was his, and yet, if he'd not recovered, Stephen would have owned everything entailed.

Even the barns would have been Stephen's.

When he reached the nearest barn, the scent of hay grew stronger, results of the recent harvest. Hermes whinnied, possibly asking for a treat. The mare, Hera, watched them, and the other horse, a gelding, nudged at the gate.

The flame-coloured cat meandered over to visit Reid. He gently shooed him away with his boot, but knew the pest wouldn't leave. It never did.

He hated animal hair on his clothing. Always had. But someone took care of it after he changed.

The stableman, Nettles, strode out, face shuttered, a bucket in one hand and a crop in the other. 'Hermes?' he asked, not looking up. 'Or the gelding?'

'The stallion.' Reid took the bucket. Within

seconds, Reid's favourite horse was released, and ran up to him. Reid held the grain for Hermes and patted the horse's neck.

The stablemaster was already returning to the barn.

He glanced down at his trouser leg; a fluff of cat hair had floated free from its owner and attached itself to him. He moved the cat away again, and brushed the hairs off.

The stablemaster spoiled every animal crossing his path, except rats.

'Nettles,' Reid called. 'Has Orange caught any mice lately?'

The man paused, stilled by his employer's voice, hesitant. 'A fair amount. She's the best mouser we've ever had.'

'Hand me the crop,' Reid said. He thought of adding *please* but figured it might startle the stableman.

Nettles's feet didn't appear to want to return. Reid strode forward, trading the bucket for the crop in the stableman's hands. 'Thank you.' He spoke the words quickly, turning them into almost one syllable.

Nettles studied him. 'Pardon, sir?'

'I appreciate your helping me back to the house after my accident.'

'You were too foxed to walk.' He paused. 'I

thought…' He peered at the ground. 'I didn't realise you'd been hurt so bad.'

'That makes two of us.'

The stallion followed the pail. Nettles was basically trapped. He would have to talk with Reid.

Reid shook the crop. The cat pounced on it. Reid stepped aside quickly, letting the cat jump upward.

Reid swung out the tool again, letting the feline play, and trying to move fast enough to keep it from her teeth. 'Nettles, this is the ugliest, most spoiled cat I've ever seen. She'd be gone if it wasn't for the rats.'

'The mice will be trying to move in when winter weather sets. Best to keep her.'

Reid danced the end of the crop along the grass tops, and beyond them to a bare spot. The cat pounced, and a cloud of dust erupted at her feet.

He used the end to scratch Orange behind the ears, but she jumped around, trying to bite the leather tip. 'You hear that, Orange? The only reason I let you stay is because of the horses. We have to keep their grain safe from vermin.' Orange swiped a paw at the rod. 'And you don't care.'

'She does like a mouse now and again,' the stableman said.

'Orange is a pest.' He glanced down at her, and she peered at him, one fang showing from beneath the scar on her lip. 'Aren't you?'

Teeth bared, she nipped at the whip.

'Where are the other cats?'

'Asleep somewhere. Your mother keeps sending scraps out, and Orange is the only one that ignores them. Wants to hunt. Wants to be friends.'

He used the tip of the rod to keep Orange occupied, and, after the bucket emptied, moved closer to the barn with the stableman, discussing plans for next year's foals.

Guinevere continued stitching, trying to ignore Stephen's droning speech. He had found a newspaper, and read the articles to them, adding commentary. He had a way of making everything in the paper sound tedious.

She noticed the Marchioness had put aside her embroidery and moved to the window. The older woman frowned at the sight beyond, but then her expression lightened.

'Stephen, would you be a dear,' the Marchioness asked, 'and fetch a book for me, and read to us? It's in the library. I have a perfect one. It's a story about some thieves and a princess.'

'What is the title?'

'I fear I've forgotten.' She shook her head. 'But you'll recognise it instantly. It's on top of the others, unless the maid put it away. If she did, would you please search it out? I think it has the word *princess* in the title. Or perhaps it's something else. Would you be so kind? Do look for it please. I believe our guests would love the story.'

'Certainly, Aunt.'

His footsteps had barely faded when the Marchioness changed her attention to Guinevere.

'Oh, Guinevere, I hate to interrupt your stitching, but I just saw Mrs Marmalade—one of the cats that keeps pouncing on the birds—and it looked as if she was ready to attack. Would you please go down and scare her away?' Her fingers fluttered, waving Guinevere on. 'I would call for a maid, but it might be too late by then. Make haste. And you might stay a bit, because that ruthless orange cat is vicious, and keeps returning. She's at the stables.'

'Of course.' Guinevere dropped her stitching, and hurried to the door, rushing outside, secretly pleased at a chance to escape Stephen's reading, and feel the crisp air touching her cheeks.

When she approached the stables, she was surprised to see Reid and a man with him. Surely, they would keep the feline from any misbehaviour.

Reid had a rod, and kept swirling it around as he spoke, letting an orange cat chase it.

As soon as the servant saw her, he dipped his head, and smiled. 'I'll get the saddle,' he said, then moved into the stable.

She glanced around, certain this cat hadn't been chasing any prey. The beast had a scarred lip which gave her the impression of a smile, and it seemed besotted with Reid. 'I believe your mother sent me to scare away Mrs Marmalade. She thought it was attacking a bird.'

'You can tell her the birds are safe.' He glanced up at the window. 'Orange wasn't tackling anything but a crop.'

She studied the area nearby. 'It's not the right cat. I'm to scare a cat called Mrs Marmalade.'

'Same cat,' he said. 'Different owners. Orange is the stablemaster's mouser. Marmalade is the Marchioness's cat. One rodent-chaser.'

'Are you certain?' she asked, and glanced up at the window. She couldn't see the Marchioness anymore.

'Mother sent you?' he asked.

'Yes.'

He gave a firm shake of his head.

'I suppose she saw the cat jumping, and thought it was going for a bird,' Guinevere said. He didn't answer.

'Stephen was possibly caterwauling a bit and she decided getting you out of the room would shut him up.'

'She'd sent him for a book to read to us.'

'Really?' He drawled out the word and stared at her as if she should be able to comprehend his thoughts. 'She did that?'

'Yes.'

She returned to the previous subject. 'You're certain there isn't another orange cat?' she asked.

He held the tip of the crop in front of the feline nose. The cat's teeth and claws latched on to the rod, and it wrapped itself around the wood. 'What say you, Orange?'

He tugged enough to keep Orange enthralled.

'You like cats?' Guinevere watched him drag the cat around. It refused to release the shaft.

'No.'

'But you're…'

'Distracting her. If I don't, she could scratch my boots. She's a pest. And I hate rats and mice in the stables eating the horses' grain, and she hates rodents more than I. But I like her reaction to the crop. She's fierce.'

'If you're sure, then…'

'Feel free to stay a bit longer. I expect Stephen to be peering out the window any time now. He'll likely appear to see if you need any assistance—' he took a step, and the cat finally released its grip '—corralling the fierce and ferocious Mrs Orange Marmalade.'

Without looking towards it, and only with a bare nod, he indicated the window. 'And it appears she is an attraction as people keep noticing her.'

She glanced up and saw her own mother's face and then it darted away. She thought it odd. Her mother rarely moved anywhere fast, and was not a woman to spy on others. Although she could be overly curious.

Moments later, her mother's voice called.

'Guinevere.' The Duchess rushed into the area, holding her skirts in both hands, and veering to a sedate stop. 'Stephen found the book. I don't want you to miss any of it.'

Reid bowed enough to show respect, first to her mother, then her. 'Thank you, Lady Guinevere, for saving the birds.' He tucked the crop under his arm and pulled out a pair of gloves from inside his coat, and donned them, tucking the leather tight between his fingers. 'I'm sure Stephen will be waiting.'

He strode towards the barn, the cat at his heels.

'Come along, Guinevere,' her mother's voice rushed. 'The book. Stephen found it.'

Reid stopped and glanced over his shoulder. 'Yes, Lady Guinevere. Stephen awaits.'

If Lucifer had sent Reid back from the fiery flames, he'd sent along his smile with him.

She shook away the effects of it and followed her mother.

'That man has designs on you,' her mother muttered when they were inside, before moving to the stairs.

'I agree. I noticed Stephen seemed so entranced with my stitching. Goodness, it was just a hem stitch on a handkerchief. The Marchioness was stitching a peacock.'

'No.' Her mother grumbled, starting up the staircase. 'Open your eyes, Guinevere. Not Stephen. Reid.'

Guinevere stopped, grasping the stair railing. 'Mother. We have never got on well. He never asked me to dance. I never wanted him to. If he speaks with me now, it is only because of our proximity and that he's recovering and hasn't felt like returning to his true friends.'

But he had asked her to walk with him the night before, and he'd appeared genuine in their discussion. Not as if he had wanted to impress her or wished to flirt with her.

Her mother reversed her steps, standing one tread above Guinevere so they were eye to eye.

'I didn't raise you to be so innocent. Remember what I taught you about the birds and the bees.'

Guinevere remembered the story about the innocent female bird who hopelessly fell in love with the honey created by bees, but even though the honey was sweet and entrancing, it made her ill because it wasn't for her. The bees stung her, and then flew on to search out pollen. The bees always flitted from bloom to bloom, never satisfied, and they only wanted one thing, more pollen. It did not matter how exquisite any bird was, the tiny bee brains were not going to change. Pollen called to them. And more pollen.

'He's not entrancing me and he's not after the…pollen.'

The Duchess threw back her head, disbelieving. 'Young men are always after the pollen.' Her voice was a terse whisper. 'It's nature. Hard to change. You must slap Reid away with your wingtips.'

'I don't think he would feel it. He's likely never seen a wingtip he couldn't navigate, except mine.'

'You're right. But stay away from him. He's not for you.' She whispered so low Guinevere could barely hear her. 'I love Marjorie but she and Reid's father always gave him his way and he is used to it. I cannot believe how they let him wrap them around his finger and do as he wished. It might have been best for everyone if Stephen inherited the title.'

'*Mother.*'

'I would not wish so much as a broken fingernail on Reid, but still— Don't you find Stephen much more agreeable? He is so considerate. Reading to us. And he has those attractive teeth.'

'Mother, what is wrong with Reid's teeth?'

'It's hard to say. I've hardly ever seen them. Because he rarely talks to your father or me. But Stephen smiles so much and is always so pleasant to us.'

'Yes.' Of course Stephen was more agreeable. He was understanding, almost as if he saw how demanding Reid could be and wanted to shine by comparison. And he had inherited the same colour eyes, except on Stephen they weren't piercing or even intriguing. Just a shade. Bland blue. Those eyes were nothing alike. Nothing.

Reid, with his dark hair, was so much the opposite of Stephen.

'Stephen is so attentive to his aunt, too. He acts more like her son than Reid does. Is so much more respectful of your father and me. Never caused your brother to act up like Reid did. Even today, Reid left to go to the horses while his mother had guests.'

She'd not particularly cared that Reid had gone to the stables. She couldn't blame him. His cousin was pleasant but reminded her of a yapping dog with saggy ears who wanted to be scratched under the chin, so he kept finding new things to bark about, or repeating the old tricks.

Reid was different. Not innocent. Swirling with portent. A flame one shouldn't get nearer.

'Now, come along. Stephen's waiting.' Her mother continued to the entrance, not pausing for Guinevere. 'He's much more of a gentleman than Reid is.' At the landing she hesitated, fussing over Guinevere's hair, and gave her a nudge to send her along before following her.

In the sitting room, the Marchioness waited with Stephen, book in hand, lips pursed and glaring at Guinevere's mother as if they were not at all friends.

Chapter Four

Reid understood his body's response to an attractive woman's presence. He had also heard of someone's mouth drying when they experienced a moment of fear. He even recalled the headiness he'd felt after racing Hermes.

Yet, he'd never undergone all those feelings at once, and more, until Guinevere had stepped into the sunlight.

The after-effects of his experience must have remained. He'd felt like Orange, pouncing around in the dirt, chasing a diversion.

Then he wondered if he would always be altered by the accident. If it had changed him more than he understood. Perhaps it would be for the best if it had.

He peered at the empty window, hoping to see Guinevere's face, but he only saw glass.

The stableman had finished saddling Hermes

and led the horse out, and Reid was relieved at the distraction from his thoughts. A jaunt would do him well, shaking out the last vestiges of his musings about Guinevere. And it would be good to make certain that he and Hermes had the same rapport they'd shared before the incident.

He grabbed the pommel, and pulled himself astride, giving a light touch on the ribbons, and Hermes knew Reid's mind and trotted instantly.

He tried to concentrate on the journey, but it was impossible. The horse needed no instruction, and they'd taken the jaunt a thousand times. He let him move at the speed he wanted, not caring where they went.

He kept thinking of Guinevere, and it irked him.

Putting distance between him and the woman would take care of his nonsensical awareness of her. He'd leave the estate the next morning. That would be best.

He was unaware of a change in his touch on the ribbons, but Hermes cut through the trees on a return journey to the barn.

Once back, the horse whinnied and the stableman stepped out.

Hermes stopped at Nettles's side. Reid dismounted, and the man took the ribbons, and he saw the horse nuzzle the stablemaster, and Nettles didn't have a bucket of grain.

A cold slab of truth touched him, and irritation rose inside which shocked him, but he shoved it away. The horse's loyalty was because of Nettles's training and attention to duties. Not anything personal.

'I want to ride the gelding after you take care of Hermes. I've ignored him for a while. But now I need to make certain of something.'

Before leaving, he spoke to Nettles. 'I appreciate the care you give the animals. Even Orange.'

Nettles looked away, but not before Reid saw a flicker of surprise. 'Just doing my job.'

'And you do it well.'

He strode into the house. He didn't want to wait while Nettles completed the instructions. He had to check if Guinevere remained with Stephen.

He found his mother in her sitting room, staring out the window, arms crossed.

'Did everyone leave?' He wasn't sure he wanted to hear the answer. Either way.

'Only for another walk. To the stream. At least Guinevere and Stephen did. He got a catch in his throat and had to rest it.' She grimaced. 'Thank goodness.'

'What about the others?'

'Vera is relaxing and the Duke is still at the neighbours'. I believe Guinevere appeared displeased by her mother insisting on the stroll.'

'They went alone?'

She sighed. 'I sent a maid to chaperon.' She waved a hand. 'For what it's worth. Her mother didn't think of it, but I didn't feel like trotting along, and listening to Stephen extoll the virtues of *Lady Guinevere*. I swear, if he says *Lady Guinevere* one more time…'

'She can be opinionated.'

She whirled to him. 'I did not mean that. She has many virtues to speak of, but anyone can see how besotted he is. Vera has him selected as a son-in-law.'

His stomach clenched, but it didn't matter.

The Duchess could do as she wished. And so could Guinevere. It was unlikely for her to do otherwise, based on his brief experience with her.

The Marchioness's gaze fluttered to the window. 'Stephen will have handsome children. And I can understand Vera setting her sights on him for Guinevere. Only surprise is that it didn't happen earlier.'

'He's not the wonder everyone thinks he is. He drowns himself in ale.'

She tapped a finger against her lips. 'I know.

It's a family curse. But he's certainly suitable for Guinevere.'

He felt his mother said that to nick him. 'Do you dislike her?' he asked.

His mother glared at him. 'She's nice. I have always liked her. But Vera believes Guinevere should marry. We've discussed it, and I've tried to dissuade her. She thinks Stephen will be a good son-in-law. Thinks Stephen's agreeableness will make him a good match.'

'If she controls the purse strings, perhaps.' And the wine cabinet. And the carriage wheels. But it was possible Stephen would meet his match with Guinevere as a wife.

'It's unfortunate that she's not good enough for you, though,' his mother said.

He felt a slur there, somehow, as if she imagined herself quoting his words to him, and he'd never said anything of the kind.

'But she's suitable for Stephen.' She waved, as if accepting the fate. 'And he's ready to wed. It's obvious. He's smitten.'

'Stephen always looks like a sick calf.'

'He complimented her on her hem stitch. He went on and on.' Her eyes darted up. 'That's a grand feat. A hem stitch… As if every little girl doesn't learn that right after she learns a straight stitch.'

'It would be an amazing accomplishment for Stephen. He likely couldn't thread a needle.'

She grumbled. 'Don't be so harsh. You almost died. And left the title without an heir, except for your cousin.' She fixed her gaze on him. 'If that unfortunate event were to happen again, and Stephen were to be wed to Guinevere…' Her jaw moved. Then she patted her index finger over her lips again. 'I could see her being a good steward for the legacy. Her children would be…'

She chuckled. 'She might be a little like Catherine the Great, though. She was from another area, wed, her husband died mysteriously, and she kept the country. Guinevere would likely keep Stephen in line.'

'If anyone could, it would be her. But don't plan her future for her.'

'Perhaps she would be a match for you, but I don't see that happening. You'll marry some woman who is well above using a needle. She'll be too busy making sure both she and her dance steps are utterly entrancing.'

He was thankful a woman who knew how to use her brooch pin had been at his side, but his mother needed to keep her counsel. 'Don't try to push me into marriage.'

'I couldn't. That grand feat is beyond me. I gave up years ago.' She chuckled. 'Apparently, I can only push you away from it. And you have to admit, if Stephen inherited the estate, Guinevere is a suitable match for him. A duke's daughter. And marriage would mature him. She would be the mistress of this house. We would get on well.'

'Mother. Funds are set aside for you.'

'I know.' The words were clipped. 'But your father's legacy means something to me. I wanted it to be your heritage as well, and my grandchildren's.'

She put a handkerchief to her eye. 'If only we'd been blessed with more children, but your father and I wed later in life and it wasn't to happen.' She lowered the handkerchief and folded it. 'I suppose Guinevere is too old for you, anyway. She's a few years younger than you.' She let her sigh linger. 'It is sad that one gets so old at such a young age nowadays, but Stephen can't see that. All he sees is how attractive she is.'

Guinevere wasn't too old for him at all. Now, he was certain his mother was matchmaking, but it would do no good. His mother was trying to attribute flaws to Guinevere so he would argue against them.

His mother left the window, her skirts swirling, and stopped beside him. 'I tried to interest her in you, but she would have none of it. Every time I mentioned your name, Stephen interrupted me with some blatant praise for *Guine-vere*. And she paid absolutely no attention to anything I said about you.'

That did get under his skin.

She moved to the door. 'If she can't see the difference in the two of you, then it's on her. But again, she's not for you. Stephen is infatuated with her. And you would hardly want to upset your cousin.'

He didn't respond. She just smiled.

'And he visits you so regularly. I'm sure it's not only to ask you for money. And I'm sure he would be just as attracted to Guinevere if she were a merchant's daughter…like Meg. And yes—' she blinked '—I have heard that Stephen is still courting Meg in between dalliances with others. But—' she put her finger to her lips '—it's a big secret. Stephen would much rather wed someone with society connections. You and I both know that.'

'I didn't know you were aware.'

'Stephen puts on that sweet, guileless look and people believe it. You are very straightfor-ward about not being perfect, Reid. And some days, I wouldn't mind if you pretended a little flawlessness.'

'Of course.' He walked over and kissed her

forehead. 'And here I thought you considered me a saint.'

'I'm your mother. I know you.' She smiled and swatted at him. 'You're too rakish to wed. You could make some woman so happy—if she only spent a brief time with you every other day.'

'I love you, too, Mother,' he said. 'Perhaps a wife should only spend a brief time with me every third day.'

'So, you understand what a marriage to you might require?' She took the sting out of her words with a chuckle.

She left after kissing his cheek. Her footsteps pattered away, leaving him alone.

Reid perused the empty sitting room. But his mind remained on Guinevere.

He could easily understand what Stephen saw in her, and surely she was more pleasant to his cousin. Oh, he was positive of that.

Charging down the stairs, pleased to feel his ease of movement, he sprinted to the stables, and found the gelding not yet saddled. He shrugged away the stableman's apology. 'Hermes needed to be cared for first,' Reid agreed. 'I'll saddle the gelding.'

He assisted the stableman, pleased to make the chore go faster.

He put the blanket on the horse, added the

saddle and tightened the cinch, aware of the strap through his thin leather gloves.

Reid rode through the estate, making sure not to travel in the direction of the stream. Then he moved on to the crossroads tavern for a meal, asking a few questions. Mainly to see how he was greeted.

The place had been empty when he arrived but for the owner, who'd asked of Stephen, and mostly appeared asleep. A few patrons had wandered in, but it appeared they were only there to give a half-greeting, pick up post and leave.

Then he'd travelled to some of the tenants in the area, and it had been difficult to get more than a nod from the people he spoke with.

He didn't understand their reserve, but perhaps he did. They were basically strangers, and they felt it. His friends in London were different. They had good times together. Better times than he'd ever had in the country with his tenants or his cousin.

His grip on the reins momentarily tightened when he remembered Stephen's dismay at the sight of a recovering Reid. The servants' whispers of their plans without him.

Then he reached down and gave the gelding a pat. 'You've earned your oats, but let's go back.'

He returned to the estate after dinnertime,

but his mind travelled straight to his houseguest. With Guinevere in residence, it seemed like he'd arrived home, which was odd. He'd lived there since birth. Nothing should have felt different. He tossed his coat on a chair, then touched the arm where she'd jabbed him with a pin, awakening him.

But he wanted to be alone. To think about what had happened.

Before he'd awoken, he'd been aware of the conversations around him, the words and what they meant. He'd heard them, but it hadn't seemed to matter. As if he found it enlightening to hear people talk candidly and had no awareness of an ability or need to respond, or even an emotional reaction. He'd not even wanted to expend an effort to open his eyes because his mind only absorbed sounds and nothing else. Not feelings, and he'd only awakened when people spoke near him.

At one point, he was aware of the darkness. And he'd recognised Guinevere's voice, wondering what she was doing in his room, and he'd listened to her. He'd never heard music as soothing as her voice had been, and her father had spoken in that irritating, insulting way.

Something soft had brushed his cheek, and Guinevere filled his senses, and he'd started to feel emotions again. To care. He tried to open his eyes to see her, but then he'd faded again, and she'd shrieked. He'd wanted to wake to find out what had unnerved her.

She'd said a few other things next, and called him handsome, and told him goodbye. He'd wanted to ask her to stay. She didn't need to leave.

Then something had stabbed him in the arm, blasting him alert. The gouge had felt like a tremendous bee sting, and he still had a tiny red dot there. It wouldn't scar, but he almost wished it did.

A connection to his memory of her.

Arguing with her was more enjoyable than concurring with anyone else. The servants rather did as instructed. And his friends probably did the same.

He decided he didn't want to be alone in his room after all.

Reid lifted his coat from the chair where he'd tossed it and pulled it on, the fabric rippling before it settled snug against him. He remembered Guinevere wearing it, and paused, hoping to get a reminder of her perfume. Nothing. It had faded, annoying him.

Buttoning the garment, he left the room. Dinner had passed long before, and he would wager a home on the fact that Stephen would be using every moment to impress Guinevere.

Reid usually had no trouble getting a woman to be aware of him, but Guinevere reacted differently. If he'd jested the same nonsense with her that he usually spouted with women, she would have taken it badly. Even before she'd matured, she'd not been impressed by him or anything he did.

Stephen knew how to admire threads and frillies. On Reid, it would sound sarcastic. And likely would be.

Strolling into his mother's sitting room, two pairs of eyes inspected him briefly. The lamplight was bright enough, but he didn't need much to appraise the room.

They greeted him, and Guinevere dedicated her concentration on the chessboard, and Stephen's eyelashes fluttered her direction.

His cousin wasn't completely daft.

Studying Guinevere would be a pleasant way to—oh, he was losing his senses. And so was his mother to think Guinevere was getting older. She had not even achieved her full beauty yet.

He found it odd that he'd been aware of her since their childhood, but never noticed how she'd matured. It disconcerted him, and even that surprised him.

He had nothing to say. No easy banter to add to the room after his brief greeting.

He didn't want to challenge the winner to a game, because truth be told, Stephen had spent hours upon hours at a chessboard, while Reid had been enjoying life. He'd found many more adventurous ways to spend his evening hours than playing a board game, though he'd learned it enough to know he didn't like it.

'Are you well, Reid?' Stephen asked. 'Breakfast this morning. Joining your family in the evening. Results of your accident apparently.'

'I'm my old self. Much better than when I woke hearing details of my passing being discussed.'

That caught Guinevere's attention.

'It was the best option at the time, I assure you,' Reid added.

'No one knew—' she said. 'I hope it doesn't bother you still.'

'I was more irritated with the people around me who kept waking me without their knowledge.' He moved to stand at Stephen's shoulder. 'At first, I didn't know what had happened, and then I'd remember and forget again. The last thing I could recall initially was arriving at the estate.'

'Your accident was soon afterwards.'

'It's all stamped in my memory now, and I don't think I could forget it if I wanted.'

'All of it?' Guinevere asked.

'Yes.' He shrugged while Stephen slid his knight up two and over one. A terrible decision to move that chess piece. But Stephen had had to make it or he could have ended the contest in one more move.

'The last game before everyone goes to bed?' Reid asked, noting that her mother had not remained as a chaperon.

'Why, yes,' Guinevere said, surprised. 'Stephen has given me a chance to even the score.'

'A man of honour, my cousin.'

Stephen's eyes fixed on Reid, and he agreed. 'Of course. I'm playing just as you'd do tonight.'

Reid nodded in acknowledgement of the slight. 'Not entirely, I'm sure. I would have continued it longer. That was a poor move. Particularly for someone as experienced as you.'

Stephen snorted out a startled laugh.

'Distracted by your challenger's beauty, which is only surpassed by her intellect, I'm sure.' Reid bowed to Guinevere. 'True words.'

'Of course,' Stephen added, his glare for his cousin alone.

Guinevere frowned, dismissed Reid with a glance, and her hand wavered over the bishop.

'I can't win a game because you played less than your skills, Stephen. As Reid so graciously pointed out.'

He felt a pang. He'd not meant to make Guinevere feel bad for her lack of skills, and if he had to compliment his cousin to correct the error, he would.

'Stephen is the best chess player I've ever seen,' he reassured her.

'I was merely distracted by the presence of Guinevere.'

He had to agree with his mother. His cousin put entirely too much emphasis on her name.

'I believe you should move your knight to its original spot, and have another move allotted.' She took the piece and placed it in the previous square. She smiled at Reid—or at least, the corners of her lips moved up.

He remembered what she'd said about smiling at him. *Good move*, he told her with his eyes.

'After all, it is only a game,' she continued. 'And we are both tired. And I am touched that Stephen would play gently to assist me.'

'You are more than just, Lady Guinevere,' Stephen said, and moved a bishop. The thought process had taken him all of half a blink.

'I believe I'll retire to my sitting room,' Reid said. 'This game is too intense for me.'

But it wasn't the game that was intense. It was Guinevere's regard.

He'd definitely made an error by speaking, but seeing Stephen practically swooning at her across the table had irked him.

And he somehow had a feeling she would not let his comments float away, forgotten about.

She would correct him. And that pleased him.

He barely heard the sound. A soft rap on his sitting room door.

Raising his head from his hands, he surveyed the area. His boots had been tossed through the doorway nearer his bed, along with the stockings. His coat had been placed on a chair by the door. The cravat had fallen beside it.

He buttoned his waistcoat, knowing it would be Guinevere because Stephen would have strutted in, with a goose-like waggle of his head, and probably got himself thrown out.

Opening the door, he bowed and swept out his arm, indicating she enter.

She shook her head.

'Guinevere.' He could have done that as well as Stephen if he wanted, but instead he pronounced her name with an edge. He liked the crispness he could give it. 'I see no reason to raise eyebrows in our families.' He indicated she step inside. 'Or wake anyone and cause needless interpretation of our discussion. My sitting room is more private.'

'You are barefoot. Half dressed.'

'But it's the right half.' He was not going to give her a chance to decide to leave while he put on his cravat or boots or coat.

She moved into the room, and kept her hand on the door, pushing as if to shut it, but leaving it open about the width of her body.

'It was rude for you to point out the errors in the game and assume I could not win it on my own.'

'I stand corrected. In my bare feet.'

She huffed.

'Why did you assume that I needed his mistake pointed out to me?' she asked, not budging. 'Only a person who didn't know the game at all would have chosen that move.'

'Stephen wasn't doing a great job of letting you win, and it just irked me that he couldn't seem to take his eyes off you long enough to even see the pieces.'

'I would say losing a game is not his skill. Chess appears to be a talent for him, but he doesn't know how to make poor moves appear on purpose.'

'You knew?' he asked. 'You grasped he was not playing to win?'

'When it was his turn, he barely glanced at the board and spent more time chatting with me, and then he would play. I made an incredibly bad move earlier which would have normally ended the game, and he didn't seem to notice.'

She skewered him with her gaze.

'You were playing to lose?' he asked.

'Yes. I should have just captured his king and ended it, but he seemed to take such pride in his chess skills, and it didn't matter to me if I won or lost. I'd given a fair showing earlier and that was enough for me.'

He didn't believe Guinevere would exaggerate her skills, and Stephen was the best chess player he knew.

'He has only stayed because you're here.'

'You don't think he would have stayed just to make sure you're well? He apologised to me for his actions when he arrived. He said he'd been convinced you had been jesting with him.'

Reid glowered to let her know what he thought of that idea. 'Did you ever hear how he says your name?'

'Like it's pronounced?'

'If you say so.'

'Stephen may like me, but I'm generally likeable so I have no problem with that.'

'Does he truly see you?'

'You're being rude again.'

'Yes. But are you being as straightforward with him as you tend to be?'

If *Guinevere* preferred Stephen, Reid would have no problem with that. They could disparage him together as their bishops and knights danced on their happy wooden bases.

He could imagine it. Stephen would propose. They would stare adoringly into each other's eyes and have a brood of children who would inherit his estate.

Her shoulders rose, and she reminded him of a goddess. Not the pleasant, happy kind, but an appealing one nonetheless. Perhaps an ancient Roman one who discovered someone had left his lightning bolts lying around and was gathering them in her arms to reprimand him with.

'You are being unfair to yourself, and to him, in concealing this part of you,' he said. 'Besides—'

He'd almost told her Stephen would be entranced with her anyway. 'Besides, it isn't for me to pass judgement.'

'True. How would you feel if I passed judgement on you?'

'Don't you? I could have sworn you have for most of our lives.'

'Well, yes,' she admitted. 'I suppose it's human nature. And I've always had the impression you think you're better than everyone else.'

'I have more responsibility than most. A lot of livelihoods depend on me. People's meals. My mother's lifestyle.'

'That doesn't mean you can't be nice.'

'I can't. People will not accept my authority otherwise. They want leadership.'

'You can be kind, even as you maintain your position.'

'It's not possible.'

'I disagree.'

'To keep control of the world around me, and spread posies for all to sniff? Hard truths must be delivered without compromise. People must not be allowed to embroider them into other words. They must know exactly what is being said.'

'You could say what you mean much more pleasantly.'

'It will only make it harder for the listeners to understand the authority. They will question the decision. The knowledge of it. And some of them might not even be able to grasp the explanation.' He heard the irritation in his voice and quelled it.

'I know what people think of me,' he assured her. 'Better than most. As I have told you before, I had the honour of hearing the butler and maid discuss preparations for the celebration they were going to have after the physician had assured them I would not awaken. They planned to drink my best wine, to dance, and celebrate.' His eyes narrowed. 'Wine I had saved for a special occasion. Definitely a different special occasion.'

'Sometimes people do such to lessen their grief.'

'Not in this case,' he said.

'Does that not tell you anything?'

'Yes. It told me I needed a new butler but you said I should keep him. He's docile. Harmless. And does what he needs to do without fuss. You were right about not sacking him. It would be time-consuming and accomplish nothing, except training someone new—to drink my wine.'

'Perhaps you should be agreeable, like your cousin—even though, I admit, he does agree too often sometimes.'

'I'm too much like him already.'

'You are nothing like Stephen,' she said. 'I cannot believe the two of you are even related.'

'That may be the best thing you've ever said to me.'

'You don't really care for me. Do you? You might want to talk to me in the night when no one else is about, but it's more of a summons than a request.' She puffed her cheeks, and mimicked someone else speaking. '"Mmm. I'm lonely. Guinevere won't mind being kept awake half the night."'

'Did you mind?' he asked, concerned he'd not been aware of her feelings. 'If so, I apologise.'

The words caused her feathers to unruffle.

'Not really,' she admitted. 'It was a nice diversion. But I think you should consider how others feel about things.'

'I will attempt it.'

'So, will you answer my question? Do you dislike me?'

'Can we say, at the very least, I dislike you less than I dislike anyone else who expresses strong opinions counter to mine. Even though they're mostly wrong.'

'Ooh.' Her eyes sparkled mirth. 'They must think you're a gentleman, outstanding, and a veritable treasure.'

'Not entirely. But funds and a title smooth the opinions somewhat.'

She pondered his words. 'True. Fortunate you.'

'I agree.' His hand brushed his shoulder, over the spot she'd pricked, before he continued speaking.

'And what of you, Guinevere? Is it beyond you to speak your mind with everyone else as you do with me?'

'I do. I have kind thoughts for everyone but you.'

'I've never done anything wrong to you. Since that once. Or perhaps twice. And—'

'I'm sure if we spend more time together, you'll make it three.'

'That isn't said in your usual generous spirit. And since my accident I have been considering my actions more.'

'I also owe you an apology,' she said. 'If I have offended you, please forgive me.'

To hear those words coming from her mouth pained him more than making an admission of his own errors.

It reminded him that he'd been a boy and unkind to her. He took her hand and held it, clasped at his heart. 'I beg your pardon for saying no one would ever want to kiss a woman with such a big mouth, and feet as large as yours. I was a youth. That was my first phaeton. You were wearing your brother's outgrown boots, and I didn't like my new vehicle being compared to them.'

'I liked those boots.'

'I liked that phaeton until you walked around it telling everyone all that was wrong with it.'

'It could have been painted better.'

'You were right, Guinevere. Everything you said was right. Which I discovered when you pointed it out to me—and my friends.'

'And I learned from that moment on to be more careful with my words,' she said. 'I saw how you reacted, and I certainly didn't like being criticised. And my brother and his friends laughed about it for a long time.'

She mumbled. 'I'd rather hoped his best friend might notice me. I was trying to be as wise about vehicles as they were, and I thought Lord Elmire was *so* handsome with his wavy hair. I got over it, of course, and am ever so grateful I did. But at the time—'

'Lord Elmire?' He almost coughed out the words. He would never understand the feminine mind. 'You thought him handsome?'

'Yes. I did.' Her chin went up. Eyes challenged.

'Well, if you thought him attractive, and I had known it, it would have taken some of the sting out of your assessment of my vehicle. Our views were different.'

'Very.'

'Later, I suppose I should have asked you to dance at some of the events, and asked forgiveness, but I knew you wouldn't accept.'

'I was relieved not to have your attention. It is difficult to refuse a dance pleasantly, or an offer of refreshment.'

And she was so compassionate to other people. 'Oh, come now. Please do not tell me you could not do that?'

'I don't like to hurt others. I learned my lesson.'

'Neither do I, but bluntness is required in my life. And how unlike you to assume I like to injure others.'

Anger sparked behind her eyes, but she didn't answer him.

'Your opinion of me,' he asked. 'How has it been formed?'

She touched her chest. 'You cannot say that I have a wrong view of you. You agree with my assessment.'

'Not your statement that I enjoy wounding others. I don't.' He paused. 'The best way to have a good understanding of words is to speak plainly and without embroidering little hearts around them.'

He frowned and made a few imagined stitches in the air. 'I no more want to be a gracious-appearing poltroon than I could be…a posy gatherer.' He had no interest in walking around with an armful of flowers to give out to all he encountered, and he didn't really know what a posy was but surely she did.

'Or kind?' Her brows rose.

'I am kind by saying the truth. As an adult. I never again admired that phaeton.'

'You shouldn't have. But I wore those ugly boots until my mother took them from my room.'

'You shouldn't have worn them the first time.'

'I got reprimanded if I ruined my slippers in the mud, but at first Mother didn't mind about the boots, and they were mostly hidden under my old skirt.'

'No. You kept lifting the skirt hem to run through the mud.'

'If boys were allowed to get their boots dirty, then I thought it only fair I do the same.'

'Life is not like that.'

He was glad she wasn't wearing a scabbard and a sword or he would have possibly been run through.

'I don't see it that way.'

'We are at a standstill. And some disagreements can never be resolved.' But he didn't want to think they'd reached that point, or would continue to it.

He paused. 'Meet me in the portrait gallery tomorrow night after everyone is abed, and that will give you all day to think of examples to convince me of the benefits of posy words.'

She surveyed him, her arm muscles tense, and she took in a breath. 'No. I will not meet you tomorrow night.' She prepared to leave.

'Except perhaps I relish sparring with you,' he said, 'and you take that as my enjoyment of being forceful with the people around me.'

'Sparring…' She stepped outside, the click of the door closing seeming a challenge.

But then it opened again.

Her head poked around it. 'And can I tell you a secret?' she asked. 'One you must promise to keep?'

She waited. He could do nothing but agree.

'I will.'

'I expect that I'm as skilled as Stephen at chess.'

She tucked her tongue in her cheek. 'And I can probably be just as good as you are at being disagreeable. Thank you for telling me you enjoy sparring with me. Next time, I may not let you win.'

The door snapped again. He took a step to his changing room. The vixen.

The door opened behind him again, and he peered over his shoulder.

'Portrait gallery after breakfast,' she said, and the door clicked behind her.

She would not be a suitable bride for Stephen.

But she would be a suitable bride for him.

Chapter Five

Guinevere noted that she couldn't ever remember Reid having breakfast with the family until this visit.

Reid sat at the head of the table while they ate, and Stephen sat across from her. Stephen suggested over and over that they spend the day together and she'd kept brushing his ideas away.

She glanced across at Reid once, catching his eye, and he'd seemed to point out with his innocence that he'd suggested they meet later instead of earlier for a reason. To avoid his cousin.

Reid's mother had implored Stephen to help her with a musical piece she'd been studying and since he was so gifted with music, no one else could offer the same assistance as he.

Stephen irritated her after a few hours, and Reid added sparks inside her. She didn't really understand how one man could stir so much awareness and fascination. But just because something appealed to her, it didn't mean it was harmless.

When she was young, one night she'd put a flickering coal in a glass, and took it outside, blowing on it, adding oak leaves into the heat while savouring the scent. It had been fun until she'd burned her finger. She'd been in pain, but she'd managed to put out the fire and hide the evidence—and she'd had to suffer in silence because she'd been doing something wrong.

It seemed she was doing the same thing now, risking pain for a fascination. The leaves had smelled so good, but not as enticing as Reid's leather and male cleanliness.

After their meal, she stepped inside the portrait gallery, and he was only moments behind her.

The familiar room, furnished with only two chairs, a table for a lamp between them and the cabinet from bygone days, had always appeared larger to her, but now that Reid was inside, she noticed it was hardly more than a hallway.

The room had been more nursery than gallery when she'd visited as a child. Now she saw it differently, but at the time it had been an adventurous place. She and her sister had played there. His mother had had simple cloth dolls made for them, and a cradle for the toys. The two chairs would be removed, and they'd been allowed to play unsupervised, and it seemed a new plaything was always being added for them.

She spied the door behind which the playthings had been stored, left for them to have easy access to.

Without thinking, she moved to the cabinet, crouched and opened the door. There was only a folded scarf inside.

Disappointed, she reached for the other door, but she hit her thumbnail on it, and bent it. Pain surged. 'Oh, blunder,' she said, shaking her hand.

She hesitated, not wanting to show weakness, then opened the cabinet. The one where they'd found the books and they'd been able to read the stories. She saw the spines she remembered.

Pulling one out, she held it for him to see.

'I wonder what those are doing there,' he said. 'Those are from my schoolroom days. My tutor used them to teach me to read.'

She ran a hand over the cover. 'Your mother put them here for my sister and me. This was our playroom when our parents visited.'

'I must have been away at school. I don't remember your being here.'

'My sister and I relished being in this room,'

she said, glancing around, letting her memories flourish.

'Here?' He didn't appear able to believe her.

'Yes.'

'I never liked the portrait gallery. Still don't. All the faces staring from the walls. A gaol.'

'They were an audience if we acted charades. That's what we were told anyway.'

His eyes swept the room. 'I can't see Great-aunt Hester and Uncle Milford being pleasant onlookers for children's activities.'

'They were. And a maid would bring us sweet rolls more often than not. And it was grand. Once a maid pulled the hem of the draperies over the table, and added another, and told us we could play in the caves—just to take care we didn't harm anything.'

She moved to the curtains, and let the cloth slide against her hand, feeling the nubs of the weave, and her mind locking on the past.

'To be in this room would have been punishment for me,' he said. 'I rode horses when my lessons were finished.'

She dropped the cloth. 'My sister and I could have stayed at home when our parents visited. But because of the portrait gallery, we would ask to come along when we were young. And your mother would give us such confections. It was as if she would leave treasures in here for us to find. Presents, wrapped in paper with our names on them. Once there were notes directing us all about the estate, and we'd find another note at each place we ran to, until we ended up under a tree where a maid waited with tea.'

She shook her head. 'It was the usual tea, and all, but it was grand, we thought.'

'I wouldn't even know you were here.'

'Father insisted if we were to travel with them that we must be well mannered.'

'I would often get a set-down after your father's visit.'

She examined his face.

He nodded. 'Yes. Your father has never liked me. He told my father about some of my activities. I suppose he'd heard from your brother. And I had been a little out of control, but still, I didn't like your father mentioning it to mine, and my being punished.'

She heard the grit in his voice and remembered her father saying that Reid's death might be for the best.

'My father is a good man.'

'True,' he agreed. 'Doesn't mean we get on well.'

'When you were hurt, did you hear every single word said around you?'

'Enough.' His eyes shuttered. 'Thank you for saying I was handsome and that I needed a shave.' He rubbed his chin.

'I didn't know you could hear.'

She remembered her father discussing Reid's death. 'It must have been difficult for you. Listening.'

'Not at all. I didn't much care, one way or the other, what was said, or what happened. It was a kind of serenity, or only half awareness.'

'I don't believe you heard a lot of praise.'

'I could have told you what people would have said beforehand if I had wanted to. I wouldn't have been wrong. Just because they say it, doesn't make it my truth.'

'But you're not saying it's a lie. Or inaccurate.'

'People don't always know what's best for them. In fact, I might say the opposite is more often correct. Think of it.'

'My parents taught me to act on my best interests. Not of the moment. But of the future.'

'Then why are you spending time with Stephen?'

'Perhaps he is good for me. And I for him.' Even as she said the words, something sheared in her heart. The feeling of telling a lie. Of doubt in her words.

And his eyes mocked her.

'He is your cousin. Upstanding. Pleasant. Polite,' she added. 'And you can't say that he is not.'

'I would question that he's upstanding. And
he's definitely not always pleasant to me. But I
suppose one out of three isn't bad. He's the person everyone but my mother hoped was inheriting.'

'And therein lies the rub.'

'No. Again, people do not always know the
facts or how they will affect them until it is too
late. I don't want the same for you.'

'Can you tell me a truth about him? More
than what you have already said? Something not
pierced with jealousy. I don't know him well,
but he is as acquainted with my family as you
are. His parents were not as friendly with mine
as yours was, but the families have known each
other since before our grandparents were born.'

'I am not jealous of him. I would say it is more
the opposite.'

'He has only good things to say about you.'

He kept his face bland, but his eyes looked
heavenward, before fixing his gaze on her again.
'That might prove he's not to be trusted.'

'It might prove he has discretion.'

'You are letting an infatuation colour your
thoughts.'

'No. I'm not.' She wasn't enamoured of Stephen. She just wasn't. And she realised it when she spoke with Reid.

Stephen would always be second best, but safer. Reid would always be flaring coal next to the oak leaves, and she didn't need to get closer to know he was explosive for her.

'Now that I think of it,' she said. 'I must agree that people don't usually know what is best for them. Or if they do, they don't heed it.'

'You will not be letting Stephen court you, then?'

'I'm not being courted by any individual right now. And if that changes, it will be my concern, not yours.'

'Anyone but Stephen. He's not for you, Guinevere.'

'I don't plan for anything further with my friendship to him. But he is the best chess player I've seen.'

'It's one game I'll never understand,' he said.

'It's not for everyone.'

'I can agree it might be right for you,' he said. 'But what else do you want in your life?'

'I'm content with things as they are, which seems to annoy my mother.'

'Perhaps it should.'

'You have a legacy to your title and I understand that. I don't. My brother will carry on my father's. My duty is to care for the home and family.'

He glanced five different directions, all of them around her. 'Just looking for your home and your children.'

'Family. I assist my mother and help her care for our home. I'm a dutiful daughter and happy to be so.'

'I'm a dutiful son,' he said, a wide sweeping wave indicating the house. 'But what of your own legacy?'

'I've never thought of it,' she said.

'Well, perhaps you should.'

'If this is another sparring match,' she said, 'I concede loss.'

'Don't,' he said. 'When you do not appear to have victory, carry the competition on to another day.'

'If you insist.'

'In this case, I do. Besides, it will give me another chance to solve a puzzle I don't understand. There is something about you that is right in front of me but I can't figure out. It's like a word or a name I should know but don't.'

'What do you mean?'

'When I discover it, I'll be sure to inform you,' he said.

'Even if it's unkind?'

'Do you think it could be?'

'I hope not.' She held her chin high.

But perhaps Reid had a point. 'I'll think about my legacy,' she said. No one but Reid asked such questions of her, and besides, they would be going their separate ways the next day. 'Even if it is a long time before we meet again.'

Her father had decided to return to London tomorrow. Reid would be in her past, even though he'd never truly been a part of her life.

'Guinevere.'

Reid spoke her name, making it sound as if it hardly had the right amount of syllables. And it sounded harsh, as if he didn't like to say the word, which irked her.

'Yes?' She appraised him, and he didn't look angry, more bemused.

Reid walked to her side. 'Let's go see if Orange is chasing birds.'

'Do you really care?'

He paused. 'The birds would probably escape.'

'About walking with me?'

'Do you think I would have mentioned it if I didn't want to?'

She didn't answer, but went with him. 'Why?'

'Now you are beginning to sound more like me, which is an improvement.'

'I sup—pose.'

He chuckled. 'Perhaps we should remain silent for a moment, to give ourselves more time to regroup and draw our verbal swords.'

'I don't think either of us need that.'

A smile glimmered behind his lips, otherwise she would have thought he didn't hear her.

Together they walked outside, and she enjoyed it because the companionship felt different than what she would have expected.

Orange was nowhere to be found, so instead, Reid took her on a stroll along the rutted road to the fields.

'Guin, I fear you are too lenient. How will you ever take care of a household? The servants will be lax and you won't be able to reprimand them or let them go.'

He stopped in the shade of a tree, put his hand against the bark and waited for her reply, knowing she would not give him agreement. He'd always appreciated femininity, but he'd never met a woman who seemed to place so little stock in fluttering about, and still wanted to be agreeable to people. Someone who would take so much argument from him, and not want to change the subject to something frivolous or flirtatious or agree with him just to quiet him.

'Good people do not need halters to guide them,' she informed him.

'Straight talk aims people in the right direction.'

'You can employ good people and let them have the reins. They do well. It's what they were hired to do.'

'Easy to say, but motivation helps. And a person when interviewed can appear a saint and industrious, but once their job becomes routine, they become complacent. Much like a suitor could do.'

'True. And if the suitor is a wee amount irritable to begin with, can you imagine how that could proceed?' She shuddered, giving a mocking horrified glance at him.

'But who would dare be irritable when a suitor?' he asked. 'Better to keep the distance.'

'For both sides.'

He positioned himself a little closer to her and spoke as if they were in a ballroom with a thousand ears listening, and he wanted only her to hear.

'But what if the annoying suitor irritated you and intrigued you at the same time?'

'Oh, then that is a dilemma, and best avoided. You could be intrigued by a venomous snake, or a sleeping bear in a menagerie, or a cutpurse with a winning way. Best not get too close.'

'But if the bear is tame and the cutpurse is not willing to risk a noose?'

'Then you'd still best watch out for the snake.' She hissed.

'Well, I must be pleased you're not a snake, a bear or a cutpurse.' He laughed. Crinkles formed at his eyes. His lips turned up. And she was unable to take her gaze from him, her heart galloping ahead of them.

He was handsome to begin with, even though it was a dry kind of handsome. One you shouldn't put much stock in, and one meant to be cautious around. But when he laughed, she melted inside.

'Did you just pretend to be a snake?'

'No.' She let her voice rise in mock denial. 'I was merely showing you how dangerous I am not.'

He touched her arm, blasting a new form of awareness into her. 'I would think you could almost be lethal.'

He was the lethal one. He probably had Cupid for a friend, and Michelangelo's spirit had likely given his creator instructions on just how to design him for viewing. Forget wasting effort on marble sculptures. Time to put all the design into one human.

She looked to the horizon. Blast it. She was fanciful. Reid was a marquess who'd been indulged much too much and enjoyed a verbal joust. This was a chess game to him. One he was skilled at and would keep prolonging until his opponent accepted loss.

She pursed her lips, lowered her chin and let the edges of her lips rise. She patted the top of his knuckles. 'I think *lethal* might be too mild a word for you.'

He laughed again, a more robust humour this time.

Frustration poured into her, but not the right kind. She wanted to be angry. To really be upset with him, but it was impossible with the twinkle in his eyes.

'You do not argue fairly,' she said.

'And where are these argument rules written?'

'They're unwritten rules. Life is full of them. You know that.'

'I do,' he said.

'You know which ones you can bend to your advantage.'

He nodded. 'I'm fine with that. And what of you? Do you not know which ones you can bend?'

'I prefer to follow rules. It's more comfortable for me.'

'I'm sure.' He shrugged her words away. 'You wouldn't be who you are, otherwise. Old Scratch would toss you back, because you would be annoying him by trying to make everyone in Hades reform and spend their time doing charitable works for each other.'

His mouth twitched. 'I can just hear you telling people to ignore their situation and look about them and find a way to lighten the load for others because they were distressed. And if everyone pulled together—' his head cocked to the side '—hell would be a much more pleasant place.'

She paused. 'It would be quite an accomplishment to reform the rake.'

'Don't look at me so earnestly when you say that.'

'I was only thinking.'

'I know that. Be careful of it. Can ruin a good time.'

'True. And probably much easier for a hellion to alter the angels.'

'If he is a fool.' His gaze penetrated. 'Everyone needs an angel on their side.'

Chapter Six

He grasped what he'd just said, and the pleased tilt of her chin. But it was true. Annoying though she may be, the sweetness inside her soothed something he'd not known to be a part of him.

'I should return to the house,' she said.

'Why?'

'If Mother should start searching for me, I don't want to give her the impression you and I are becoming attached to each other.'

'She would survive.' He stopped, picking up a dead branch from a tree, and tossing it beside the path. Someone might be along later to collect it for cook wood.

'But I wouldn't want her to be concerned where it isn't warranted.'

'You've been courted before, I'm sure.' They resumed their stroll.

'As you said, a title and funds help, and my father has both.'

'But those will go to your eldest brother.'

'Yes, and the estate will be big enough for me to live there.'

'Your sister-in-law might not welcome you.'

'We're close. I love her dearly. But it doesn't matter.' She stopped, clasped her hands behind her back like a tutor and questioned him. 'What is the difference between living with a sister-in-law you might not get on well with, or a husband? I could leave my brother's home more freely than I could a mate's.'

He acknowledged her words with the barest lift of his brows. 'And what happened with your courtships?'

'They're continuing.'

He felt that someone had taken one of his boots and slapped it across his face.

'Someone is courting you?'

'Not anyone specifically. Carriage rides. Walks. Visits in the gardens, occasionally. When I get asked, I usually accept, and take a chaperon. I've had interesting conversations about many different topics. Some serious. Most frivolous. You have to admit, it is a change from stitchery. Mother complains that suitors are my pastime.'

Her eyes sparkled with humour, and her chin went up.

'What are your qualifications for a serious suitor that causes all these men to fall short?' he asked.

'That would be a private matter.'

'Do you even know?'

'Gentle. Kind-hearted. Respectful. Faithful. Loving.'

'Are you sure you don't want a pet instead of a husband?'

'And if I were to ask you the same thing?'

He stopped, broke a bloom from the bush and handed it to her. 'She would be understanding of my duties, and her own, and know those came first and foremost. My inheritance is my legacy and I must have it to pass to my own children. She is to support me in that regard.'

She held the flower close to her nose, but it was a weed. It had no scent except of greenery where the stem had broken. Not all things that were beautiful were perfect.

'Duties before the people they are to protect?'

'Many people depend on me for their livelihoods. The roofs over their head. The clothes they wear. I cannot put that aside, and it's important for me to have a child to train to take over in my stead. I always thought I had all the time in the world, and now I can see that might not be the case. Particularly if I would like to be there to tell him how to conduct business.'

'Are you certain he would not rebel against you?'

'He might. His loss. Truly. His loss of financial footing. A title with a withering entailed estate is not nearly as refreshing as a title with a thriving endeavour, servants, carriages and, of course, horses.'

'I can understand that,' she said. 'You do have a considerable responsibility. Much like my father.' She returned the bloom to him. 'My parents always tell me that I'm fortunate that I was born female and in the role I have. My father and brother handle the responsibilities. I am cherished by my family. Some days my biggest decision is if someone calls on me, whether I should go for a carriage ride in the morning or afternoon, or what I should embroider on a handkerchief.'

'Don't you want more? A sense of accomplishing a larger goal?'

'I'm happy to leave those to other people. Besides, sometimes they need a little assistance, and I'm free to offer it. My sister or sister-in-law might need help with planning an event. Or feel overwhelmed. I will assist with the children when the nursery maid is indisposed or help delegate when the housekeeper visits family.'

'Shouldn't you have your own life, though?'

'I do. Perhaps my legacy is to be smaller. Think of a great singer, with a great voice, and singing in an empty room. More audience members are needed in life than singers. I am the applause, the encouragement, and I try to raise others up.'

'And you are content with that?'

'Yes. Absolutely. In fact, it's bothering me to be away from London. My little nephews are adorable, and I wanted to see the eldest on his third birthday. He's such a clever little one, and a handful.'

He could see the affection for the boys in her eyes. A gentleness that he wouldn't have minded having directed at him. He saw a different person than he'd seen previously, and one that smoothed its way inside a man, lodging in places that it couldn't be removed or forgotten.

Now his vision kept returning to the silhouette of her neck. Her skin. Its softness.

Her face might be firm when she studied him, but the rest of her exuded a womanliness that surrounded him like a cloak of desire and he couldn't move without it whispering into him.

'The brush with death has made me aware of my mortality, and the need to train someone to take over in my stead should something happen.'

'Then you are fortunate to have someone as intelligent as Stephen as second in line to be the Marquess should you not have an heir or time to groom him. And this seems to prove my point. The people in the background have their own roles.'

'You have a point. But Stephen isn't really the person I wish to follow me.' He tossed the words to the side, knowing they would wilt before she took stock of them. Much like he'd done with his romances of the past.

'Have you no words of uplifting audience applause for me?' he asked.

'No. You've had too much in your life.'

'How can you be so sure?'

'I have seen you on occasion since I have known you practically the whole of my life. The praise you criticise me for giving to others is the same deference you demand from those around you. I daresay you do not recognise anyone who isn't subservient to you. You barely acknowledge my father and he is a duke.'

'I respect his position.'

'But you do not like him.'

'Is that a crime? He was always spouting some nonsense to my father that I was too young for this or that, or I should be disciplined more, or should be made to apply myself to lessons. I didn't need to study more. My man-of-affairs needed to be studious. My staff needed to do their job, and if I directed them well, I had more time to go where I wished. A carriage wouldn't run well if all parts of it were wheels.'

'You have never got on well with my father or brother.'

'Your brother. As much as your father believes he trained him…' He shook his head. 'He is likely to fritter away what's left of your father's fortune once he gets his hands on it.'

'Father is guiding him well.'

'To applaud others? That will not keep the coffers full. It is one thing for you to do, but—'

He would have thought he'd just stepped on Orange's tail or put another flock of fowl under Hermes's feet.

'Shall we return to the house?' She was three steps on her way before she finished the question, only it was less of a question than a slap.

And he'd said it was appropriate for her. Only he could tell she'd not taken it well. It was an agreement with her statements, but she wasn't understanding it that way.

* * *

Their steps were the only sounds shared between them.

And he felt it best to retreat while her temper cooled.

When they arrived at the outer doorway, his fingers skimmed her elbow, stopping her. 'I would like to call on you when you're in London, and see how this frivolousness is proceeding. Perhaps I erred.'

'Can you be pleasant?'

'What I consider pleasant might not be the same as your definition.'

She let out a soft, regretful sigh, and blinked, before dropping her head and raising it to give him a spectacularly demure smile, and one with a delightful touch of wickedness. 'True. And what I consider an interesting evening might not include you.'

She might as well have said, *Checkmate.*

'I would hope to change your mind.'

'I would hope that as well, but I would not expect it.'

She walked inside.

He'd intended to return to the stables, but he couldn't step away from her. He had to see her safely to her room. Or just look at her a moment longer.

He followed her, and someone said, *I apologise*, and he knew the words came from his mouth but it didn't sound like his voice.

She addressed him, chin up. 'Accepted.' Then she clapped her palms together. Slowly. Three times.

Reid raised an eyebrow. 'You should have been your father's firstborn son.'

'I would have still been considerate.'

'Oh, hell, no. You would have fisted your sweet little hand, and it would have collided with my jaw. And broken a few bones. In your hand.'

'Only if I hit that hard head of yours.'

'You're more like me than you want to admit.'

'Oh, no. People like me.'

He cocked his head. 'The right people answer to me.'

'You could be correct in the statement that if I were a man I would have clouted you, though I hope not. And if I had broken my hand, I would have made sure to have done so on your jaw. A courtesy. So, you would have had trouble speaking and a chance to think before you did so.'

'It wouldn't matter if I'm conversing with you, as you pay no attention.'

Her father stepped from the sitting room. 'Guinevere. Reid. What are you two fussing about?'

'He said…that… I should have been your firstborn son. That I would manage your business well. I applauded him for his observation.'

'Why did you say that?' he asked Reid.

'Because she thinks she's being pleasant all the time, and she's likely to stab an injured man if she thinks he should answer her, insist on setting a time for a meeting and silently letting him know she will not show up if it is not at the time she directed, and offering applause with as much force as a man could punch another.'

The Duke glowered. 'Guinevere is a gentle soul. Don't suggest otherwise.'

'With all her gentleness, she is determined to get her way.'

'She is nothing like that. Guinevere is a—'

'Father.' She raised a hand, stopping him, and then addressed Reid. 'I am only direct with a few, few people who require it.'

He appraised her. 'And you just quietened your father, His Grace.'

Neither spoke.

He addressed the Duke. 'I suspected something different about her earlier and I couldn't work it out until this moment. It was on the tip of my tongue, but I couldn't see it. And no one in society knows it. Even her. You raised an iron fist in a delicate frame. She is a secret weapon of strength that no one has defences against.'

Taking in a breath, and focusing his full attention on her, he said, 'Lady Guinevere, I *have* obviously offended you, and I beg your pardon. Until I said the words, I didn't realise the strength of character that you have. The strength of your mind. Whatever it is you are doing, continue to do so.'

The Duke's eyes switched between her and Reid, and he appeared to have swallowed a word he wouldn't utter in his daughter's presence.

'We will be leaving tomorrow,' the Duke said.

'Are you sure you would not like to stay longer,' Reid asked, but it wasn't really a question, and her father had already answered it with the tightness of his expression.

'Positive,' her father answered, his eyes glinting like a ray of light on a sword blade.

'Then let's have a bonfire tonight,' Reid said. 'I can have the servants bring trays of food to serve us, and drinks, and we can watch the night sky together. Perhaps we'll see a shooting star. It will be a treat for Mother and the Duchess. Mother hasn't had dinner like that since before Father passed.'

He felt he was asking for his life, and he didn't understand why it was so important for him that he see her that night. She was Guinevere, now all grown up and appearing an illusion of womanliness—the daughter of a man whom he had never liked and with whose family he had had a passing acquaintance because a friendship wasn't possible. And a woman whom he suspected was the cleverest person he'd ever met.

'Let's watch the stars. With a large fire blazing. All of us,' Guinevere said.

She took a step towards His Grace, and Reid could see the tension leaving her father as he considered her words. 'Well…'

'Perhaps it will give the Marchioness and Mother a pleasant memory to have of this time. It began so unhappily, and it would be pleasant to end it with a quiet celebration.'

'I'll have preparations started,' Reid suggested.

'Fine.' Her father waved a hand, dismissing Reid, and left.

'You are a rare person.' Reid spoke softly.

'Is that meant as a compliment?'

'Compliments do not do you justice.'

Something was happening when he stood near Guinevere and kept entreating him to return to her. One more harmless look. One more meaningless disagreement. One more moment.

All because she had stabbed him with a pin.

A prod that had awakened him and continued to stir him. He recalled the shock in her eyes when she'd been above him, and the surprise he'd felt. When he saw her now, he viewed her as the first woman he'd ever seen.

'That is what else I couldn't grasp earlier, Guinevere. It fits with the attraction of chess. Of strategy. You are more than a match for any man, and whether you admit it or not, you've not wanted to tie yourself to a lesser being. That's why you've not wed.'

'You're decidedly silver-tongued when you wish to be.'

'Years of practice.'

He walked by her on his exit and saw the smallest wisp of her hair move when he spoke. 'And you have not needed practice. You were born knowing how to charm. You could even talk a man into questioning everything he's ever believed in.'

He stared into her eyes. 'Neither he nor you would even know it was occurring.'

Guinevere watched him leave, the shoulders broad, and the walk relaxed, unhurried, fluid. Some men kicked their feet out to the side when they walked, led with their arms, had a rolling gait, were hurried or slow, and Reid did none of that.

There wasn't anything particular about his movement, except his assuredness, and she didn't understand how he accomplished that except by not adding actions into it.

And while it never occurred to her that others might be thinking while walking away from her—as her own mind usually wandered to her conclusions about the conversation or the day— she did with Reid.

When he disappeared from view the feeling of aloneness that surrounded her in his wake jarred her.

He'd played on her father's sympathies to get his way, knowing it would be hard to refuse giving the Marchioness and the Duchess a chance to relive happy times and memories.

She put a fingertip to her lips. Not many men could match a duke for assuredness, but Reid did.

And a marquess was of lesser rank than a duke, but you really couldn't tell it by watching Reid.

She thought of a duke's younger son who half-heartedly partnered her whenever they encountered each other at a dance. He did everything indifferently.

Reid didn't. He put more intent in the raise of

an eyebrow than the other man put in an hour of conversation.

He completely grasped his power as a marquess.

And she was fairly certain she would have made a benevolent, caring duke. Perhaps better than her brother would, now that she thought of Reid's statement. Her father had been spending extra time with his heir, and she suspected he was being corrected. She could have managed just as well as her brother, and doubted she would have needed any additional cautions.

She would have managed with kindness. Consideration. Gentleness.

People, except Reid, tended to see her point of view easily. Yet sometimes he seemed to be aware of too much. More than she anticipated.

She believed he saw more intensely into her than anyone else did, and she wasn't sure she liked the possibility of him being able to know what she was thinking.

He could learn from her or she could learn from him, but she didn't believe either ever would. Not the way those boots clicked when he left the room.

Guinevere sat with her parents in the clearing just beyond the gardens. Reid had spoken two sentences, maybe less, and everything appeared in place, including the setting sun. A night of serenity.

Chairs had been arranged around the fire. Two tables had been brought from the house and were laden with trays of food and drink.

Embers crackled, and the aroma of burning oak wafted in the air. Then the servants took the heaping platters and offered the cheese, sweet meats, biscuits, and made sure everyone had a glass of wine.

No servant needed any instruction, and all stood nearby to assist as needed. In fact, it seemed that every household servant had been organised to wait on them. A bit much, she thought.

A cool breeze kept the fire from feeling too warm, and the night surrounded them in a velvet hug accented by the pleasant scent of woodsmoke wafting in the air.

Reid didn't sit, but stood at the perimeter, away from them—not a member of the group. The silent host.

And yet, he didn't feel silent.

His awareness of the group, the servants and everything going on around him was obvious to her. He wasn't speaking, but he was communicating his wishes to the staff possibly only by his presence.

When he saw her gaze linger on him, he stared into the night. But it was as if she'd issued a request because his seeming random movements around the edge of the group brought him to her elbow.

'I expected Stephen to be here,' she said, relieved that he wasn't.

'I believe his invitation was lost.' Reid stood at her side. 'That—and I told him about a mare for sale which might be a good purchase for the stables that I would let him select. Besides, he knows you're leaving in the morning to return to London so he has decided it would be good to see Town again.'

'Do you think he will visit my home once I'm in London?'

'I'm sure of it.'

'I don't want to play another chess game with him.'

'Then you will have to be firm. He doesn't always take polite refusals as refusals, but as weak acceptances.'

'What of you?' she asked. 'Will you visit?'

Faint strains of music seemed to grow from nowhere. The only answer to her question. At first, she thought herself overhearing someone else's festivities—until the sound grew. A violin playing a slow song.

Then a man in billowing trousers, and shirt to match, stepped from the woods, and moved closer to the fire so that all could see him. He reversed his direction as the last soft note faded at the end of his bow. His arm swung again, and this time the music splashed into the air.

He sang about a hen who cackled every time she laid an egg, making the music mimic the sound of the chicken. Every day the hen worked longer and produced one more than the day before. All was well until the little hen began presenting the world with her bounty in the wee hours of the night, and an owl screeched from the night sky, and the last cackle stopped midpoint, and the sound which ended the song wasn't a cackle, but a deep *whoo...whoo...whoo* from the violin and musician.

Everyone applauded. He bowed and then he began again, but this time more slowly. A lady moved from the woods into the firelight, her skirt gathered tightly at her waist. The amount of cloth in her garment should have weighed her down, but she held it from her body and danced around the fireside, and it flowed, her feet as free as if the skirt were wings keeping her aloft.

As the songs continued, the music seemed to draw Reid closer to Guinevere.

She kept her words low, trying to read his expression in the darkness, touching his forearm. Firelight reflected from his eyes and appeared to add a warming glow over him. If this was their goodbye, she wanted it to be a kind one, not like the conversations they'd had as youngsters.

'Thank you for suggesting this. I've never had a picnic in the night, and the entertainment is splendid.'

'The man often provides music for the village when they have a celebration, and his wife was happy to come along.'

She missed his nearness as she moved away, surprised that something so brief, so unexpected and so impersonal could have been so intense. But even more surprised he'd not given her an answer to her question about visiting.

The couple bowed after several more songs ended, and the Marchioness thanked them, requesting they stay and help themselves to the feast if they wished.

'I suppose we must be going in,' the Duke said. 'I want to get an early start in the morning.'

Her parents took several steps towards the house before her father stilled, searched her out, and his mouth opened. She was certain it was to suggest she come inside with them, but the Marchioness spoke, telling them how much she'd appreciated their time together, and expressing joy for the wonderful friendship they had, and then asked him another question, diverting him, and the three moved forward.

The Marchioness had deftly guided her parents back to the house, leaving her alone with Reid.

Reid stepped beside Guinevere, holding his arm for her to take.

'I hope the servants will be able to see well enough to clear the tables in the darkness,' she whispered, feeling a need to break the silence between them, almost wishing she'd not asked the question and somehow more hurt that he'd not answered her than she'd been when they'd clashed in the past.

'If they carry anything but bare platters and empty wine bottles into the house, I'll be surprised. The abundance of food may have appeared to be for our benefit, but they're not going to miss out on an opportunity when it's presented.'

'That's wonderful.'

He muttered a response, but she wasn't certain if it was agreement or disagreement, and she didn't want to pursue it.

The music started again, and Reid stopped her, and indicated she look behind them. Wood was being added to the bonfire. In the shadows, she could see servants beginning a dance.

'I'd never heard a lone violinist play,' she whispered, because even though it was impossible for the sound to carry so far, she didn't want to interrupt the music.

'The violin. So many different variations in the notes. Beautiful in the right hands. My favourite instrument.'

'Your favourite sound?' she asked.

He shook his head. 'No.'

Standing behind her, but so close that he brushed against her shoulder, he spoke softly with a deep richness that caused sparkling awareness within her. 'That would be a woman's voice.'

'You are such a rake.'

'I'm truthful.'

Leaves and twigs on the ground rustled with his footsteps. 'Now, tell me,' he said. 'On occasion, don't you appreciate the sound of a male voice?'

'Now that you mention it,' she said. 'And don't take that as a compliment.'

'Why not?' he said. 'Flattery is, for lack of a better word...flattery, and praise.'

'You could give lessons in flirtation. But you didn't answer my question. I will take that as a no. I completely understand. It is enough that we, finally, part friends, and not with unkind words between us. And I think it's best for both of us.'

'Friends?' he said.

She sensed a hesitation in his voice. 'Aren't we?' she asked.

Again, he didn't seem to want to answer, but he appeared to want to lighten the mood, or he merely wanted to change the subject, or perhaps he regretted his words.

'Let's tell the horses goodnight,' he said.

She stared in the direction her parents had taken, hesitating.

'If the Duke is concerned, I have every confidence he will send someone out,' Reid said. 'The servants are still going all around, and we'll be visible in the shadows.'

'True,' she said, moving to the stables, and stopping at the fence.

'Wait here,' he said, and moved to the dark doorway, going inside. In a few moments, she heard a latch being pushed, and the larger opening swung wide. He stood outside, and whistled, watching for the horses. Afterwards, the stallion ran out, followed by the gelding, and the mare, Hera.

'You woke them.'

He left the door and walked closer to her, then climbed up and over the fence, stopping beside her, studying the animals. 'I doubt they were slumbering, and they usually sleep just as comfortably standing. One of their hind legs locks, and it appears they're tilting forward, and they'll just nod off for a few minutes.'

They seemed happy to be out of the barn, exercising their legs.

He rested his arm on the fence, and relaxed against the railing, watching the beasts. Absently, he brushed the back of his thumbnail against his face. 'Hermes's sire's parent once belonged to my grandfather. The gelding and Hermes are both prime riding horses. Hera isn't, but she's trained to pull carts.'

He straightened. 'Hermes will always have a home here because he reminds me of the stallion my grandfather had. You should be aware that he's the man I patterned my life after.'

'Were you close to your grandfather?'

'No one was close to him, but we were…similar.'

She could remember seeing his grandfather from a distance when her parents had visited. A spindly man of above average height, and a hawkish glare. But she didn't remember ever being in the same room with him.

'We would ride together,' Reid said. 'He was devoted to horses. He did give me instruction, though, often. He felt his attention should be on me. He didn't believe my father would give me the guidance I needed. Father thought my grandfather too overbearing to him, and too much of a jackanapes for a marquess. They didn't get on.'

He whistled and patted the fence, and Hera trotted over. He scratched her behind the ears.

'Grandfather was always directing Father this way or that. According to Father he had to stay at Grandfather's right hand all the time, jumping hither and yon, and making sure to keep Grandfather happy. Apparently, as a child, he even summoned the servants for him. My father considered himself a glorified footman for Grandfather, and that I was truly the heir Grandfather had wished for.'

'Did you mourn your grandfather?'

'Yes. I was sad to see him go and I missed riding with him, and I'd felt proud of his directions. He was my grandfather and I could do no wrong in his eyes, even though his own son could do no right. My father was lighter when he didn't have to keep the old Marquess happy any more.'

'Your father was a good man.'

'Beneath the surface, we are all flawed.' His voice had iron in it, but then it lightened. 'Except perhaps you, Lady Guinevere.'

'Oh, I am just as flawed as the next person.'

'And modest, too.'

'Reid?' Something about the way he said it seemed critical.

'Tell me a flaw you have.'

'You've seen my anger demonstrated.'

'I would not even call that a temper. But perhaps defence when wet hair was swabbed across your nose, after practically being dunked head-first in the water.'

'I do think my anger is a fault.'

'And on that, you and I disagree. But I think I do see a failing in you.'

She shored herself up. 'Enlighten me.'

'I'm hearing a bit of that ire you mentioned seeping through the generous spirit you demonstrate, and which I don't see as a problem, but as a truth. Perhaps an asset. Your flaw may be in too much modesty. In not asking more of yourself.'

He didn't continue the thread of conversation.

'I'll leave the horses out, and but we two-legged creatures should get inside.' He took her elbow.

She felt she'd just been refused a dance with

the only man she wanted to be with. Ever so gently.

Reid walked her into the house, perfectly behaved as if the twenty eyes of ten chaperons viewed them. He took the lit lamp sitting just inside the doorway and guided her to her room.

'Happy travels, gallant Lady Guinevere,' he said, stopping at her bedroom.

'You, too,' she said, upset with herself for such an inadequate response. Her words sounded insincere, too rushed. But she'd wanted to speak with him a moment longer.

He paused, stopped and appeared to be able to study her in the darkness.

Taking her fingertips, he kissed them, and then lowered her hand, but didn't release her. 'I feel you saved my life.'

'I will accept that. I suppose you owe me a great deal.'

His voice rolled through the darkness, and swirled around her, coating her in its sound. 'How would you like to collect?'

She felt the stillness, and the warmth of the flames she'd seen earlier flared. 'Do I have options?'

'You may. It depends on what you suggest.'

'Pay me in kindness. You must be gentle to others.'

He exaggerated disappointment. 'That is too much of a price for my life.' His soft chuckle rolled through the night, lodging in her. 'I was hoping for something a little more adventurous.'

'Then I will have to think about it.' She pulled her hand free, but could not go through the doorway to close him away. 'Be careful what you wish for.'

He smiled, the barest glimmer. 'Don't think too long about it. You may lose sleep.'

Then he took a step back and bowed to her, and left, returning the way they'd arrived.

The door sounded hollow after she opened it, moved into the room and closed it behind her. Or maybe it was the echo in her heart. She saw herself as following in the fictional steps of her namesake and never finding happiness with the man of her dreams.

And she suspected she'd been offered a confectionary shop of treats, and she'd refused each of them for ever.

'Wait,' she said, rushing out, and hurrying a few steps towards him.

With a conservation of movement she'd never noticed on anyone else, he appraised her. 'You have another wish?'

Her first words locked in her throat. She

forced through the second choice. 'You didn't say whether you'll visit me or not.'

He stared over her shoulder, briefly, bowed and turned, and she felt that if she'd called out to him again and again, he would not have stopped, but he did anyway. Surprising her.

'Lady Guinevere, even though it may be the most challenging thing ever requested of me, I will consider the payment you requested. And as for the question on visiting you, I cannot answer it.'

Then he left, and she went back inside her room, heart thundering with an awareness of Reid, awash in the sadness that he had walked out of her life and knowing he would not be at breakfast.

Reid stood in the darkness, hidden from the servants, but he could see their outlines around the fire. Guinevere resided as strong in his thoughts as if she stood at his side, but distant as the moon.

He'd not told her the true flaw he saw in her. The one that made her, the mostly perfect woman, unsuitable for him. Although he could hardly complain. It wasn't as if he were anything near the proper mate she would expect.

He tried to let the motions of the staff distract him.

They weren't even pretending to gather foodstuffs, but were jesting with each other, and sampling the wines. He'd given them the celebration they wished for, and he'd been alive to watch it.

Then he saw the stablemaster arrive and ask if enough food had been prepared for him, and chatter started in earnest, and pretence of anything but enjoyment left. It was as if they'd given themselves leave to do as they wished.

He didn't listen any more, but let the words meld into the forest.

Something inside him felt different. He seemed to be having the same kind of awareness of Guinevere that he'd had of everyone after his accident.

He could see her, be aware of the conversation they had, and yet he could not reach out and touch her.

He knew his heart beat, and it pulsed an awareness of Guinevere into him. But she wasn't a woman for a dalliance, not that he hadn't halfway put the suggestion in the air, and had it been thrust back at him with a suggestion of niceness.

Niceness? That had not been what he'd been thinking of.

He supposed he'd deserved it for planning an

evening with family sitting around a bonfire. That had been a first for him.

He'd had nights with friends around a fire. The servants were far better mannered than he and his friends had been, but perhaps if the staff didn't have to rise early in the morning, they would have been rowdier.

Guinevere and her family lived a sedate life, even in Town. One that he supposed could be accepted for short occasions and then dusted away for a more boisterous night with people who lacked reserve and pushed the limits further for revelry, sometimes well beyond the bounds of good taste. Well, in all fairness, the people he often associated with did not approach or accept anything of proper taste as worthwhile of more than a jest.

Guinevere would have been appalled at their humour. He sometimes was, but he still enjoyed it.

His grandfather had always advised him never to marry unless he found a woman he could give his heart to. And then he'd said that it was best because then he could take out the unreliable thing and leave it at home with his wife for her to guard it for him while he did as nature intended. Discretion, his grandfather commanded, was vital to a contented marriage, and honesty. A wife should know in the beginning she would not be informed of every event in her husband's life and should have the decency not to ask too many questions.

Reid could not see shushing Guinevere into a pleasant marriage.

A gulf existed between him and Guinevere. She'd known him her entire lifetime and that was the amount of time she'd used to build up the reserve between them. For good reason. He would have instructed her to do the same if he'd been advising her.

Guinevere's name was mentioned around the campfire, and instantly Reid's full attention snapped onto the conversation.

A few murmuring comments about how no one would be surprised if a marriage was in the future for her and Stephen.

Reid's reaction surprised him. Bubbles in the boiling cauldron his body became—sizzled, the intensity rising to the top and bursting—pushed aloft by heat of something foreign to him. Jealousy, perhaps.

Reid decided to answer Guinevere's question in person.

He'd heard enough. He left.

Chapter Seven

Three days after she'd arrived in London, she was studying the main chessboard, when the butler arrived at the family sitting room door, his usual rap on the wall sounding several steps before he appeared.

'The Marquess of Hartcroft has enquired if Lady Guinevere is home,' the servant said.

Her mother held up one pointed finger, causing her bracelet to slide on her wrist, and waved him out while speaking. 'Let us have a moment,' she said. 'I will direct you.'

The butler closed the door behind him.

'Did you...? Were you expecting...?' Her mother studied her face.

'No. Not really,' Guinevere said, but she glanced down at the chess pieces on the board. She'd not known Reid would visit, but she couldn't stop the smile and the warmth in her cheeks.

'Take care.' The words came out with the violence of a slap.

'Mother. I always take care. Always.' She lifted the queen.

'You will never have as much power over your life as you do at this moment, and it is fading fast,' her mother said. 'Use it wisely. Reid is…'

'What…?'

'Are you using Reid to pull a proposal out of Stephen?'

'I would think I could merit a courtship without using anyone.'

'Well, don't be doing the opposite. Reid is a little too assured. You know your father and I have never liked him. Never.'

'Perhaps I could talk with him and see.'

'Don't lead the man on, when you have entirely no wish to court him. Stephen is so much more agreeable. Guin, you've always thought before you acted. You've been so mature for your age.'

Guinevere didn't answer.

'I really wasn't pleased yesterday when Stephen visited and you practically ignored him.'

'Mother, he was here to see you and Father. He said that plainly.'

'No. He wasn't. Are you cognizant that Stephen is more agreeable?' But she didn't pause long enough for Guinevere to answer. 'But Reid is the kind of poison that draws the eye.' Her head quivered sideways in a shake. 'It's not good for a man, and especially not Reid. He's been spoiled his whole life—by the circumstance of birth, his appearance, his grandfather and his parents.' She rose from her chair, her sketchbook forgotten.

'Mother. Perhaps we could see what he wants. Before we last parted, he asked me how he could repay me for saving his life. And, if we let him in, we could see what he is here for.'

'Oh, that's how it starts,' her mother insisted. *'Thank you for saving my life. Now all I want is to destroy yours in return.'*

Her mother's hand flew up, fingers outstretched, almost hitting the harp that had stood in the corner for Guinevere's entire life. 'And Reid almost died. He doesn't have any choice but to think of heirs. And likely marriage, and will for another few months, and then once the ring is on his wife's finger and he's got that chore taken care of, he will have her trapped like a butterfly in a spider's web.'

'Mother, you're jumping to conclusions.'

'Logical ones. Logical ones.' Her mother paced, her gown fluttering around her slippers.

Guinevere bit the inside of her lip. Best to let her mother wind down.

'I was fortunate to wed your father and I don't want you making a mistake. I almost married the wrong man, but your father swept in, and, well— My parents guided me in his direction, and I am ever so thankful.'

'You never have a cross word.'

'In front of others. Your father is still more agreeable than most.' Her mother shook her head. 'You must listen, Guinevere. A suitor can be a good man ten days out of thirty, and only see his sweetheart ten days a month. Which days will he choose to visit a woman he wishes to marry? A husband can be a good husband twenty-nine days out of thirty, and his wife will be his wife all of those days, and he can still make her miserable the whole of the month on *one* day.'

Her mother gathered in air for another on-slaught. 'Think about Stephen. He's agreeable. Visits his aunt. Gets on well with your father and has never broken your brother's arm.'

Guinevere studied the queen, not speaking.

'In truth,' her mother said, tone softening. 'About the best a woman can hope for is to find a man who's adequate about twenty-five days a month. The *best*.'

'*Mother*.'

'I don't mean to disparage the male world, but a marriage is not going to be perfect all the time. It's not. Your father is wonderful, but we have our disagreements. We just keep them hidden.'

'Are you telling me it's time I wed—or warning me away from marriage?'

'I'm being realistic. Reid might not even be a good husband more than a few hours a month, and Stephen is much better natured. Yes, some talk of his bad habits has been spoken, but Reid has made himself a legend with his behaviour.'

Her lip quivered. 'I cannot bear the thought of how unhappy Reid would make you, when someone like Stephen is definitely interested. He has asked your father if he may call on you and of course your father and I agreed.'

Guinevere almost choked. 'Did I have a say in the matter?'

'Of course. Certainly. But Stephen is not going to keep knocking for ever. Nor are the other suitors. If you ignore their attentions, they will move on. If you encourage them, you will discourage others.'

'Perhaps that's for the best.'

'Of course it is.' Her mother's voice dripped

treacle. 'And you have to ask yourself whether you will be happier with the suitors, or without them. If you're going to wed, go for the most days of happiness. There is no perfect person in a marriage,' she said. 'But there are agreeable ones.' She readjusted the bracelet on her arm. 'And Reid is—Reid. And you cannot change that.'

'I'm sure.'

'If you err in marriage, you'll never have the position you would in society if people are always talking about your husband's exploits.'

'Mother. You've spent entirely too much time thinking about this.'

'And you should spend more time thinking of marriage. This is a little different than what I said to your sister, and you know her husband is only good for providing beautiful grandbabies. She didn't listen.'

'I'd rather have thirty days out of thirty—or no marriage.'

'Wouldn't we all, Guinnie? But that's hoping for too much.' Then she snatched the chess piece out of her daughter's hand. 'A few years ago, you didn't give any proper attention to Lord Marcus, and he married that artist, and I've heard she's happier than she's ever been. Last year, you scarcely noticed Chalgrove and he's wed now.

How are you going to feel when all your friends have married and you're stuck with what's left?'

Her mother slapped the piece back onto the board, pausing as she left the doorway. 'You cannot risk being seen as a woman who toys with men's affections. It is beyond time that you settled with a good man like Stephen. I told him that and he agreed.' She sighed. 'And you might end up a marchioness if that cousin of his keeps tempting fate. Stephen could inherit the title.'

The Duke's butler was taking entirely too long to tell him that Guinevere was not at home. This time.

The day before, it had been a quick endeavour. The butler had informed Reid immediately that she was away.

Finally, the butler appeared, even starchier than before.

'If you will follow me to Her Grace and Lady Guinevere.'

Reid stepped forward. The butler said her name properly. He didn't linger over it. Said it and was done with it.

Inside the sitting room, Guinevere greeted him and her mother barely raised her eyes, a charcoal and a sketchbook in her hands. 'Hartcroft.' Lady Glouston had taken any trace of sweetness out of his name. She'd once called him Reid. But not with the same sharpness. Well, perhaps she had.

But what did one say to a family friend who no longer called him by his first name? Ah, well. 'Good afternoon.'

'I am sure you are not here to see me,' her mother said. 'But my daughter.'

'I hoped to go for a walk with her.'

'That would be pleasant.' Guinevere sat, both hands crossed in her lap, back straight, and reminding him of a tutor with an errant charge.

He could almost hear the sound of her mother looking heavenward.

Behind her sat a table prepared for a chess game, with elaborate figurines, and it appeared that a game was in progress, except the queen was askew. Then he noticed another table to the side. A second game. He remembered her brother showing him the pieces years before, and he'd forgotten about them.

'They were my father's,' the Duchess said, following his eyes. 'He was a patron for an artist and you would not believe the conversations they had before the carving started. The smaller one is a simple set we gave the children when they were young.'

He examined the elaborate set closely, but

then he looked at the children's game pieces which were of good quality, but not the master-piece of the other set.

'Please be seated. I'm sketching her, and I need her to remain still for a moment.' Her mother gripped her charcoal, and then made a deft stroke.

He moved to sit on the sofa beside the Duch-ess and saw she was creating a picture of her daughter. He found himself silent, seeing Guine-vere through different eyes. Her mother's.

He didn't know the woman in the sketch. Had never seen her before. Her mother wasn't an in-experienced artist and had captured another per-spective of Guinevere.

Instantly, his eyes moved from the paper to the woman. Yes, it was the same person.

He studied the portrait, seeing a woman he'd not viewed before—not a child, an adversary, a friend's sister or a duke's daughter. A woman who would have captured attention when she en-tered a room, but he wouldn't have approached. This woman had no interest in empty flattery. In fact, she would never have to listen to it because enough true praise could be delivered to her.

Then he realised he lied to himself. Not only would he have spoken with her, but he would have tried to be the first at her side. He couldn't have stopped himself.

'You do your subject justice,' he said to her mother.

She shrugged away his words. As if a compliment from him wasn't a true one.

'Mother is accomplished,' Guinevere said. 'She plays the harp. Sings. I have no talent for those things.'

'But she inherited her chess skills twice over from her grandfather,' her mother interspersed. 'Guinevere is one of the best chess players I have ever seen. She and her father have one game going at almost all times, and she is using the children's game because she likes challenging herself.'

Guinevere's cheeks brightened, and she appeared to have been caught with a bolt of lightning that didn't belong to her. Her gaze was too wide.

Of course. She'd been letting Stephen win.

Silence.

'Are you sure you wouldn't rather play chess than go for a walk?' the Duchess asked.

He knew when he was being set up to lose. 'It would be disastrous from the beginning,' he said. 'It's not my game.'

'Ah,' said the Duchess. 'It is my daughter's. And she doesn't like to be defeated.'

'She doesn't like to lose?' He asked the question of Guinevere.

Guinevere's fingertips trailed over the fabric of the armchair. 'To a competitive opponent. It doesn't concern me if I feel I am helping a lesser player strengthen.'

'I would definitely be outmatched on the board, and I wouldn't want a challenger who let me win.'

'I will remember that,' Guinevere said.

The Duchess's charcoal crumpled beneath her fingers, and she placed her sketchbook between them, gave him a glare and said, 'I'm finished for today.'

'Would you like to go for a stroll, Lady Guinevere?' He'd said her name properly.

'Yes,' Guinevere answered.

Lady Glouston went to the bell. 'I'll send my maid with you. She's quite talkative in the mornings when she does my hair.'

Then the Duchess appraised him. 'Lord Hartcroft. Are there thirty days in this month, or thirty-one? It's so hard for me to keep count of them all.'

'Thirty.'

'Well,' she said. 'Sometimes short months are a blessing. Like February. It's brief. And cold.

And that harsh weather takes a lot of forgiving. Seeps against you and doesn't let go.'

Based on the tenseness of Guinevere's jaw, he didn't respond.

Guinevere's maid brought her coat, and as she preceded him down the stairs, he was not only beside the woman who'd jabbed him into awakening with a pin, but the one who was an excellent chess player. The woman in the sketch.

She wore a brown spencer, which did seem a bit warm for the day, and a bonnet with a feather that curled over it which fluttered when she moved.

When they stepped outside, she sighed, and looked at her maid. 'I cannot believe I didn't bring the gloves that match this outfit. Do be a dear and fetch them for me. And it must be the brown ones. It must. Don't forget.'

The maid dashed back into the house, forgetting she was a chaperon and only thinking of her servant duties.

Guinevere held her parasol, still unopened, and tucked it under her arm, to push a lock of hair under her hat brim.

'I didn't think you'd visit me.' Guinevere studied him, hand pausing in mid-air. 'When we last talked, I thought you were turning your back on me, so to speak.'

'Doesn't mean I can't change directions.' He hadn't been turning from her because he didn't want to see her, but because he had to put distance between them or he wouldn't be able to.

'Stephen called on my parents yesterday.' She pursed her lips, biting the bottom one.

Reid wasn't surprised. In fact, the opposite would have amazed him. 'When I reached London, he wasn't at my town house as he usually is, so I hoped I'd been wrong and he'd stayed in the country.'

'No. Mother intends that he should court me.'

'My mother pretends she wants him to court you, also. When he left the countryside, Mother used the time to recall your attributes to me. On and on, and innocently told me what a wonderful helpmate you would make for Stephen.'

She closed her parasol and held it at her side.

'She is matchmaking,' he explained. 'She knows that if she wishes for me to discount a female as a companion—in the past, she has only had to push me in that direction. I found it interesting she was treading so lightly, and at the same time, trying to point out your virtues.'

'Or she is desperate to get you wed and I'm a last resort?' Her eyes questioned him.

He laughed. 'She was desperate years ago. I thought she'd given up, but recent events may have renewed her interest.'

Her eyes widened, and briefly the parasol end pointed in his direction. 'I can't think why you wish to court me, unless the brush with death made you think of the necessity of heirs.' She spoke softly, words only for the two of them, and then the parasol dipped over her shoulder as she spoke.

'It did.'

'And then you thought of me?'

'Of course.'

'You need a wife, in truth. It's obvious to me. Mother was insisting when we were at your estate that you hardly have a choice in the matter.'

'I have choices.'

'Yes. Of course you do. But your feet are being held to the fire, so to speak, in your mind where marriage is concerned.'

'Is that a reference to my wrongdoings?' he asked. 'You once mentioned the devil returning me.'

'No. In earlier times people supposedly were forced to walk over hot coals to prove their innocence. In theory, they would be protected by a higher power if they weren't guilty and wouldn't feel pain. Of course, everyone always felt pain. A good way for people to set their neighbours up for a guilty verdict. *Oh, let's test him by putting him to the fire. Blink. Blink. If he's innocent, he won't feel a thing.*'

'We humans do go to great lengths to prove our compassion for one another.'

'You've got to walk over the hot coals because you've decided you've not been upholding your duty to your estate. You need a succession plan, and partly because he wasn't as upset at the thought of inheriting as he could have been, Stephen isn't your first choice.'

'If he'd been distraught, he wouldn't have been my first choice. I think the prospect of my death and not living up to the promise of it, so to speak, brought out the worst in him.'

'You can only have another selection by having a son,' she continued. 'You need a wife for that because the law doesn't recognise a child not born of a marriage. And, without my being immodest, I have suitable lineage. Besides, you've never truly got on well with my parents, and a marriage to me would rather be a sneer at them.'

'That's too drastic. Besides, if I want to annoy your father, all I have to do is be in his path. And he is the same for me.'

She gave a twist, bent her knees, moved her chin forward and smiled. 'And it only took you how many years, and a brush with death, to think of me. I'm so flattered.'

'Guinevere, are you wanting compliments?'

'I bet you can dish them out like peas on a plate.'

'I'm fair at it.'

'I'm not finding fault. But I do feel rather like an old boot that has been left about and now that winter is near, it's time to put on the woollen socks and get the leather in shape.'

'Guinevere. You're so agreeable. I can hardly fathom why you've not wed before now. You old boot, you,' he whispered. 'How's that for a pea on a plate compliment?'

'Well, it's original.'

He'd moved again. Closer. Surrounding her with the scent of shaving soap. 'I won't do the ten tasks of Hercules. Either you are fond of me, or you aren't. Which is it?'

'Would you walk away again if I said I wasn't fond of you?' She ran her tongue over her lips.

'Yes.' Then he studied her. 'But it would be my loss.'

'I would hope.'

'And will you answer my question?'

She put her hand on his arm, running her fingers along the coat. 'I'm entirely fond of you.' She held out her fingers in a pinch. 'But I was really fond of those old boots I used to wear. And I got rid of them.'

'Lady Guinevere. You are strategic.'

'I would hope.'

'And I didn't tell you the flaw that I perceive in you.'

'What an original way to begin our walk.' She pressed her tongue against her cheek. 'I doubt I could stop you from informing me.'

The maid barrelled out the door and they both moved away, conversation interrupted. She held white gloves. 'Milady, I could not locate the gloves anywhere and I searched and searched.'

Guinevere put her hand to her head. 'Oh, now I recall. I dropped them behind the wardrobe. No matter. I'll wear the white ones.'

Before she could say anything else, he took one glove from the maid.

'Can we keep a secret?' he asked, voice stilling them all with its intensity.

Both she and the maid waited, a reaction to the baritone timbre of his words.

He held the glove for her to slip her fingers into, and she did. He tapped it into place, taking his time, making sure each bit of leather touched her skin. Giving it an extra tiny tug and running his hand over it to make sure he'd not missed anything. Both women watched, entranced.

Then he took the other, and repeated the actions, slowly putting it on her hand.

'I've never put gloves on a lady before,' he said.

Then he offered his elbow. 'Shall we take a stroll, Lady Guinevere?'

She hardly spoke while they walked, not wanting to ask him about her flaw in front of the maid because, likely, he'd tell her.

In fact, she realised, he had many more strengths in that game than she ever would. He'd played it longer and with more success. She was the novice.

Her mother thought she'd just fallen for Reid's long legs, which, in truth, made no difference to her. But when her mother had asked her exactly what about Reid made him suitable, she'd been unable to answer. In truth, though, there was nothing to even notice about Stephen, and too much to be aware of about Reid.

When they reached her front door again, she waited, waving the maid to continue. The chaperon wasn't supposed to leave her but she strolled inside, serene, happy to be following Guinevere's bidding.

* * *

Reid watched the maid disappear into the home, pleased to have another moment with Guinevere.

'Well, what of my flaw?' she said. 'It's curiosity, isn't it?'

'Are you interested in Stephen as a suitor?' he asked.

Her eyes widened. 'The only reason it would concern you is if you wish to court me. Perhaps my flaw is that I like to have suitors. My mother says Stephen would be a perfect one.'

'I don't even believe he is an adequate acquaintance for you.'

Standing under the portico, he glanced at the parasol, then captured Guinevere's eyes, knowing he had her full awareness. Then he held out his palm.

She deliberated a second, unsure.

She delivered the parasol to him.

'What a useful courtship tool this is,' he said. 'You could hold a suitor at bay with it, or perhaps pull him closer. Or—'

He opened it, and then seemed to shake something from it, but in truth, giving himself an excuse to shield the two of them from the world as he held it extended between them and the other houses.

His head lowered, his eyes shut and he tasted her lips for a brief moment. Gentle. Soft. Moist. The lusciousness of the heavens. His breath stopped and he pulled away.

Now he knew what it would be like to be inside a goddess's bolt of lightning.

He closed the accessory, opened the door and stood aside for her to enter, placing the parasol in her grasp, then closing his fingers over the handle. 'One suitor is all you need.'

'I've heard there's safety in numbers.'

'Is that why you sent your maid into the house?'

Without waiting, he left, while he could still move away.

Just a touch and he knew in that instant that he would have to fight himself to keep from saying her name as Stephen did.

Chapter Eight

Stephen visited my home after you left. He has suggested we wed.

Reid crumpled the paper, surprised it hadn't burst into flames from the heat of his anger. Someone had said a maid from the Duke's household had delivered it earlier.

Reid had kissed Guinevere. Practically proposed and she'd jousted with him and possibly already received a proposal from his cousin. Well, good luck to both of them. May they have many happy little opinionated daughters, and spineless sons, and spend many evenings playing chess.

He didn't finish reading the paper but thrust it towards the fireplace and the flickering coals. It hit the grate and bounced onto the floor.

Stephen had been practically dancing around

the house after he arrived, and Reid had been able to tell by the smile lurking behind his cousin's eyes that he'd ridden to London for one reason and one reason only. And his chest had been bursting out, as if he'd just bagged the prime partridge of the season. As if he'd bested Reid in the quest for Guinevere's hand.

But she would always be Lady Guinevere to Reid…until she wasn't. Until she was his cousin's wife.

He might as well plan on letting his cousin's children inherit the title as it was unlikely he would ever wed.

The only person he'd considered halfway interesting as a wife had allowed him to kiss her, knowing full well she had an interest in his cousin. Despicable. Unthinkable, and just plain wrong.

He heard humming in the hallway. His home was Stephen's home when his cousin was in London, when Stephen needed a place to perch and didn't stay at the Albany. That might need to change.

He stepped out into the hallway. 'So, are you here to court *Guinevere*?'

'Of course. Her mother has indicated that she would consider me a fine son-in-law.' Stephen slicked back his hair, then adjusted his cravat.

'You piece of tripe.'

'You arrogant arse.'

'What about Meg?'

'It's not a problem. You can love more than one woman at once, and besides, she's not seeing me now.' He raised a palm. 'And I've turned over a new leaf. I don't know what kind of plant it is, but it's new.'

'A leaf is a page in a book.'

'Well, then I've opened a new book. A book of love for my Guinevere.'

'You were betrothed to Meg and she ended it because she found out about your dalliances and your habits.'

'I've told the Duchess that I am not nearly good enough for her daughter, and I regret the error of my ways.' He smiled. 'I threw myself on her mercy. Her Grace was impressed. Thinks I'm grand.'

'Well, your mother doesn't.'

'Well, your mother doesn't think so much of you either. Thought you should wed, but no, you were too busy going to events and being a rake.' He put a hand to his cheek. 'Oh, wait, you aren't a rake. You are a marquess. One who needs heirs. Guess you'll have to search out someone besides a duke's daughter. You might have the title but I'm going to get the Lady.'

Then he ran his fingers over his chin. 'I need to shave closely before I visit Guinevere tomorrow. I wouldn't want to scratch her.'

'You know, if you were killed and I was hanged for it, your younger brother would inherit the title. Now there's a solution.'

Stephen laughed. 'Want to come to the wedding? I'd so like to see you there.'

'She should know about your dalliances. She'll find out eventually.'

He didn't want to inform her unless she specifically asked. She'd consider him jealous.

'Eventually. I'll confess if I must. In tears. On the wedding night, perhaps.' Then he shrugged. 'No. The next day. The morning after. It will ring the truest then.'

'If she marries you, she deserves what she gets.'

Reid took a step to the rear and slammed his sitting room door.

He swept up the crumpled paper and ripped it in half. Then he saw more writing below the big space after the first sentence.

He uncrumpled the other half.

I must tell my parents I cannot marry him. Can you meet with me at midnight? I will be in the garden.

He read the words a second time.

He folded the halves and put them in his waistcoat pocket. He went to the door and strode to Stephen's room. He opened the door. 'Did you propose?'

'That would be my concern. Not yours. But I will be calling on her at tea tomorrow and letting her know I wish to make her my bride.'

'Best of luck tomorrow.' For Guinevere.

'I wish I could say the same, saphead.'

'It doesn't matter if you say it or not.'

It was blasted hard to see in front of him, and he'd carried a long cane in case any dogs mistook him for a cutpurse.

At the edge of the Duke's home he'd damn near tripped over some bush, and he'd had to move a frond aside, and discovered the plant had sharp leaves.

But when he touched the garden gate, it opened easily and without a squeak.

Inside, he saw a silhouette, sitting on a garden bench.

She rose, her shawl fluttering like a fallen angel's wings.

'I could have simply called on you at teatime,' he said, moving close enough to be able to speak softly. Windows could be open. Sounds carried easily on a quiet night.

'Except you might find Stephen here, and I'd rather have the meeting end pleasantly, and for some reason, I don't think it would if you put in an appearance.'

She reached up, putting fingertips to her head, and he saw she gripped the corner of her wrap. 'I didn't want my parents to know. It appears Mother wants me to wed Stephen, and plans for me to see him tomorrow. She thinks he will suggest marriage, and she strongly prefers I say yes.'

'I have it on good authority that Stephen will propose.'

She muttered, tugging the cloth back into place on her shoulders. 'So polite of him to let everyone else know before he discusses it with me.'

'I've found him to be thoughtful that way. And you don't plan to accept?'

'No.' She bit out the words. 'It feels that I'm being nudged off a cliff into matrimony with Stephen, and I like him less with each push. Mother has already told me that Father can make certain Stephen has an appointment to get a Special License. It's what she has planned.'

He moved towards her, took her arm and helped her to the bench, sitting beside her. Her voice was much too loud for the night. He wanted to keep them alone and hear her whispers and feel they were the only two beings in the world.

'And what move do you have in mind?' He held the cane but rested it against his knee.

She puffed out a breath, but didn't answer right away. 'It irks me. Mother has been increasingly assertive about my being unmarried. She isn't happy about it. Listing suitors. Questioning me after events to see if I'm considering a serious courtship. I know exactly what you meant when you mentioned that the Marchioness is also pushing you to wed.'

She twisted the cloth in her hands, and he placed his fingertips over hers, stilling them. Her tension appeared to fade.

She paused. 'And when my mother was out of the room at your estate, the Marchioness warned me about Stephen. She said he can appear overly constrained, and on occasion forgets and tends to fall into an abyss which lacks the moderation he has tried to embrace. I've heard similar rumours that he was entirely indiscreet, which is why his sweetheart, Meg, didn't wed him.'

'I would think you've heard more rumours about me.'

'They are not so much hints, but more statements of fact. Are they correct?'

'I would imagine they are. I've never cared what society says about me, except I have been careful not to mislead any woman with my intentions. At times, I felt proud of the poor reports.' He spoke carefully, honestly, but with gentleness.

'I have always cared what people say about me. But it doesn't seem that they've been considerate. I feel I'm being painted as fickle, capricious and indecisive. That's what Mother believes.'

'I would have said you were overly decisive.'

'Thank you.'

When she relaxed her arms, the shawl fell from her shoulder, away from him, and she retrieved it. 'I am positive I don't want to be coerced into a marriage. It has its upheaval as well.' She leaned into him, and he put an arm around her, aware of the innocence inside the body of a tempting woman.

'Mother was at an event, where a married woman created a stir admiring Byron. Mother was aghast, and left. She muttered about it for days. Everyone spoke of it. Two different maids told me, promising me to secrecy.'

'I heard about it. Everyone did. I remembered how much the woman was in love with her husband shortly after they wed. Then afterwards, I danced with her. She appeared taken with me, and I kept my distance. It made me question the sincerity of marriage. The risks—'

'I could never chase a man so blatantly.'

'I know you couldn't.'

'True.'

Now her fingers closed over his hand holding the cane. Startling him at the feel of femininity. The intensity of his body's reaction surprised him. He should not be so aware of Guinevere.

He let the cane fall against his knee and brought her hand to his lips and kissed the back of it, but he didn't release her.

'Don't turn to me as an escape from Stephen. Just tell Stephen to go away. Yes, you'll hurt his feelings, but he will recover.'

'I wish you didn't need to wed,' she said. 'If you didn't, you would be the perfect suitor for me. If you were my betrothed,' she said, 'it would keep my mother from pushing me to anyone. It wouldn't have to lead to marriage. In fact, it would be a barrier between anyone who might want to be a suitor.'

'It would be a sham of sorts?'

'Not truly. More of a placeholder.'

'And a betrothal to me would certainly make a declaration. You think I'd still be going about town and would leave you to your own devices.

No one would beleaguer you about getting wed, and you like my mother.'

'I like your country estate as well.'

He chuckled. 'You'd be betrothed to me for the house?'

'It has good childhood memories for me. The gardens are so lush and well-tended. I could visit more often with my parents, and you wouldn't even have to be there, which could make it optimum,' she jested. 'And I could become acquainted with Mrs Orange.'

'I hate that cat. But it is a good mouser.'

She sighed aloud. 'I must have been more irritated with Mother than I expected. Trust me, I have heard Stephen's name mentioned in every other sentence she speaks, it seems. *"Wouldn't Stephen like this preserve?" "Doesn't Stephen have straight teeth and nice wavy hair?"'*

'Stephen has wavy hair?' His eyes narrowed. 'Guess his hasn't been singed off.'

'I suppose that was unkind of me to say, if not untrue…'

'But you weren't speaking behind my back.'

He turned and, with his free hand, brushed his knuckles against her chin. 'It would be best to wed someone who agrees with most of your opinions.'

'I know. And Stephen appears to, but I don't think he really does.'

'I wouldn't bet my life on it. Or even better, his.'

'Mother will be upset when I refuse him. And I don't like her to be angry but I have no choice. Is that what you consider my flaw?' she asked. 'My wish to stay unmarried?'

He'd known she would ask. 'You're content to sit at a chessboard. You attend dances, but it is almost an afterthought to you. And perhaps that is why your mother is pushing you to wed, but she doesn't realise it. But the failing is not that you're happy to remain unwed. What I see is that you're content to let life move by you.'

'I take exception to that being considered a failing. I consider it being happy with my world.'

'Normally, I would agree. But in your case, I see it as a placid acceptance. An unwillingness to challenge yourself because you simply don't have to. Everything is at your fingertips.'

'It's my life. To live as I want. Just as yours is your own.'

'I thought the same,' he admitted, 'until it wasn't any more—'

His words ended abruptly; he followed, musing, '—and I saw that I need to wed soon. Simple as that. Ring. Duty. I accept it. I was thinking of a short betrothal. Less than a fortnight. A marriage. No waiting around. Decision. Done. Over.'

She didn't like the idea of him proposing to someone else, yet simple jealousy was no basis to begin a marriage. She must accept his choice to find a bride and support it. He wanted to do the right thing. 'How many ladies would you say are on your marital prospects list?'

'I would imagine there are some out there who would make a suitable wife for me and remember they said vows. Being a marchioness would entrance them. They might think of it as sacrificing themselves to have a son of rank... and an estate.'

'And you plan to propose?'

His eyes jolted her, in some deep place. And she really couldn't see his expression, but she could feel it. Feel the intensity.

'I may have a plan to propose to one of them, but I don't know if it's the right thing for her, and I don't know if she'd accept.'

'You can only find out one way.'

'Want to discuss it with me on a trip to Scotland?'

His breath brushed against hers when he said *Scotland*, reminding her that he was so much more than any of the other suitors she'd considered.

'I don't think your estate is that grand.'

'Are you sure? It has happy memories for you. Where else will you get an estate with such a fine portrait gallery?'

Something fluttered the leaves above her head. Perhaps an errant breeze. But it felt as if the rest of the world had moved, and the leaves had remained steadfast.

He drew her close, cloaking her in his presence.

She relaxed against him, secure and more coddled than she'd ever felt before, but a hint of grief at what couldn't be surfaced. 'What about love?'

'Love is easy. Simple. Lasting love is the conundrum. I have seen it professed, and seen it evaporate more quickly than the fog. But it's not necessary in a marriage.'

He had told her more than she wanted to know.

'It's wonderful in theory,' he said. 'I understand the belief of it. But it's more important that both people have the same direction. The family. The legacy.'

She'd known he was honest, but now that he spoke, she wondered if she knew him at all.

And presumed she didn't.

'For me,' she said, 'I have believed love should be foremost, and perhaps that's why I've not married.'

'Other people fall in and out of love at the drop of a hat. At every event I attend, I hear at least one mention of a dalliance. When I go to the clubs, I hear more than hints. And when I attend the next dinner or soiree, I notice the secretive glances. The knowing looks. I can't agree with my grandfather that men should be permitted to be unfaithful. I would rather wed a person unable to love, than someone who is too free with her heart.'

'Is that…? Is that why you asked me to wed? You think I can't have that depth of feeling?'

'It wouldn't matter. The flaw I mentioned that I see in you, that you don't agree with, would be an asset in a wife. A contentment.'

'Oh, my.' She shut her eyes. 'I disagreed with you at first, but you have an amazing argument for convincing me I could be wrong about…contentment.'

She brushed her fingers over his chest.

'Reid,' she whispered. 'This is worse than when you told me no one would want to kiss me. I didn't even insult your conveyance this time.'

He pulled her close, and his breath warmed

her cheek, and travelled on a tantalising path throughout her body. 'Guinevere. I would happily do more than kiss you the rest of our lives. So, don't push that thought between us.'

She wondered if she had a life of her own. Perhaps she should go to Scotland with Reid, but her heart plunged at the thought. Moving into a not-well-considered marriage could be like standing in the rain and wondering where the water came from.

She studied the sliver of moon. Irritating thing. It gave her no answers and hid its face.

'I wouldn't want to wed without a love that I believed was only for me. I suppose that is why it has been so difficult for me to consider it in the past. Sometimes I believed the men were courting my parents more than they noticed me. A duke for a father-in-law is not a bad thing.'

'I could argue that. I know your father.'

'He's a kind man.'

'Not with me.'

That concerned her. Perhaps her father could see Reid more objectively than she.

But then she realised how little a man could truly have courted her with the Duchess standing nearby.

'Your parents have protected you. Chaperons. Watchfulness. The friends you have are your own, but you have likely only been able to choose them from the selection put in front of you by the Duke and Duchess. The events you attend aren't bawdy affairs, but genteel moments, and no one wants to anger the Duke. To you he is a loving father, but he can be vengeful. And he wields more power than most other dukes.'

'Oh.' It was true, though she'd not grasped it before Reid spoke. While she'd been encouraged to go to events, she'd been mostly in sight of her parents the whole time.

'If it weren't for the fact that Stephen contains his missteps under his roof, and keeps himself in the country, I doubt he would be welcomed by your parents. I am not, however, encouraged to be near you.'

The truth of his words settled. After Reid's recovery, her parents had noticed her fledgling friendship with him, and had possibly decided to return to London more quickly than they otherwise would have.

When her sister had married, she'd overheard her mother swear not to make the same mistake of letting Guinevere wed an unsuitable man, which she'd thought ridiculous at the time. Now she understood it.

Her mother had determined to watch Guinevere even more closely than she'd controlled Cleo.

'Well…' The ember of knowledge inside her felt smaller than the tiniest tip of a needle, but blazed hotter than any fire she'd ever played with. Her fingers tightened involuntarily on Reid's and she felt her world change.

The layer of protection around her shattered, only she didn't know what the other side would bring if she ventured beyond it. She was tempted to elope with him. Tempted.

But reason prevailed. She would be marrying him as an escape.

She rose, putting distance between them. 'I can't go to Scotland with you. It would be wrong to run.'

He unfolded his legs, lifting the staff when he rose, but remained standing by the bench. 'The archbishop would not risk offending your father by allowing me a Special License without waiting to make some discreet inquiries. He would know there has been no public courtship. He would likely put me off, so he wouldn't anger your father. They are friends.'

'I meant the marriage,' she said. 'I have enough strength to send Stephen away, and if it angers my parents, then they will have to get over it.'

Her thoughts didn't whirl inside her head, but presented themselves as squarely as marks on a chessboard. She was angry at her parents, whom she deeply adored. And she could see the coddling layers that had been around her, and how accepting she'd been. She'd believed herself making her own choices, but the only true determination she might have made was in remaining a spinster.

Until Reid had said the words, she'd not comprehended how sheltered she'd been at the soirees and in society. Most everyone she knew had appeared in her life through her parents first.

And how could she direct her own life with so much hidden from her.

'Your parents truly are good people, Guinevere,' he said.

'I know.'

As if she'd been summoned, a door opened, and a light shone out.

'Guinevere, your bed is empty.' Her mother stood in the shadows.

He put out an arm, holding the small of Guinevere's back.

'Your Grace.' He bowed.

'It's time you came in now, Guinevere.' Her mother opened the door wider, her voice a grating rumble. 'It's past everyone's bedtime.'

Reid gave her a bow. 'I would like to call on your daughter tomorrow, Duchess.'

'I suppose it is best for the two of you to meet in the main sitting room with a chaperon. In daylight. You may visit tomorrow. After dinner.' Silence while she took in a deep breath. 'We will see how that evolves.'

She walked to Guinevere and took her arm. 'Guinevere is ruining her life. She is getting a reputation of being fickle, and now I see it is preferable to the one she is bound to get.'

She stopped and glared at Reid. A low grumble escaped from her lips before she tugged on Guinevere but addressed Reid. 'Marjorie should have reprimanded you more when you were a youngster. But I doubt it would have helped.'

'May I say goodbye privately?'

She glared through the darkness before leaving. 'Briefly. And I do mean *briefly.*' She snapped her fingers and left.

Reid spoke. 'I will visit you tomorrow and see how your parents are reacting. If we need to, I can have a carriage readied, and you can slip out at night and we can go to Scotland. I cannot promise you the marriage you would like, but I can promise you freedom.'

She clutched at his arm, needing his support to keep standing. 'That's not how I want a marriage. Or freedom. Not at all. Not to be rescued. That's wrong.'

He walked her to the closed doorway, then his fingers slid under her chin, sending new shivers through her stronger than any shooting star. His lips touched hers, warm and fulfilling. His mouth held hers for only a brief moment, before he released her, and she thought she heard a soft, *Goodnight*, but she wasn't certain.

She held the latch to remain upright, and glanced back up at the moon, which was disappearing behind a cloud floating over it.

She'd just entered into a friendship destined to fail because he was a man who believed in honesty, and she did as well. But she wasn't ready to be as straightforward as he was.

The kiss had whirled into her. No wonder she had been concerned about being close to anyone. The power of Reid's kiss had expanded inside her. It had seemed to take over her whole body. Weakened her. A woman weakened by kisses could never make strong decisions.

She would be setting herself up for heartbreak. Reid wasn't a gamble, because if one wagered, one had a chance of winning, no matter how slim. And Reid was a marquess who was used to doing things as he wished. He was as unwavering as her parents.

Perhaps she was also as determined as everyone about her.

Her mother was pushing her to Stephen, and she would not be attached to him in any way.

And did she look around, did she choose the most likely person for a long, devoted marriage? she wondered. No, she picked the least. A man used to doing as he wished.

Or had he chosen her? Chosen her with the rare twinkle in his eyes when it passed behind them. The almost grin that caused bursts of unfamiliar feelings in her breasts. The stature created to show the world how man should be formed, and which drew the eyes in a way no artwork ever would.

She grasped that she was stepping close to her own fire, but if her life went up in flames, then she wanted to be the one that ignited the coals.

Chapter Nine

The walls of her home felt frigid every time she walked by her mother or father. She wondered if they comprehended their ice.

On the surface, little had changed except for downcast headshakes from her mother; and one early morning oration, which lasted until her father's voice tired, on the sanctity of marriage, the value of family, and he finished with a blast on the perils of inattention.

And one reluctant agreement from her parents.

A servant alerted them that Reid had arrived as they were finishing dinner. Her mother's and father's eyes locked on her. 'You may be excused to the sitting room, and you must send him away,' her father said, tone sombre as if he were saying a last goodbye before sentencing her to the gallows. 'We are honouring your wish to do so. You made your decision and decided your life. You will abide by it.'

She signalled to the servant, and waited for Reid in the formal sitting room which had the one musical instrument in the abode. A harp which had been her grandmother's and which her mother called *the beast* but said she could never get rid of it because it had belonged to her mother-in-law. But she'd reassured Guinevere that it would never be hers. The beast would stay with the title.

Reid appeared in the doorway, dressed in black, with a grey silk waistcoat, and a simple cravat.

The world stopped and gave her a chance to absorb the sight in front of her. A man, simply, and yet no woman of her age would be able to justifiably call him only a man. Her vision didn't just take him in, but it translated the vision of him into bursts of memory. The recollection of touching his unshaven face. Of knowing that when she'd viewed him in bed, he'd been in repose, storing his energies to return more vibrant than ever. Of an awareness that he was watching her with the same intensity that she comprehended him.

Her hand burned, as if she rubbed it over his cheek.

His eyes took care of all the necessary greeting formalities. He strode in, taking control of the room with his presence.

Reid examined the harp, but she knew his attention was on her.

He ran a finger along the instrument, sounding a note, letting it linger in the room. 'I remember this. Your brother brought me here and we tried to launch an arrow from the strings. We ripped a hole in the drapery, but we arranged the folds so that it was inconspicuous.'

He strolled to the gold brocade, studying it. 'I can't see the gouge.'

'It was mended by an excellent seamstress. Mother could not work out how it tore so. A maid discovered it and they wondered if it were not a flaw in the fabric until they saw the scratch in the wall behind it. Father said not to ask questions and she assumed he did it.'

'It was his arrow, if that counts. And the point was dulled. He likely noticed that.'

'I didn't remember that you visited here with my brother.'

'A few times. He thought we should be mature. I wanted to do as I wished.'

'Have you changed?'

'I learned to like the excesses of maturity.' He

neared the harp, sweeping fingers wide across the strings, then waiting until the sound died.

'I didn't expect your parents to admit me,' he said.

'They are good people. And don't consider you the problem but a result of an error in raising me. They feel I was given too much latitude— even though I feel I spent my time at Mother's elbow.'

'My father often quoted your father's admonition that I'd been given too much freedom and needed to be reined in so that I would make a proper marquess. Your parents are rigid in their views, but the kind of people who keep the polite world on track.'

'Is there anything wrong with that?'

'No. But everything cannot be solved with a smile and a pat on the head.'

His lips turned up in a tight line, but even though the gesture was only meant to point out his disbelief in the platitudes, her chest warmed in response.

He studied her, but the appraisal didn't make her uncomfortable. He appeared to be trying to look beyond her to her thoughts and how they were formed.

This time the barest smile. A true one, and possibly directed at himself, while he examined her with respect. Then he moved the strings, creating a series of notes, one after the other, but his awareness remained on her.

'Do you play?' he asked.

'Oh, heavens, no. My grandmother hired someone to entertain at her soirees, and Mother learned at Father's request but she finds it insufferable.'

A slight nod answered. 'And how do you feel about it?'

'It is pleasant to have it sitting in the corner. A rare thing of beauty to be seen and not heard. Like a wife could be, or so I surmise you believe. Much like a new piece of jewellery. An object to be purchased, bring temporary happiness, admired and left in place while chatter resumes.'

'The only jewellery I wear occasionally is the ring my grandfather gave me. On my little finger. The one he made his seal with.'

'Have you given jewellery as gifts?'

'Of course.'

'Are the women in your life now?'

'Only in passing. I don't even remember whom I gifted or what I gave.'

'If a woman walked up to you, wearing a gift you'd given her, would you remember it?'

'Probably not. I tended to let the jeweller choose something for me. I told him what I wanted—a necklace, ring or brooch—and mentioned the woman's name if he might know her and suggested a price. The man-of-affairs took care of the particulars.'

She held out her hand, examining the ring. A gift from her mother. She'd never received any jewels from anyone else. 'I remember every person who ever gave me jewellery.'

'I would expect no less from you.'

'It's not as impressive a feat as you'd think.'

Their eyes met, and she knew he would not ask for the names of who'd given her presents.

'Have your parents been difficult?' he asked.

'Mother told me I must make a decision in regard to Stephen, but I already had. Just not the one she hoped for.'

'Well, Stephen wasn't happy when I saw him last.'

'Immediately after he arrived, I explained I was not interested in any type of courtship and would not be dissuaded. I didn't want to upset him.'

'He always upsets easily. As far as I've been concerned.'

'Apparently he does with me, also.'

Moving forward, he touched the empty spot on her left ring finger. 'My offer to go to Scotland still stands. You have family ties that will blend well with my own.'

'I would never marry based on that proposal. And I wouldn't have to go to Scotland. Mother might even see that you have an appointment for a Special License since Stephen is off the list.'

'You would be perfect at my country estate.'

'But you wouldn't. Be perfect. Or at the estate.'

'I have old scars, caused by my own errors. And maybe a new one.' He held out his fist to her, and she saw the healing marks on his knuckles.

He turned away and returned to the harp. 'The mirrors were to be draped because of my passing. Someone had forgotten to remove the one in the library at my town house. I walked in and saw it. That mirror will never be used again. I am not entirely certain the covering being left in place was a true mistake.'

'You know that to break a mirror is to bring misfortune. The Romans believed it to last for seven years.'

'Be thankful I broke it. Not you.'

'I don't know if it would be a good thing to wed after breaking a mirror. Seven years is a long time. And I would hope my marriage would last longer than that, so it could be more misfortune than a mere seven years.'

'You don't believe a superstition hundreds of years old?'

'Not at all. Of course not. But I don't need anything to tell me you're not a saint.' Then she shrugged. 'I have seen you at events. We weren't friends. And you were endearing. To the ladies.'

'Not all of them. Not you.'

She peered closely at him. 'If you'd not had the brush with mortality, I don't believe you'd be inclined to wed.'

'What is the problem as to how I arrived at the conclusion?'

'That it might not be the right thing for you.'

She moved to his side and glanced up at him. She reached out, but at the last second, she didn't touch him, and her fingernail gave the lightest vibration on the harp's strings. 'I would have your household. And you would have your heirs.'

'They would be your children as well.'

Then she felt her cheeks warm, and an awareness of what one day in proximity to Reid could do to her. That might be more than she bargained for.

'Marriage,' he said. 'Say the word.'

'Impossible.' She clasped both his hands.

Eyes captured her, locking their gazes together. 'I know a challenge when I hear it.'

'I know one when I see it. And that's what a marriage to you would be like.'

Reid watched every nuance of her expression, but he couldn't see her thoughts. He could almost see his future passing in front of his eyes, a sea of emptiness. 'Life isn't always easy.' He spoke more for himself than her, and steadied himself with an awareness of her grasp.

'My mother is upset with me. Saying no to Stephen. Meeting you in the night. I told her you had suggested we elope, but I could not. Instead, I want to leave London, and help care for an elderly aunt.'

The same intensity of feeling of seeing the mirror draped plunged into him. Aloneness.

'My great-aunt Eleanor is a spinster. Has been writing the most morose letters to Mother. And Mother thinks that next season, after a year with Aunt Eleanor, I may be more amenable to marriage, and if not, she says she will accept it.'

Reid saw the woman, but in experience, she was little more than a youth. But there was hope.

'Was I your first kiss?' He spoke without thinking.

'Yes.'

He pressed his eyes together tightly before speaking. 'I'm sorry. I never thought of—'

'Don't be concerned. It had to happen eventually. I would hope.'

'I could not believe you so protected.'

'I allowed the security around me. I didn't mind. Kisses lead to other things, or so I was told, and those other things are best avoided until marriage. And our childish argument hadn't made me confident of my abilities in that area.'

Again, his conscience reared its head, causing guilt, but at the same time, an unfair happiness infused him. He'd been the beautiful Guinevere's first kiss.

She walked to the curtain and straightened the drapes again. Then she undid all her fussing over the coverings and spread them wide.

'If I'm to go away, or to be pushed into marriage, then I should know a bit of what I'm missing or what I'm being directed to.'

'I might not have suggested an elopement had I known you were such an innocent. You should have a courtship.'

She strode to him. 'Then you are relegating my thoughts to being so green as to be unable to learn from others' mistakes.'

'No mistake teaches you as much, or as powerfully, as the one you make yourself.'

'Only if you choose to learn from it. Have you?'

'Only time will tell.'

'I think not.' She smiled, and rested her hand on his coat front as she let out a breath. 'I think not. I don't think you've learned from them. Or you wouldn't have said that. You would have said *yes*.'

'My accident changed me.'

'It made you consider a bride. But is that a change, a path or merely a diversion?' She bent her knuckles and held her fingernails together. 'Did you only notice me because Stephen did?'

'That does not dignify an answer.'

'It dignified a question.'

He didn't speak.

'But it doesn't matter,' she said. 'He is out of my life now. And I suspect, shortly, so will you be.' She retreated and stopped near the door. 'I was tempted. Truly. Tempted.'

Normally he would have considered the temptation to be a positive thing, but he could tell by the way her hands kept lightly fisting that she wasn't pleased.

'Don't tell me the goal you have for your life is to be mistress of an estate. If it were, you could have accepted my proposal.'

She might be a masterful chess player but

he'd never seen a gambler with a better stare than hers.

'You should aim higher than such a goal.' He challenged her. 'To sit about while a housekeeper and nursery maid take care of the unpleasant duties.'

'Said the Marquess with the butler, house-keeper and man-of-affairs.'

'You don't understand the chore of it. They need direction. You've had your parents at hand to take over when needed.'

'True. But no longer. Now, I will be spending time with my elderly aunt to help with her employees. She needs assistance. And you have had others do all the labour for you. Do you even saddle your own horse? Or would you know how to ready a carriage?'

'Of course. But I employ people for that. My time is best spent on other things.'

'Could you manage half as well as they do? Do you truly grasp what the underlings in your life must do? But don't answer. It's easy to say you comprehend something. It's another thing when tested.'

'There is no marquess test. You either pass or fail.' And he wasn't positive he'd not been failing. Not in a way anyone else would be aware of. In hindsight, likely anyone could have done as well as he had.

'How can you fail at being a peer? A stable-man, that is something you could be unsuccessful at.'

'Managing horses and carriages would be simple compared to my job.'

'I challenge you. Travel to my aunt Eleanor's,' she said. 'Wait a bit, then follow me. For a month. Be the stablemaster there.'

'I can't leave my work.'

'You almost left it for a very long time.' She looked askance at him. 'More than thirty or thirty-one days.'

'That was unavoidable.' Most men would have hesitated at the stare he gave her. She didn't seem to notice it.

'You didn't address my point,' she continued. 'You're surrounded by staff. Can you manage without them?'

'It would prove nothing to act as a servant.'

'It might. Are you only able to follow the path given to you? You told me it was my flaw to be content. Is yours the same? Are you truly capable to see the entire world around you, or is it something you only think you comprehend?'

The emotionless countenance. A challenge. A dare.

She bit her bottom lip. 'I know I can set the pieces in motion for you to be accepted as a stablemaster. My father's steward hired the last one for my aunt, but he left several years ago.'

'You're wagering a lot, and your reputation could be damaged. There's no way you keep a secret such as that.'

'I only expect Maggie, my maid, who is loyal to me, to be sent along. Do you know her?'

He shook his head.

'It is a wager, but I'm doing the same thing with my own life,' she said. 'I'll be proving my mettle. I've seen my aunt's staff and they're relaxed. Act as a stablemaster. The barns are decrepit, and there aren't any horses. A stablemaster with no horses? You could try it. How hard could it be?'

One phrase in her words caused an explosive reaction inside him, and she didn't even know it. *How hard could it be?* She'd gouged him.

'Are you wanting me to prove my worth to myself, or to prove it to you?'

'I've only seen you as a man who knows how to attend soirees, gather with his friends and direct servants,' she said. 'You have nothing to prove to me. To anyone. You don't have to prove anything—ever—to anyone.'

He gathered his temper and shoved it aside before answering a question she'd not asked.

'If you thought I would give the devil a hard time, how much difficulty do you think I could give a saint?'

She reached up, giving her oval filigree necklace a nudge before she straightened the chain, much like a soldier would have polished a medal. In that instant something glimmered, and it wasn't the stone or the chain, it was the determination in her eyes.

'I'm not a saint. I'm flawed.'

'So are the saints.'

She approached closer. Their bodies touched, sending sparks of awareness.

'My parents might be doing the same as your mother did,' she said. 'That's part of the reason I want to leave London. What if they badly want me to wed? What if they are pushing me to Stephen in order to get me to wed? Or to get me closer to you?'

He took a long step back from her. 'Who *are* you, Guinevere? Do you think everyone is playing a game?'

She didn't speak, but she didn't blink either. 'My mother did not act as upset as she could have when she found us outside together. She was more irritated when I suggested that I wanted to visit my aunt. I think they would be pleased to see me betrothed to you.'

'Your parents really don't like me, Guinevere. Never have. They wouldn't do that to you.'

Her voice strengthened. 'You just gave yourself a very poor recommendation.'

He met her gaze with one as direct. She was blasted right.

'I will take your dare and provide horses.'

Wedging another ledger into the satchel, he didn't really know what he'd agreed to. Or even why he'd agreed to it. There were other women he could easily court and... Easily. That was the word that lodged in him. Guinevere wasn't easily pursued. The other ones could be less naïve or more—but a few kisses, dropped hints, and they would accept him on his terms.

'Your trunk is ready, milord.' His valet entered the room, eyes seeming almost hidden beneath the bushy brows, and holding a tray. 'And the drink you requested.' He sat the filled glass on Reid's desk, and the decanter.

'Have a hackney ready to arrive in the morning. I'll spend today with my man-of-affairs and prepare a trunk with my roughest clothing. Nothing but the sturdiest. Be sure and have the wooden golf clubs with it. I plan to be gone... perhaps a month.'

The valet's movements were indiscernible, as was his rarely varying expression. 'I will be happy to do so.' Beckham would have announced a burning building or that shaving water was ready with the same emphasis.

'Be sure my carriage driver takes the letter to Mother so that she doesn't concern herself. I've told her I'll be with friends. And if Stephen badgers you to find out my location, misdirect as you see fit.'

He'd given Stephen and the servants the impression he was off to drink his way north and visit every tavern along the way. 'I am making up for what I missed earlier.'

'With all due respect, you would have to agree you did not miss much.'

The quiet words hit the air and seemed to increase inside Reid's head. But he had missed Guinevere and she'd been right in front of him.

'True.'

Raising a silver pen, he tucked it into the small pocket of the filled satchel Beckham had prepared, then slipped the strap through the buckle and forced it closed.

Beckham waited.

'That will be all,' Reid said.

Still, Beckham lingered.

In the years Beckham had laboured as a valet, Reid and the manservant had never shared any talk other than the necessary amount for the workday. Perhaps they'd shared a few absurd remarks here and there because their humour matched, but little conversation passed between them.

'That will be all,' Reid repeated, grasping the glass.

Perhaps Beckham had a jest to share.

Reid took a sip, waiting, as he savoured the strength of the drink, the taste rolling across his tongue like nectar.

The valet cleared his throat.

Reid studied the servant's demeanour.

'Did I tell you how sorrowful I was to learn of your accident?' The valet shifted his perusal to the remaining liquid, and then he gazed directly into Reid's eyes.

Reid stilled.

Beckham's words were measured. 'I was also saddened to learn you are leaving.'

Reid was touched. A servant who wanted him to stay.

'To travel north, and—' Beckham waited. 'I would prefer to keep my employment. This is the first drink I have brought you since the mishap, and I have been surprised.'

Reid stopped, somehow lost in the conversation. At least the valet hadn't seemed pleased at the prospect of losing him.

'How much spirits—' Beckham seemed to be drawing all the air in the room into his lungs '—had you had that morning?'

Rage infused Reid's body. 'The horse stumbled.' Reid resisted the urge to curse at the man. 'Get out. Now.'

The angry haze in his eyes cleared as the door shut behind Beckham.

He examined the liquid. His first taste since returning to London. It was not chocolate. It never had been when he was in London until recently. And he'd known he needed to spend more time considering his finances instead of laughing and drinking with his friends. Most of their fathers took care of their business, and he'd comprehended himself letting down his legacy—and began to study the transactions made in his name.

Then he'd lost sight of what his heritage was.

He'd gone to the estate with plans to discover the truth. And he had. After he'd arrived, he'd been up all night, studying ledgers, stunned. Then he'd remembered the spirits stored there and the knowledge he'd discovered had seemed much easier with drink in hand. Too much drink in hand.

He'd decided to go for an early morning ride, and that had almost killed him.

Placing the container on the table, he stared at it, feeling his life reflected from the amber, seeing many nights where deals were made, true business was conducted and fortunes were increased. The revelry was part of the game. The game was tactical, and pieces were moved about when one could hardly stand.

He touched the rim where his lips had rested, then he raised the brandy, watching the fluid swirl at eye level.

Was he stronger than the liquid?

He thought of Guinevere.

Blast it all. He had no time for this nonsense.

He slammed the glass down onto the table, then he lifted it, and slung it into the fireplace. The sound of the glass shattering vibrated in his body as he strode out of the room.

He was stronger than the liquid. He didn't have to prove anything to anyone.

But himself.

Chapter Ten

Rain pelted his hat, but the caped coat kept him dry when he stepped out of the hackney. Even in the darkness, he could tell he'd fared better than the man at the ribbons. The man's hat flopped around his ears.

Reid took the satchel and the portmanteau. The driver scurried to help with the trunk. Striding through the puddles, Reid moved to the entrance, hearing the man sloshing along behind.

Reid shook the water from his shoulders and waited in the shelter of the portico for someone to let them in, hoping he'd not been given the wrong direction, feeling the rush of excitement at seeing Guinevere again.

A man, whose hair had been shorn at the sides, opened the door, and stepped sideways for Reid to enter, but the driver stayed outside.

Reid was let into an entryway which smelled

as if it might be hiding a wet dog, and a herd of bovines. The only ornamentation was a sconce holding a melted candle which should have been replaced, and a lit lamp on a side table. The man held a smaller light.

If this was the well-maintained part of the home, he hated to think what his quarters would be like.

'I'm the new stablemaster,' he introduced himself.

'I heard you might be here.'

'Find an umbrella for me, and a lamp, and fetch some candles to take to the cottage. I've a hackney driver staying the night, and we'll both need supper brought.'

'Don't be telling me what to do, Your Lordship.' The frail man had a stare worthy of someone twice his size. 'A stableman does not direct the highest household staff.'

Reid paused at the reference, trying to figure out how he'd been discovered, until he saw the sneer on the other man's face and comprehended he was being mocked. Reid had given instruction from habit.

'I will have one of the maids get a lamp and umbrella for you,' the butler said. 'And I will only allow this to be provided because it is your first day. I suggest you learn afterwards to keep supplies in your lodging and do not trouble the household staff for such trivialities.'

'Food?' Reid asked, not wanting to go hungry, and being afraid to speak more without giving a command.

'In this household, we are proud of our generosity to unfortunate travellers,' he said. 'And you would fall into that category.'

The butler left, and Guinevere came into view. She chuckled. 'Your Lordship,' she almost chirped.

He smiled. 'There's dust on the sconce, Your Ladyship.'

'So we both have some learning to do.'

Bathed in lamplight, Guinevere stood at the top of the stair, as regal as her name, her dress flowing like a royal robe. His body weakened enough to assist him with a bow. 'My lady.'

'How were the roads?'

'Only passable,' Reid answered.

'I hope your accommodations are suitable,' she said, hesitating, then hurrying down two more steps. 'I know they could be better. The maids have cleaned them and done as best they could.'

She moved to the last stair-step, voice softer. 'I didn't know if you were going to arrive. I thought you'd changed your mind.'

'I did.'

And he had. A thousand times. But that last time had been too late. He'd already arrived at the door of the house.

'I'm pleased you're here,' she said. 'The cottage is ready for you.'

'I'll find it,' he said.

She moved closer, her presence fading the scents of the damp house and replacing them with a springtime-fresh womanly fragrance.

'How are you faring?' he asked. He needed to keep space between them. But he couldn't force himself to leave. He'd sat trapped in a carriage with broken springs for hours to see the sight in front of him, and to be in her presence.

'Better now that I'm growing more familiar with what needs to be done. Maggie is with me, but I wondered…almost, if I'd made the decision so I could step farther from my parents' guidance. To choose my own direction.'

'You definitely didn't err by not marrying Stephen,' he said. 'You'll never look back on that with regrets, only relief.'

He studied the countenance in front of him, a gaze more intriguing than any he'd ever seen before, and understood why he'd let her distract him.

When Guinevere had left London, he'd not

sought out his friends, or dulled any of his senses, and he'd experienced every whisper of every reflection that surrounded him. He'd seen options and choices, and a different way of considering life. Instead of being directed by the whims of what sounded amusing, diverting or new, he'd thought about where he wanted to be and how he should get there. Perhaps it was strategy.

The same kind directing Guinevere in a chess game.

He remained close a moment longer, to feel her presence. She didn't infuse him with the recklessness he'd felt in his younger years when he saw a woman and thought of nothing else but pursuing her. Yet, she pulled him towards her with an even stronger power and calmed the bursts of energy that had bounded within him and made him restless.

But he wasn't sure it was only her. Something had changed after the accident, making things seem meaningless that had once meant a great deal, and matters which hadn't been high on his priorities now enveloped him.

Guinevere foremost.

He felt strong emotion for her. But he feared he couldn't trust it.

If he would wake and his old life would whirl

back, she would be hurt. He couldn't risk letting her care too much if he couldn't be the man she thought he was.

'I would like to see you tonight,' he said, 'but it wouldn't be a good idea. The driver will be nearby. He can't return on the wet roads. But tomorrow night?' he asked.

'I have…missed you,' she said.

'From the look on your face, you didn't expect to.' The surge of happiness that filled him surprised him, and put the hint of a laugh into his voice. 'Life is full of amazements.'

His own stablemaster arrived at midday, loaded with supplies and followed by Hermes, with Hera pulling a riding chair and one of the other servants driving it.

Hera and Hermes acted as if he were another stable hand. They greeted him the same as always.

Curtains were moved aside at windows, possibly with everyone in the house seeing what caused the commotion.

The riding chair Hera pulled had two big wheels on either side of the seat. The narrow profile gave it an advantage over the heavier carriages, and it was one of the simplest ways, next to riding, to cover country roads less travelled.

He doubted Guinevere or her aunt had ever ridden in one, but his mother had sometimes used it, and found it easier to take a jaunt into the nearby village.

Guinevere rushed out of the house, dressed every bit the country miss, the brim of her bonnet in place to protect her from the sun, and her parasol in her hand. He bowed to her, and she smiled.

It felt they were playing. Her part of the endeavour was of innocence and lightness. He wasn't sure exactly where he sat on the game board.

But this game could hurt the players. He saw to the end of it and the deep cuts it could leave in her life if people began talking about her, and she lost standing over it. He couldn't risk that for her, and yet he couldn't walk away.

'A riding chair?'

'It's an easier way to get along rough roads if you're not inclined to go on horseback or walk.' The low chair would handle only a sole occupant at the reins, and a large wheel on each side of the low-sitting chair gave it stability. 'A sedate, smaller and safer version of a phaeton.'

She laughed. 'A phaeton for a lady who prefers safety over adventure.'

'Would that not be you?'

'In the past.' She studied the chair. 'But now it almost seems too sedate for me. I may have changed.'

He started to tell her she'd not altered from the woman she'd been, but he didn't, because he wasn't sure.

'This evening,' he said, 'after Hera rests and eats, I'll see that you and your aunt have a chance to drive the vehicle.'

'I don't know if my aunt can manage it. It might be too much for her.'

'I'll go along on Hermes to assist if she has any problems.'

'Will you do the same for me?'

'Of course, milady,' he said, and tipped his hat. 'It is my job.'

'Thank you.' She ducked her head. The brightness that filled her cheeks infused him with an unfamiliar weakness. She was the one blushing, and he felt like the inexperienced lad.

'It is good to have you here. The new surroundings have been a challenge, though my aunt doesn't seem to mind what I do. So, I've been changing a few things as I see fit. I had no choice. Maggie refused to stay if I didn't. She's distraught about leaving London.'

She peered at her hands. 'I didn't realise how it would affect her life to bring her with me.'

'The house wasn't up to the standards expected.' He studied her.

'It has vastly improved,' she said. 'Your cottage took most of my time the first few days. I started the staff on it initially. They didn't want the extra duties. But I was careful to be fair and to let them know what was called for. I was direct, but not unkind.'

'They already knew what was required. You should have reprimanded them.'

'I couldn't. I was new, and I wanted to give them a chance. They just needed direction. Not condemnation.'

'Good employees get lax and require a stern word.'

'Haven't you ever wanted to please anyone just because you admired or respected them? Your mother, for instance?'

He raised his brows and glanced at her enough to show her that mothers fell into a separate category.

'Besides her, then?' she countered. 'Your grandfather?'

He remembered how he'd felt as a lad towards his grandfather. 'He was rather a gruff old bear. Demanding. I admired that about the Marquess. Everyone hopped around him.'

'But was he really demanding to you? Or was

he attentive? I was under the impression that you were the perfect heir in his mind, and he wanted you to follow in his every footstep.'

Reid paused, remembering his grandfather's tirades, but he'd never noticed before that none were truly ever directed at him. Well, perhaps a few had been, but they were well-deserved.

'Most of the time, even when I misbehaved, he chuckled about it,' Reid admitted. 'Said I was the image of him.'

'From what I hear, you are.'

He let the silence linger as she waited, overly wide-eyed, for his response. 'Lady Guinevere, I think you would not give a servant such a sincere look as you're giving me.'

'Oh, I would,' she said, humour bubbling beneath her words. 'If they had indeed ignored my suggestions.'

'Perhaps you do speak directly to them. Just in a different way than I do.'

He glanced around. 'But whoever tends the gardens has been doing well for a long time. You cannot create this in a week, or day, or month. The grass has been clipped well. I noticed it this morning when I stepped outside.'

'You're right,' she said. 'But that is the only staff member who needed no instruction. I didn't give the gardener any guidance at all. He must love his duties.'

He noticed one of the servants who'd stepped outside with a basket in her hand kept watching them.

'The employees believe my father sent me here to oversee Aunt Eleanor's care. I fostered that idea. The butler is uppity, and I can see up his nostrils every time I direct him, but my aunt considers him irreplaceable and always jumps to his defence.'

His reaction to the excitement in her voice stunned him. He wanted her to keep talking, just to listen to her.

She laughed. 'I have been struggling to understand what needs to be done, and Maggie has had to guide me.'

'But you've taken charge.'

'My mother is a caring woman, but this did give me a chance to step out from under her rule.'

'You shouldn't be pushed into marriage.' His conscience attacked him, remembering his attempts to do just that. 'Unless you'd decided to go to Scotland with me,' he added. 'That wasn't a push, it was a proposal. Which you declined.'

'I didn't mind you asking,' she said. 'If you didn't mind my saying no.'

He took in an exaggerated breath. 'You said no? I must have missed that.' He couldn't help himself, he reached out and touched the edge of her bonnet brim. 'I told you that you can direct people without even letting them know it's your idea.'

'I wish that were also true of the servants here.'

'Give them time. They don't know you well.'

He was the one who needed a chaperon, but he'd guard himself carefully. Hers was peering out the window.

'You should get inside,' he said. 'I need to get to my tasks, and we're the centre of attention.'

Guinevere agreed, and he made sure not to watch her returning to the house. They were already being observed, but he would take more care in the future.

Guinevere wasn't the only person who'd stepped into a new life. The one he'd found when he'd awoken was a different existence than he'd had only days before.

The physical labour he'd done since morning in order to ready the place for Hera and Hermes didn't feel like a holiday. Blisters instead of bell pulls.

The tasks were challenging, tiring and earning him a new respect for his staff, and an awareness of just how much effort it took to upkeep the world around him. Guinevere had been correct.

The stable, even as small as it was, was a challenge, also. It had been ignored for a long time. He moved out to cut an old board he'd located, then he retrieved the saw he'd found the night before. He'd use the board to replace a rotten one holding Hera and Hermes in. They had better manners than he'd suspected or they wouldn't have remained in the enclosure.

Making repairs on a stable was a definite change from his daily life, and not something he was going to continue. Without question he would return to his estate and his town house. His life of a marquess was the correct one.

He was giving Guinevere an inaccurate perception of who he was.

She had to be aware of her father's duties, but her father took the slower, measured path. He was a duke with his wealth amassed, diversified and in the hands of his capable staff.

Reid's father had taken an easier route, living off the funds his father had created, and always trusting others, and never contemplating too deeply.

His grandfather had grumbled about the expenses, the yearly totals and the costs of everything. Reid had been unaware he was being instructed to care for the finances in ways his father hadn't done. But he understood it better since he'd been researching the funds.

His family's livelihood rested on his decisions. No one else could manage the estate but him, and the family seemed to grow all the time. Even Stephen's finances were in Reid's hands. He didn't want his aunt to be a pauper.

His daily life couldn't be conducted in a stable. He had to remain among society to gain knowledge to make the decisions which would support his world.

But he'd not been able to stay away from Guinevere. He'd longed to be with her again.

The happiness in her eyes lulled him, and he pushed all his doubts away, letting himself remember the eagerness and exhilaration in her face.

Guinevere was challenging herself. She'd found a new chess game to play, directing her aunt's household, and this one enthralled her.

He'd promised himself to be better after the accident, but he didn't know if he'd achieved the vow. He was playing an even bigger game now than one of a night of cards. He was acting in a charade, and he'd lied to himself if he'd thought it to prove his mettle.

It was to be closer to Guinevere.

Chapter Eleven

Reid had finished getting Hera and Hermes settled, but while he'd worked, he'd mentally made a list of all the items needed to make the fences sturdy again, the animals comfortable and to correct problems time and inefficiencies had created. He'd never before deliberated on how much his staff did.

One man alone couldn't finish all the corrections in a short time, and he didn't think he could let his two prize animals stay without their being able to run freely. He could still exercise them, but the field wasn't secured, and it was so overgrown that someone needed to cut the saplings out of it.

A gentle rap.

He knew who it would be, and stood to open the door.

She had on a brown woollen cape, with the

hood resting on her back, and he immediately forgot his irritation with the way the fences had fallen into disrepair.

'I noticed you hadn't been outside,' she said. 'And I hoped I might be able to use the new conveyance.'

'I believe the *new* vehicle once belonged to my grandparents,' he said. 'My grandmother was spirited, and believed she could manage a horse, and she could.'

'That's wonderful,' she said. 'I would like to try.'

'I'll get it ready,' he said, and moved to saddle Hermes, and then to hitch Hera to the cart.

She waited, and he noticed her feeding each an apple while he readied the other horse.

'Making friends?' he asked.

'Trying to, but I don't think I needed the apples.'

'You didn't,' he admitted. Hera, and even Hermes, seemed entranced with her, but he couldn't blame them. Except he was a little irritated with Hermes, his favourite.

'I'll go with you on the stallion,' he said. 'If you have any trouble with Hera, then I'll be there to assist.'

She was a natural at the reins, and he rode beside her.

When the excursion was over, she put the brake on, and it screeched, piercing the ear. He caught himself before telling her he'd have the stablemaster look at it.

He dismounted, and realised his job wouldn't be over after he'd ridden with the aunt on her journey. He would need to unsaddle and unhitch. Hermes definitely wanted to go for another trek, though.

'When I first rode Hermes after the accident,' he said, 'I was waiting for something to go wrong. I possibly could have prevented the accident had I not been foxed. But I also wondered if Hermes felt the lord should be deposited on the ground for not taking better care of things. For not being more considerate to him.'

'He wouldn't—'

'He might. I don't think he would try to injure me, but if he could accidentally dump me on the ground because he didn't think I was behaving properly, I could see him doing it.'

'A horse wouldn't try to deliver a comeuppance.'

Reid argued with a sideways stare. 'You really don't know Hermes. It's not the only time I've had a mishap with him, but it was the most serious.'

'I don't think it could get worse than that accident.'

'Or better,' he admitted. 'It was hard to overlook you when you jabbed me in the arm.' He studied his surroundings. 'I wouldn't be here if it weren't for you.'

'Are you enjoying it?'

'This is not my life.'

'You don't like the countryside?'

'In London, I have a valet. A cook who prepares food to my requests. No mice skittering across the floor at night. No drafts at the windows. Even my country estate is much better equipped than this one. With no disrespect, it's a palace compared to this setting, and it's so much closer to London.'

'I've enjoyed it more than I ever believed I would. Only the first few days were hard. I think it's splendid here. No one watches me like a child. My life at my own home was pleasant with so many events to attend. But it's different here. More pleasant and peaceful. The rooms are not as comfortable, but I like it. My aunt seems so appreciative, and I've been able to know her better.'

'So, no mice in the house?'

'Not that I'm aware of. Aunt has a cat that sleeps at her feet most of the day.'

'She should send him to the barn.'

'I don't think she likes the feline out of her sight.'

'I've never been that fond of a cat. Or a pet. Except the horses, and I don't think they count. Transportation.'

'Even Orange?'

'He's acceptable. A good mouser.'

'The animals are surely more to you than that. A cat as a rodent chaser. Horses for transportation. Is that the only way you see them?'

'Mostly. I'm proud of Hermes and Hera. I know they're the best that anyone can have, but still, they're useful and require excellent and sometimes costly care. It's particularly an extravagance in winter when no one is travelling. They need more food in the cold weather when there's slight natural forage.'

He noticed she didn't want to go in the house, and she lingered, and he couldn't tell her to leave. He liked hearing the sound of her voice and having her at his side. It was true he wasn't fond of the residence, the staff or his chores, but he'd wanted the chance to be with Guinevere.

He put an elbow on the fence and spoke quietly. He didn't want any servant overhearing. Guinevere moved closer.

'This has made me see my life differently,' he

said. 'I see how much I take for granted. Things provided by my forebears. Perhaps my father knew more than I gave him credit for. And more than my grandfather would acknowledge.'

'Your father was genuine, and a true friend to my family.'

'In Grandfather's eyes, he never measured up.'

'Do you think it was possible?'

'Not really. I understand it better now.'

'You're more compassionate since your accident.'

'I may be. Perhaps it was time.' A few days before the accident, Reid had realised he'd never seen his father's hunting box, and didn't even know where it was located, and confronted the man-of-affairs. He'd thought the man had been making odd choices with the funds. Then the man had confessed he'd only been continuing instructions. Reid had investigated.

He'd returned to the estate, searching through the stored ledgers, learning that the original expenses for the hunting lodge had been incurred Reid's entire lifetime, and collaborating the steward's words that the annual trip his father had taken away had been a meeting. Every year, his father had given additional funds to a woman. The steward had continued after Reid's father had passed on.

'I was furious at my father all night before the accident, and I had to keep it from my mother. In my anger, I drank a lot.' He'd almost taken that secret to his grave without meaning to.

'None of us are perfect,' he said. Then he caught the concern on Guinevere's face and wanted to jest away his words. 'Except you're near enough.'

She stilled, studying him, letting the words settle into her thoughts.

A servant stepped out of the main house, and moved to the chicken pens, probably gathering the eggs for the day. The woman glowered at him.

Then he comprehended his stance. The way he spoke to Guinevere as an equal and stood close to her. The servants wouldn't accept his behaviour as appropriate for a stableman to a family member of the house.

Perhaps it would have been best if he'd spoken more loudly and remained farther apart. No one would believe him a marquess, but anyone could credit him captivated by Guinevere.

Reid stepped into the room mostly furnished in items reminding him of fruit fallen to the ground in the orchard and left to rot. His stable-master palace.

He shrugged, ducking his head under the doorway, and slipped into the bedroom. The wardrobe took up the majority of the room, and the bed was closer to sleeping on hay than he imagined real fodder would feel. The shaving mirror was small, the first one he'd truly looked at since the one he'd broken. It didn't sit well with him that it had a crack in it. The washbasin overpowered its stand.

He lifted his satchel, pulling the papers out and then placing them on the only table in the room. He would need to keep up with his finances while he was away, and he'd instructed his steward to send him once-weekly posts, discreetly, with the stablemaster as the recipient.

Then he stared at the papers on the table. Another thing he'd not considered. A stableman would not have a marquess's private papers. He checked the door and found no adequate latch, but he would take care if someone entered.

Without thinking, he looked around for a bottle. Then he shrugged the thought away, remembering the pitcher under the washbasin table.

It had been twelve days, and he wasn't going to count them any more because he'd seen Guinevere.

Twelve days they'd been apart, and they had been the longest days of his life. More like years.

Never before had he considered the time when he was away from a sweetheart. It hadn't mattered.

But no one else had been Guinevere.

His thoughts stilled inside him.

When he left, it would be difficult, and he didn't know how often he would be able to return for a visit, or if he would. Until then, he would cherish each moment, and each memory, he had with her.

A gentle rap sounded on his door, causing his lips to turn up. He let her in.

'That was exciting,' she said, her glow of happiness infusing into him. He stayed close, absorbing her presence.

He knew what she was talking about, and it had concerned him. 'Not to me.'

'When Aunt shook the reins and shouted out for Hera to gallop, it completely surprised me. I thought the chair was going to bounce her out. Thank goodness you had Hermes ready and could catch them and slow her.' She clasped his arm in her exhilaration, her touch stilling him in a way he'd never been before.

'I will never, ever, ever suggest she go for another ride in that chair,' he said. 'As far as she's concerned, Hera is lame, foaling or foundering.

Whatever it takes. And Hermes is even more out of the question. He thinks like your aunt.'

'Can we go for a walk?' she asked. 'The sky is so beautiful tonight. The crescent moon is so bright you can see the shape of the entire circle.'

He could hold her. Clasp her. Kiss her. But he couldn't. 'Someone else could be doing the same, and it would be bad for your reputation if someone saw us. Word would get out faster than any wildfire. We can't take the risk.'

He held himself aloof, keeping his body in check, or trying to. Not hugging her close.

She put her arms around him. 'We could be quiet. And just sit under the stars.'

The memory of their first kiss lodged in him, nestling in a place he'd never be able to remove the memory of. Then he stopped. He had used his next to last fragment of willpower.

Reid took her cheeks in his hands.

'We can't.'

'Why not?'

'You're a virgin.'

'We can't sit under the stars because I'm a virgin?'

'No one could see you outside with a man, away from chaperons. It's too risky. It might look as if you were hidden here to have a child.'

'But they would work it out—eventually.'

'No. They'd just say you'd been mistaken or something similar. I wondered last night what your mother was thinking to risk speculation about you.'

'No one will speculate about me like that,' she said. 'You forget, I *do* have a reputation. As a fickle woman who made certain to keep men at arm's length.' Her voice lowered. 'I had a fear of being kissed. And I was so careful not to be alone with a suitor.'

He held her shoulders. 'Guinevere. I apologise again. I didn't even remember saying that until you reminded me. I only recalled how haughty you were about the vehicle. It was my first one I had any choice about. I was so proud of it.'

'Well, that explains it.' Her laughter made the last words melodious. 'But you can make it up to me.'

She looked up at him, lips moist, eyes alight, arms slipping around him.

He gave her a brief, chaste touch on the lips, and then pulled away, or so he'd meant to. His head had moved to allow more space, but his arms had moved around her, nestling her close.

Awareness of her body hummed in him, removing everything around him but her lips, their fullness and the promise of them.

If he'd made her uncomfortable about kissing

in the past, it would be unpardonable to neglect the blooming beauty of her now. That was what he told himself but he knew he couldn't keep her at a distance.

Her breath brushed against his mouth, and he could hear their clothing rustling together, and smell the clean scent of her.

He tasted the softness, the flavour of honey and the sublime promise of Guinevere.

Clasping her even closer, his tongue found the seam of her lips, and united them, an interlude that blotted time and surroundings, making his body alive and yet erasing everything but Guin.

He felt her the length of his body. Awareness of her womanliness infused him, making him feel as if she were his first kiss. And he could have sworn an oath he'd never kissed anyone but her and believed it.

He pulled away, his senses blinded except for her presence, his hardness compelling him closer to her.

'Guin.' He wouldn't have recognised his voice, changed by the promise of the moment. He forced himself into control, or at least much closer to it than he'd been.

'That is what a kiss is to feel like.'

Her sigh echoed in his ears. 'I waited far too long.'

'Perhaps you waited just the right amount.'

She stumbled back, shaking her head, then clasped his shoulders for support. 'I should never have listened to you.'

'Not about that.'

She studied him. 'Well, I forgive you. For now. If you kiss me again.'

She burrowed back in his arms, lingering, and their lips united. He took his time, losing himself in her taste, his hand trailing her face, and down the long slow curves of her body to rest on her hip.

Then he stopped, moved away and stared at the wall. 'No. We can't. This can only lead to one place and it's not fair to you.'

And he wasn't certain it would be fair to him. To hold Guinevere and to lose her was a price he wasn't sure he wanted to pay. But he knew that his body would lie to him with all the persuasion of a multitude of angels, and in the morning, he'd wake with a devil of a pounding conscience—and memories of Guinevere that he could never forget.

He didn't want to wake with any possibility of grievance to her on his mind. He'd sworn to change. Promised each angel on his shoulder and each one in the heavens, and he'd meant those words. Meant them.

'I can't, Guin,' he said.

'Oh, you can. I'm certain of that. I may be innocent, but not that innocent.'

'It all seems perfect now, but six hours from now, it's evaporated, and the only answer is to repeat the experience or run from it. I don't want either. And you have to think about the consequences in the light of day.'

She marched around to stand in front of him. 'Because of you I missed out on probably more kisses than I can count. I see no reason to continue to do so.'

'I'm not talking about kisses.'

'Well, either—or—and. Take it how you wish. I missed out.'

'You're a virgin. That has to mean something. It does to me. If you've waited this long, you should wait. In case you do decide to wed.' He touched her chin.

'It doesn't seem important. It seems almost a mistake now to have been so careful.' She increased the distance between them, head down.

He put a hand on her back and she found herself in his arms.

'Well, you should have decided that before we became friends. Before me,' he said.

'Are you saying you wouldn't?' She looked into his eyes.

'Yes.'

'I'm hurt.'

'It hurts me not to have you in my arms, to spend the night with you and wake with you. But it has to be more than that. The commitment. It has to be there for you.'

'You're supposed to be—not like that.'

'I wasn't. I've changed. The accident.' Though he didn't know if that was entirely the truth. If he had been with Guinevere the week before his accident, he suspected he would have said the same thing to her. She was Lady Guinevere. The one he'd always stayed away from, and perhaps it wasn't just because they'd known each other from childhood. Perhaps it was because she'd always been different to him than everyone else. Something to be noticed from afar. To be cherished.

'Couldn't you become noble after me?'

He chuckled. 'It didn't work out that way.'

'Why did you come here, then?'

'You invited me. And I wanted to see if I could drink chocolate for breakfast. And I wanted to understand more about the things around me. I wanted to step into another world, and you put it in front of me. How could I say no?'

'You can say no fairly easily. You've proven it.'

He regarded her with all the intensity he felt,

his appearance chilled. 'What if it was my revenge on your father?'

Her face tightened, but then she shook her head. 'I don't believe you. If you were getting revenge, you would not be pushing me away.'

'You're very trusting.'

'Not that trusting.' She touched the stubble on his cheek, and all his pretence faded. With the brush of her hand, she smoothed out the furrows inside him.

All the times he'd been sworn at, he couldn't remember. All the times he'd fought with someone, well, they were just arguments that went too far. But he'd kissed Lady Guinevere, and pulled himself away from her, and that was the most painful thing he'd ever done.

'Makes me see my life differently if marriage to me is a way of punishing someone else. I'm thankful you didn't tell me this on the way back from a Scotland trip.'

He kissed her forehead, while holding her at a safe distance.

He walked her to the door. 'You have to go, Lady Guin. Neither of us are thinking clearly. And if you stay any longer, I fear there's a chance of losing your friendship, and I don't want that. I will watch to see that you get safely to the house,' he said at the doorway.

'You want to be friends with me?' she asked, moving outside.

'Yes. From a distance.'

'I would rather be close with you.'

Chapter Twelve

Breakfast. Delivered by a dour woman who obviously wanted to give the uppity new stablemaster a bad morning. She could have sent an underservant.

'You best be coming to the kitchen from now on to collect your meals, and then bring them here,' she said. 'And don't expect no special London treatment. We are regular folk here and proud of it.'

He surveyed the stale roll unbefitting a horse, and porridge which clung to the spoon so tightly he was thankful he'd had a knife so he could cut the bread into bite-sized pieces. Hunger forced him to eat.

He hoped Guinevere was faring better, but he was certain she did. No one would serve a duke's daughter such poorly prepared food.

And he missed her. He was concerned for her,

but he held himself from seeking her out. He could never cause questions to surface about her, and he had to keep his distance. A little familiarity to her would be overlooked by the servants, but only a very little.

And chores awaited him. The horses would need attention. Water. Food because the pasture wasn't secure enough for them to graze. And some manure shovelling to finish a delightful sunny afternoon.

Everyone appeared to be shunning him, but he supposed the new one always had to prove himself.

Society was different, but emotions were the same no matter what part of life you were from. They varied by person, but travelled the same veins.

After he'd taken care of the horses and managed to take a cold bath, he moved to the front of the house and admired the grass again.

The gardener had taken care with his duties and the foliage in front of the house. That and the perfect temperature was too tempting for Reid.

Besides, he was going to have a long trip in front of him the next day.

He was leaving. He'd decided. The experiment had failed. Or succeeded beyond his dreams. He wasn't sure which but he was going to leave.

But the grass called to him.

He sent the butler to gather everyone at the front of the house, and collect chairs for them to sit in. Rutledge balked, but Reid used his size, his years of being a marquess, and when the man still refused, Reid held out a coin which apparently spoke best and more persuasively than he could. When Rutledge reached for it, Reid flipped it up, caught it and said, 'If everyone appears, and an empty bottle is secured for me.'

'Everyone?' Rutledge grumped.

'Yes. Except Lady Eleanor doesn't have to. It is her home.'

But Eleanor arrived with everyone else, even though he was uncertain to let her touch the clubs.

Rutledge appeared last holding a wine bottle high.

Reid took it and gave the butler the coin.

Then he addressed everyone. 'This is the objective. To make the bottle ring or have your ball land against it.' He directed one of the young men to place the bottle at the edge of the grass.

He took the two carved L-shaped wooden clubs and handed her one of the leather-wrapped balls half the size of his fist. He kept one for himself.

'Some people play by hitting the ball into a

small hole in the ground, but we'll play a different version.'

He addressed the group. 'Lady Guinevere and I will demonstrate a match against each other first, and then the competition can begin.'

The servants didn't smile. Their day was being interrupted by the upstart. It would not be good to give ground to a stranger.

'If you break the bottle, you lose instantly. We each get a swing in turn, and whoever gets the first clink wins the first game, and we continue on until we're tired of it.'

'This sounds like a game invented by a drunken sailor,' Guinevere said.

'Don't know,' he said. 'But it was once criminal in Scotland, around the time of James II, because archers preferred to practice it instead of their military skills. It was considered an unprofitable sport, and I have to agree.'

'Way to make something sound more interesting is to make it illegal,' Rutledge said. 'But that doesn't mean we've got any compunction to break the law.'

'It's not unlawful now, and the way we'll play it is more a jest of that game than the true game of golf.'

'What if you knock the bottle over?'

'Doesn't matter, as long as it remains sound.

The loser has to pick up the glass if the bottle breaks and loses for the entire night. All his wins are forfeited. Keeps players from hitting the ball too roughly.'

He took his place at the edge of the shrubs surrounding the garden. The wine bottle was almost in the middle of the grounds. 'Lady Guinevere and I will demonstrate the competition. Again, we each take a swing in turn, and the first one to hit the bottle wins. If we both hit the bottle after the same number of tries, it's a tie.'

Then he locked his legs, eyed the target and swung the club, hitting the ball—which stopped when it clinked the bottle.

'My apologies, Lady Guinevere. I have heard of others who diminish their skills to lose a game, but I am not one of them.'

'But you've done this before. You're obviously going to be better than I.'

'I would hope. And I will accept that reluctance as your forfeit.'

'No.' She stood in place, swung and connected with the ball, sending it too far past the bottle.

'We are both fortunate this was a demonstration,' he said, 'or you would have lost.'

Then he handed the club to her aunt. 'Now that the game has been explained, it's time to begin the tournament. You are next against Lady Guinevere, Lady Eleanor. Show her no mercy.'

He snapped his fingers and sent one of the younger staff members to stand the bottle up.

'The staff will divide into teams of two each and the winners of those teams will play until we have a champion.'

Reid watched as the game continued with the servants taking a turn. The cheers and jeers lightened the day.

Guinevere stood beside him to watch the others play. He should have left to go back to the stables, but he couldn't. He remained standing with her, listening to the laughter and the joy around them.

No one swore, except the cook muttered a curse under her breath when she swung and completely missed the ball, and the spirit of the camaraderie was similar to the ribald evenings he'd spent with friends. He felt like a patriarch, overseeing a household, but this was a different sort than his London town house held. In truth, he couldn't imagine his servants relaxing enough to do such a thing, but perhaps he would try someday, assuming he could let them touch the clubs.

Guinevere took another turn.

Leaving them at play, he finally slipped away

and saddled Hermes, and travelled the road. He needed to have the distance between them. It would be best if he didn't think of her. Nor stood so close the wind wafted the scent of her perfume over him.

Once he found someone who could watch over Hera, he would be gone.

'Milady, do you fathom what the servants are whispering about?' Maggie took Guinevere's shawl from her after Reid had left and everyone had dispersed inside the house.

'I would suppose they're always whispering about something,' Guinevere said, brushing a lock of hair back from her face. 'It makes the drudgery of duties go faster.' She repeated the words her mother had said to her.

'They're noting you and the stableman. He's much too assured for his own good. And so familiar. I daresay your mother wouldn't have sent you here if she'd known the man your father's steward sent to provide transportation for you would have such a winning way.'

Guinevere didn't say anything, but watched as Maggie worked out the truth.

She put her hand over her open mouth. 'It's him,' she whispered. 'It is, isn't it? It's Lord

Hartcroft, the man who visited your home and your parents don't approve of. The one injured. He's the one you were speaking with. Reid, the man you had me deliver the note to. It is one thing to let him court you secretly—'

Maggie's voice rose. Guinevere held her hands out, fluttering them to shush Maggie, and she quietened, but the velocity increased.

'—it is another thing to practically move him into this house. I thought you were interested in helping your aunt. Not a—a dishonourable situation.'

'Don't write to Mother or Father.'

Maggie stepped forward, almost pleading. 'Milady, if I don't, they'll sack me. You have to tell him to go. You have to.'

'He's only to stay a fortnight or two.'

'Courting you?'

'No. Ridiculous. He's only testing his mettle.' Maggie snorted.

Guinevere hesitated. Was she, in fact, courting him? Had she used this as a strategy to get him closer. Perhaps she hoped he might fall in love, or perhaps it had started as a sort of revenge to the man who'd jested at her about her kisses.

But, oh, what a mistake Reid could be. The lord who never courted women with chaperons, and he'd not wanted to court her, but wed.

'Your father and mother have never liked this man. Never. Even when he was a lad. He would lead your brother astray and the Duke put a stop to it. He even caused your brother to hurt his arm when they were challenging each other.'

'My brother could get into trouble on his own.'

'Lady Guin, Lord Hartcroft caused your brother to get so sotted, and then they were trying to trip each other as a game and Lord David got hurt. Your father made Lord David stay by his side for a month. They refused to let Lord David associate with him.'

'My brother was just as much at fault as Reid.'

'That's not how your parents saw it. Your brother did well, except when he was around Lord Hartcroft. Lord Hartcroft was clever enough to get out of trouble but he wasn't clever enough to stay out of trouble. *Moderation* is not a word he knows. Don't you recall your mother and I talking about how he was always getting into some scrape?'

'Vaguely. But it was childhood antics.'

'Not always. He knocked a Viscount's son from a carriage once. It's a wonder no one was killed.'

'It was over a gambling wager, wasn't it?'

'No, it was over a woman they both fancied.'

'I think his accident changed him.'

'Could be. Could be,' she mused. 'Now he's acting a stableman to court a duke's daughter without a chaperon.'

'You make it sound—'

'Alarming? Perilous for you?' Maggie took her fan and fluttered it so that wisps of hair blew from her face even though the room was cool. 'I never would have expected this of you, Lady Guinevere. How did you get your father's steward to hire him?'

'He didn't. Who questions a man showing up for chores?'

Maggie squawked. 'I just hope he leaves soon and your parents never, ever find out. They will be so disappointed in you.'

Guinevere dropped her chin and kept Maggie in her vision. 'They wanted me to wed Stephen. And I'm not fond of him. Did you ever notice how overexuberant he can get over stitches, eggs for breakfast or any bonnet I wear? If he complimented my bonnet one more time when we went on the walk, I was going to ask him if he wanted it.'

'Well, that was their mistake in trying to match you with him. Don't make it two. If you're not very careful, this will turn in a bad way. I feel it in my bones.'

* * *

'It was thrilling. More fun than chess,' Guinevere said as she slipped in his doorway. She'd not knocked, nor had she waited long enough to ascertain that everyone was asleep. But he couldn't complain and risk erasing her delight.

He put down the pencil he'd been using since he ran out of ink.

She was taking too large a risk, and he knew if he stayed they would both keep taking them, in so many different ways. It was as easy as falling off a horse, but the problem was getting back up again.

And sometimes you didn't get a second chance.

He walked to her, savouring the feelings as his thoughts embraced her, his awareness heightened.

'Where did you discover such a game?' she asked.

'In Scotland. This was a version I created which makes it easier when my friends are drunken and can barely see the ball or hold the club.'

She twined her hand in his, and then melted against him, filling his senses with the scent of roses. 'Everyone enjoyed it so, and the servants were much more agreeable at dinnertime. Even Aunt was happier.'

He led her to the chair, and took the one across from her, increasing their distance.

She told him about how the evening had proceeded after he left, and he could have asked her to leave, but knew he'd not be able to concentrate on his tasks whether she remained or left. Better to have her in front of him, sitting sedately, than dancing in his imagination.

'I'm happy everyone had a good time,' he said when she paused.

'I never anticipated your friends to relish such a playful sport.'

Guinevere was seeing him as someone he wasn't. The game—he truly played a version of it with his friends. But the other combatants gestured in the rudest ways imaginable to distract their opponents, and sometimes the person swinging the club would be staggering, and might fall after swinging, causing even more laughter.

The competition between him and his friends didn't start or end with the game. It was in the one-upmanship of their stories, and their lives. Everyone tried to have the best horses, the sleekest carriages, the best trained staff and the loftiest connections. They jousted with each other at every turn and with every idea at their disposal.

But his time with Guinevere was not a competition in any way.

Guinevere would be a perfect bride for stature. Perfect.

The innocent. Taking him out at the knees, or heart.

He would leave soon. He would. Before he wasn't able to walk away.

He gathered his strength and listened to the melody of her words.

Imagining her being wedded to someone else sent a stab into him. He hoped she remained a spinster, at least for a long enough time that he was no longer entranced by her. But that would mean she would never wed.

She ran a fingertip over the wood of the table. 'Maggie knows who you are.'

He'd wondered how long it would last. 'It was only a matter of time, I suppose.'

'It's not necessary that we be concerned. Maggie is going to keep it a secret,' she said.

But it was time to stop the risk. He couldn't be around her and not show his feelings. He evaluated the next words he said, knowing they had to be spoken. 'It's time I left anyway.'

'Another week?' Her voice reminded him of a lost child, but she wasn't. He was the one who'd been unaware. The true innocent. Unaware of what Guinevere could do to him.

'No. I should leave. You've had a chance to get to know me, somewhat. You should know this is not for me.'

'Somewhat?' Her brows rose.

'Yes. This is not who I am. It's been a pleasant diversion, but this is not my life. You are becoming the woman you were meant to be. You saw a need to improve your aunt's surroundings and you didn't hesitate—you reacted. When you saw me in bed after my accident, you didn't trust what everyone was telling you—you reacted. When your parents pushed you to marriage, again you reacted.'

'But do you understand what other people must do to make the world right for your needs?'

'I have blisters. Sore muscles. But this isn't the true me. I can do so much more in my true role. Besides, I don't want to cause any trouble for you by being here. The staff seems to be watching us. And it would not be good for word to get back to London that you are spending time with a stableman.'

'A stableman who seems to have my best interests at heart.'

He tightened his jaw. 'Even on my most unsettled day, I pray I would have turned you away if you'd offered more than a kiss. I would have wed you in Scotland but I understand that a duke's daughter would expect more than an elopement over rough roads.'

Again, he took her hands as he had many times before, and he lifted her knuckles, kissing them one at a time. 'I adore you in a way I have never adored another woman. You pull my soul to you. But you're only seeing what you want to see. And I can't even tell you who I am because I don't know who I will be a month from now.'

Her hands slipped from his as easily as water slid through his fingers.

'Is this goodbye?'

'I cannot know what is going to happen...' Other than his life being pulled out of him when he left her.

He put a kiss on her cheek, the soft skin calling its siren's song to him, and he used all his strength to increase the distance between them.

'I'm taking my satchel, and I'll leave on Hermes. I located a boy in the village and he's agreed to stop by to check on Hera each day until my stablemaster arrives to take her back to my estate.'

He couldn't wait until morning to leave. If she'd visited him after the sun went down, and

kissed him, his defences would be shattered, and
he didn't know if he could be strong enough.

He'd been her first kiss, and he wanted her to
always remember their time together with purity
and innocence. And so did he.

'Are you leaving the job, or me?'

He studied her face. 'I'm leaving for me. You
don't know me. I'm pretending to be a stableman. I'm acting the part of a servant, and I'm a
marquess. This is a pretence for me, and I have
duties to return to.'

Then he looked at the blister on his palm. 'I
am not a game piece, waiting until you make
your move. I'm not a diversion. A kissing experiment. I very much regret what I said to you
when you were a child. I do, and I would change
it if I could. But it's best I leave now while no
one really knows I was here. Even you, I think.'

He moved forward, touching along her jaw.
'Let me see you to the house, and we'll have one
last moment. One kiss under the stars, and one
kiss goodbye.'

Chapter Thirteen

The morning arrived with all the promise of any other, and no chance of fulfilment. Hermes was gone. She peered into the cottage. It appeared as if Reid had already gone, except for the haphazardly straightened bedclothing and his things lumped by the doorway. A portmanteau with shaving gear and clothing stuffed inside. His trunk filled carelessly.

She'd not told Maggie about Reid's absence, but the servants weren't taking any new mail so Maggie hadn't attempted to contact Guinevere's parents.

And there was the chance he would change his mind. A slim chance. Excruciatingly slim, which diminished as the day wore on, and a young man arrived from the village to care for Hera before returning back to his home.

That evening, she retrieved Reid's clubs, and

talked the servants into playing another game. It didn't take much persuading. She didn't join, but watched. Their chatter didn't divert her attention, and the sense of loss she felt carried through with her to the next day.

Even as the second day without Reid wore on, she couldn't help listening for hoof beats.

At teatime, she heard the sound she'd been awaiting and her heart thrummed more rapidly than the hooves. She ran down the stairway and to the front door, but as soon as she exited she recognised the rider wasn't Reid.

She waited, hearing the butler's footsteps behind her.

'I will take care of this,' she said, when she recognised the new arrival.

Her luck could not get any worse.

Stephen jumped off the horse and waved his hat in a sweeping, low bow. 'My Lady Guinevere.'

'Why are you here?' she asked. She feared Reid had sent him. 'My father would not appreciate your visiting without his approval.'

'I tried to call on you, hoping you'd changed your mind, and your mother informed me you had not. She said you were at your aunt's. I suspected it was a plan to keep you away from Reid. But she said it wasn't.'

'Well, I am here. But you are not welcome.'

Stephen briefly grimaced. 'I thought I might find my dear cousin here. He seems to have disappeared and I am the search party. I went to his country estate to search and found his carriage. Two of his horses are gone. And why would a man leave on a long journey and take two horses…but not a carriage? Makes no sense if he is travelling. Particularly soon after a lovely lady left London.' He smiled. 'A lovely lady left London—has a ring to it, doesn't it?'

'Well, he isn't here.'

'His stablemaster would not give me any idea of where he went, but then I asked Reid's mother if she knew where the Duke's aunt resided. She did. Then I happened to see the boy from the stables and I mentioned this location and asked if it had been hard to transport the horses here. *Voilà.*'

'Reid is not here.'

A horse neighed, and Stephen glanced at Hera. 'I believe I will put my horse with his, then.'

'Go away, Stephen. I told you I wasn't interested in marriage or courtship. At the time, I suggested friendship, and I see even that was overreaching my abilities. I cannot abide being followed.'

'He's not here?' He glanced around. 'Well, I don't see Hermes but I see Hera. I believe I will wait. He will surely be returning for his horse.'

'I told you politely I was not interested in furthering our friendship when you asked me to wed you.'

'Well, I was curious to see whose friendship you might be interested in furthering.'

She addressed the butler. 'Do you have a weapon here?'

'No, milady. We once had a dog but he ran away. We have those clubs, but we'd prefer not to break them.'

She considered her options and glared at Stephen. 'Reid will throttle you if he finds you here.'

'He might try,' Stephen said. 'And he might succeed, but he is not going to want your father to find out about this. I will be thinking of how my dear cousin can recompense me for all the agonies he has put me through over the years.'

'You're intent on blackmail.'

'I wouldn't call it that. I would call it payment for saving your reputation by not telling all of London.'

'He is liable to recompense you with broken bones. Yours.'

Stephen laughed. 'It might be worth it for his reaction when he appears and sees me. And I would so hate to tell everyone how Reid is having a wonderful time in the countryside, at… um…the Duke's aunt's home. I'm not leaving.'

Guinevere needed time to think.

'You are not allowed in this house,' she said.

'I'll unsaddle my horse, then, since I daresay your stablemaster will not help.'

'Oh, he would love to help you,' she said, 'but he's not here. I don't know when he will be back. And I will instruct the servants that you are to fend for yourself and will not be expecting meals other than the porridge. In the meantime, you can clean up after Hera. No one will allow you entrance into the house and I will not be speaking with you.'

Dusk approached when she saw another vehicle, relieved to hear the wheels.

She again darted down the stairway, and when she stepped outside, her heart thudded to her shoes.

The ducal crest shone on the side of the coach. She waited.

Her father's groom stepped down from the perch and opened the carriage door. Her father understood the value of an entrance. He descended slowly and gave her a broad smile.

'Maggie wrote to your mother and told her—'

Guinevere gulped.

'That you were doing a remarkable job of helping my aunt. She said you are a treasure. A gem of a niece and you've taken over the staff instructions needed. We were proud.'

He strode to her.

Then he heard Hera whinny, and his glare narrowed. 'Aunt doesn't have any cattle. That horse appears familiar. Do I know her? And there's two of them.'

'You may.' She pointed to the cottage. 'Stephen is here.'

Her father took in a deep breath that seemed to stare at the heels of his boots. His eyes frosted. 'Guinevere. If the two of you have been here together, there will be no argument. You must wed.'

'He arrived today, and I could not get him to depart.'

Her father's head lowered, lines deepened at his eyes. 'He followed you? He took it upon himself to follow my daughter? You did not request it?'

'No. I never expected him to arrive. I was furious. He's in the cottage. And he won't leave. And he has been accusing me of being here with Reid. And Reid is not here.' She touched her chest. 'I think Stephen is intent on blackmail. I was going to set the dog on him but there isn't one.'

Her father snapped his fingers, pointed to the drivers and then to the cottage. One driver jumped from the perch and stood beside the other. Both stared at the doorway.

'Stephen,' she shouted. 'Come out, you annoying worm spore. My father is here to give you your payment.'

'Your Grace.' Stephen came out, seemingly having just awoken, hands raised in front of him. 'That's Hera in the stall. Reid's horse. And there's a portmanteau in the cottage. Things strewn about in it.' He motioned inside. 'They're not mine. Come in and see for yourself.'

'Hera is in the stall,' Guinevere said. 'Reid is not here no matter what Stephen says. Stephen would not believe me when I told him the truth. And he would not leave.'

'No. No.' Stephen gesticulated. 'It was a jest. I was waiting on Reid to return.'

'Your Grace, that disreputable human arrived today.' The butler stepped from behind her. 'And your daughter wanted a weapon to hit him with but we couldn't spare one. And he wanted payment for his silence to you.'

Her father unbuttoned his coat and tossed it to the ground. 'No one blackmails my daughter.'

'Wait.' Guinevere stepped in front of her father. 'Please, Father. Please, let me.'

'Guin, I could not let you soil your hands on him.'

'I will use a shovel.' With that she ran to the stalls, got the spade and filled it with fresh manure. It was heavier than she'd estimated. The first blade full went on Stephen's saddle top and she refilled it halfway and walked out with a lighter scoop.

'Saddle your horse,' she commanded.

Stephen paused.

'I would do so if I were you.' The Duke's voice tolled like a death knell, and his two drivers glared at Stephen.

Stephen walked by her and she tossed the contents on his boots. 'Tell your horse I beg its pardon for the stench, but it should be used to it by now.'

'I will be happy to see the last of her,' Stephen growled as he moved to his saddle.

'You give my little girl one hint of grief and I will have more than your head. I may anyway,' the Duke shouted after Stephen.

Stephen readied his horse and left, the dust rising behind him.

Guinevere put the shovel away and dusted off her hands.

'Thank you, Father. I did not know how I was to rid myself of him.'

'He had two horses here and didn't take the other one when he left?' her father asked her as Hera whinnied.

She didn't answer.

The Duke directed a stare at the butler. 'Who does the second horse belong to?'

'The new stableman, Your Grace.'

'Oh, well, that explains it.' His lips turned up. 'The stableman. Of course.' He took Guinevere's arm and spoke to the butler. 'Would you leave us? I have a few things to discuss with my daughter.'

Chapter Fourteen

Reid held the plate in one hand and the buttered bread in the other while he read from the stack of papers in front of him. Figures he'd comprehended earlier faded from his memory, replaced by the vision of Guinevere.

He'd hated to leave her. But he'd not seen any other choice.

'The Duke of Glouston to see you,' the butler announced, interrupting Reid's concentration. 'And Lady Guinevere. I have shown them to the sitting room.'

He sat the plate on the documents and rubbed his hand over his stubbled cheek.

'He wished me to tell you that he has returned Hera to your country estate and since he did not find you there, he has travelled here.'

Reid blinked.

'He is calm, sir. And she appears skittish. Not Hera. Lady Guinevere.'

'Very well.' Reid stood and dusted a crumb from his waistcoat. He pulled his coat from the back of his chair and donned it, fastening the buttons.

In the sitting room, he found two serious demeanours.

The Duke stopped pacing, and glowered at Reid. 'You and I need a discussion.'

Reid didn't say a word.

'Father visited his aunt's and found Stephen there.' Guinevere met his eyes,

'Stephen?' Reid said. That wasn't at all what he'd expected to hear.

'Yes,' the Duke answered, his voice rising. 'And he was searching for you.'

Reid didn't answer. *That* he expected. After all, he had been in the country with Guinevere.

'What were you thinking to let your cousin find out where Guin was?' The Duke strode forward.

A mix of anger and confusion hit him. How was the Duke aware that Reid had known where Guinevere was?

And Stephen hadn't been here. He didn't know what the Duke and Guinevere were talking about.

'I didn't. And what does Stephen have to do with this?'

Guinevere stepped in front of her father. 'Stephen visited my great-aunt. It was unpleasant. He wouldn't leave, so I sent him to the stable. And then Father arrived.'

Reid wasn't certain he heard correctly. 'Stephen? My cousin Stephen?' The anger that had simmered now flashed into rage. 'I will throttle him.' He took a step towards the door, forgetting for a moment he didn't know where the wastrel was.

'No need,' Guinevere said, voice wavering. 'The matter was resolved.'

'We need another matter resolved,' her father said, relocating beside Guinevere, and running his fingers through his thinning grey hair. 'The wedding. I stopped on the way and made an appointment for you to get the Special Licence. You don't have to thank me.'

Reid felt fury caused by the insensitivity towards Guinevere. 'I'm not. I asked her. She said no.'

'Well, she's agreed now.' He stared at Reid. 'I've never liked you.'

'The feeling is mutual.'

'Enlighten me, Reid. Can you name me one good thing you've done in your life? Just one?'

'Not throttling you right now.'

'Pshut.' He turned to his daughter, waved a hand and crossed his arms. 'See. That's the best he can come up with.'

Reid spoke softly. 'It's more of an accomplishment than you realise.'

'If you two do not marry, I will destroy you in this town,' he said, intent on Reid. 'I will use every last bit of my power, my friends and all that I have at my disposal to run you so far into the ground you'll never get anywhere or anything you want.'

'Father, you cannot. That is totally unjust.'

'Consider it strategy.'

'Father—'

'You're not hushing me this time. Your mother and I have followed your wishes, given you the absolute best, let you wander where you want, and you repay us with deception.' He glared at her. 'You will wed him. No more games. And I do mean there will be no more games. Not at my home. You learned chess too early. I ruined your life by letting you touch that board.' His chest heaved.

He scowled at Reid. 'And she doesn't even need to watch the pieces. She could play the game blindfold. And sometimes, she will play against herself. How can that amuse her? But it does. And probably what she was doing at my aunt's. Having an entertainment.'

Reid scrutinised her, but she didn't meet his gaze.

'Yes. I play well. I'm not ashamed of it,' she said. 'It's not difficult for me.'

'Her uncle, my son and I all joined together to test her skills one day,' the Duke said. 'We consulted. We had another board in a different room. We spent hours planning our play, and she thought it great fun as she did her stitchery, gave a glance at the board and trounced us. She gets that from her mother's side of the family.'

The Duke smiled. 'Guinevere will give you the details of the appointment. And I will be waiting to take you both in my carriage. Get the proposal out of the way, and hurry along.'

He scowled at Guinevere. 'And I should never have let you go to Reid's estate for his funeral.'

Reid stared at the fireplace, and the small empty spot where the mirror hung that had been draped and had not been replaced.

'You know of my past, Guinevere, but it is a past. I have not had a drop of strong spirits since before I travelled to your aunt's home.'

She assessed him.

'It has always been a skill in my family,' he

said. 'How we can consume more than many others. I'm sure your father is aware of it. My father was skilled, too.'

He moved to the empty spot on the wall, remembering the mirror. 'I didn't think anyone noticed. How much I consumed. It didn't seem excessive to me. But when Stephen drank the same amount, I judged him overindulging.' The light from the window flickered into his eyes.

'My valet mentioned it, and I respect his opinion,' he said. 'Other people had warned me before, but I'd not taken them seriously. I'd dismissed them as wrong. I listened to Beckham, although Hermes had tried to tell me in his own way, I suppose.'

'Should I be concerned?'

'No. The ground wasn't soft. The dark before I woke was bleak. Not caring about what happened was strange. I don't miss it.' He shook his head. 'My own errors are too easy to make and even easier to dismiss when I've consumed a lot. And life seems less complex, but drinking away the complexity doesn't erase it.'

'Is there anything else that I might discover and be surprised of? Children? A hidden marriage? Laudanum?'

He shook his head. 'None of those. But that doesn't make me wholesome. I don't want you to marry simply because your father is demanding a decision. It's not his to make. It's not his life.'

'But you asked me to go to Scotland with you.'

'Yes. I know. But that was before I worked as a stableman. Before we talked. My life has changed a lot in the last few days.'

'All the way to London Father worked out ideas on ways to cause grief to you.'

'What of you?'

'I have no choice. I have to wed you, or show up at the appointment with someone else, and there is no one else. And on the carriage ride here,' she said, 'the veil seemed removed from my eyes, and I saw the situation, not the beau.'

He didn't see how she could separate a marriage to him…from him.

She tensed. 'I understand you need to wed in order to have heirs. I considered it, and it's a sincere, and understandable motive. We don't have a choice. Today, he's the Duke of Glouston first, and my father second. The Duke is speaking.'

'So is the Duke's daughter.' Ringing for Beckham, he spoke to Guinevere. 'Whoever he is, I'm having him sent on his way. He's not invited to the wedding.'

* * *

Guinevere sat in the carriage beside the stranger she thought she knew.

'You can still change your mind,' he said. 'Until the moment the vows are spoken, you can leave.'

'Then what?' she asked, watching as they met another vehicle.

'We will worry about that as it happens.'

'I'm not that person,' she said. 'I worry in advance. And I plan.'

'I didn't see this as being part of your strategy.'

'It wasn't.' She could never have expected Stephen to show up at her aunt's, or her father. But she should have understood that the trip could go wrong. And, maybe in some part of her she didn't want to accept, she had.

'What if this was my plan all along?' She didn't have her reticule. Her gloves. A handkerchief or any of the necessities she usually travelled with. She'd left them all behind.

'Then you could have avoided it all by going to Scotland with me. Don't second-guess yourself using the wrong theories.'

'My flaw,' she said. 'The one you mentioned before. It shouldn't matter to me where I live as long as I have my chess pieces.'

'Is that true?'

'No. They don't seem important right now. They did earlier, when my father threatened to lock them away. But I think it was the act of having it taken, rather than what was being taken, that disturbed me most.' And she'd not liked all the threats he'd made about Reid, and a social battle would hurt everyone, including the Duchess and Marchioness.

Perhaps she was wrong, though. Perhaps she'd not wanted the game taken.

'Chess is the only thing I'm really good at.' And she'd really done nothing to earn the skill. She'd been born with it. 'I may have trapped myself with an errant move.'

Yet, it wasn't that she felt trapped. She didn't feel she belonged at her parents' home, or even at the home she'd tried to make for herself at her aunt's. A ship who could see the shoreline and ports, but didn't belong in them.

They would both have what they needed. He would have a wife for heirs, and she would have her own home. Only from his expression, he wasn't as sincere about providing heirs as she'd expected.

'At my aunt's, I'd started to see—for the first time—what others did. You know what I said to you about being the stableman? Well, it was true of me more than you,' she said. 'I needed to understand how a home functioned. You had true duties to get back to. I didn't. I'd be at my aunt's for a long time if Father hadn't arrived.'

'Why did he decide to visit you?'

'Stephen had been inquiring about where you were, and when you'd left. And he'd asked someone if they knew I was at my aunt's, and Father had heard. He just wanted to make sure everything was fine.'

'So we have dear cousin Stephen to thank for this.'

The way he said the words irritated her. 'I put manure on his saddle and boots and sent him on his way.'

'Good on you.'

'It felt good seeing him leave and being the one who told him to go.' But she didn't know if she'd have a say in her own life, now that she was getting married. 'I expect to continue to make decisions.'

'I would hope so. We're each getting married. Not getting a new servant.'

Somehow, that didn't make her feel better. 'We can't back out.'

'Yes. We can.' The seat depressed as he moved closer. 'We can.'

She let out a deep breath. 'Too many people might be hurt. Both our mothers.'

He took her hand and kissed the knuckles.

No matter who she wed, it would be a risk. She knew that. 'My sister and brother both married their sweethearts for love,' she said, trying to reassure herself that no magic broth existed for a good marriage.

'Your brother is not as perfect as you think he is, Guin. We were friends.'

The carriage pulled to a stop.

Taking her hand from his, she squared her shoulders.

He saw the movement. 'If you don't want to marry, I will not wed. I'll take my chances with whatever disgrace, or disappointment, might happen, and tell your father I refused. I'll make certain you have a home. You can even stay with my mother at my country estate.'

'You would do that?'

'Yes.'

'We'll wed.'

'I might tell your father we didn't go through with it. Tomorrow.'

'No,' she whispered.

He winked. 'Then let's go get the paperwork done.'

Chapter Fifteen

The veil was removed from his eyes, and he'd felt no nervousness about saying the vows. No qualms about the commitment. The deep responsibility lodged in him. He'd made a vow. To his wife.

The ceremony had nothing to do with providing heirs. It was for the two of them only. A few brief words for a life-changing moment, but he supposed most life-altering moments were hardly longer than a finger-snap.

He wanted to move forward in the right way, but wasn't sure of the procedure. He didn't want to spend his life with a wall of glass between him and Guinevere that almost no one could see, but they would know was there. The one he'd ignored between his ever-so-perfect parents. Devotion and deference when friends were about, and politeness when they were alone.

He'd rushed head-on into disasters, sorting them out as he went, and he'd rushed into the situation with Guin.

Situation. A strange choice of word for him to choose, and not at all what he wanted the marriage to be. A union.

'Well,' he said, assisting her into the vehicle, 'since your father made the appointment with us to get the Special License, I would expect we don't need to inform your mother of the news, and I will have a message sent to my country estate.'

He rapped the top of the vehicle to alert the driver to leave and pulled down the shade halfway so he wouldn't watch out, wanting to feel alone with Guinevere.

Nervousness at the ceremony would have been preferred. Instead, it had felt like the eerie quiet before a storm that might never arrive or could hurl in with a devastating wind.

'But there is something else you need to know,' he said.

She raised her eyebrows.

'Chess is not my game,' he admitted.

'I've found that true with most people.'

When the carriage rolled to a stop in front of his town house, he told the driver to wait, and he helped her alight.

Inside, he introduced her to the butler. 'The new Marchioness, Lady Hartcroft.'

The butler did all but sputter, before composing himself, bowing and saying he was pleased to meet her.

'Please inform the other staff members,' Reid said, 'and gather them here quickly. I want to introduce them to my wife.'

Then Reid took her outdoors, again, leaving the door open behind them, waiting on the other servants to gather. 'I didn't carry you over the threshold. I forgot.'

'Superstitious nonsense,' she said.

'It may be. I don't know and I don't care. But I did break a mirror. I'm not taking any more chances.' And he couldn't. Not with her.

And he wanted the servants' first vision of her as his wife to be in his arms, held aloft, and adored.

When the staff had gathered in the entrance, he lifted her, carrying her over the threshold, and crowding the servants so that they had to cluster closer.

'My Lady Guinevere,' he said, putting her on her feet. Their happy faces pleased him. Next, he asked them to introduce themselves to her, and give her a brief history of how they came to arrive in the household.

At her elbow, he watched her as she listened to each servant, and thanked them.

She didn't have to concern herself with winning them over, she would easily with her demeanour, but he realised that they would follow her instructions anyway because they were so well trained.

Then he saw her to their sitting room, with his bedroom on one side and hers on the other. She studied her new chambers, and he didn't believe she was aware that she was biting her bottom lip.

'I suppose I need some time to get used to living here,' she said. 'And I'd like to make some notes on what I might need brought, and to compose letters to friends telling them of the changes.'

'I understand,' he said, exiting.

He truly did. He needed to think about composing some letters of his own.

At his desk, he tried to push aside all thoughts of his lady wife who now lived under his roof while he considered how he'd go forward in life.

He'd married Guinevere. The true jewel.

His life was all sorted out now. As precisely laid out as plans for a fortress on the edge of a cliff. A cliff with a few gaping caves underneath with crumbling walls.

He made a note to commission chess pieces

from an artist as a present for Guinevere. The king and queen could be patterned after himself and Guinevere. The knights, Hermes and Hera. The bishops, family. The pawns, staff. A belated wedding gift, or Christmas, or an anniversary, and one he suspected she would appreciate more than any jewel.

His wife would be so happy to have a chess set created for her.

It would help soothe some of the concern he felt. Perhaps he'd not told her the entire truth, but he'd not fully seen it until after he'd brought her home as a marchioness.

But he kept imagining her, and he could not keep her waiting.

He'd given her enough time to get settled, and he couldn't stay away any longer. The sun was setting and he had to see her.

Walking across the hall from his library, he knocked at her bedroom door, and heard her call out to enter.

She was standing, waiting.

He saw each plane of her face highlighted, bathing her in a glow he'd never seen on anyone else. Perhaps he'd been blind to it before Guinevere, or perhaps it hadn't existed on others.

He strode closer, letting his forefinger trail down her shoulder to her wrist, savouring the touch. Letting the femininity of her enter his body, and infuse itself, simply with the barest touch.

'Are you tired?' he asked.

'More the feeling of a grain of sand in a whirlwind.'

'Glad it is behind us?'

'Yes. Very. I feel as if I could sleep for a week. Travel. Decisions. Plans for moving.'

'I apologise, Guin. Sleep is not what a wedding night is for. I know I've heard that somewhere,' he said, moving closer, taking her in his arms. 'Please stop me if you've heard otherwise.'

She burrowed herself against the silk waistcoat, his clasp holding her close. A form appearing and feeling as delicate as a puff of the wind she'd mentioned. His Lady Guinevere.

'Well, perhaps I feel I could stay abed for a week,' she said.

'What a man wants to hear from his bride.'

Arms around her, he ran his touch over her back, aware of the fragility of her body, the gentleness of her backbone against the fabric of her dress and the womanly strength he held.

Every night, he would have to thank each star in the sky for his good fortune of opening his eyes to Guinevere.

He doused the light, and threw open the curtains, letting the moonlight in.

Watching her was like being inside one of the golden beams of light visible on rare occasions when the sun created its best magic.

He didn't believe in superstition because no fates would have deemed him worthy of Guinevere.

She'd been so protected. He'd been her first kiss, and she'd brought him back into the world. He owed her so much, and he wanted her to have everything she should have. She shouldn't be surrounded by board pieces, but by all the best things life had to offer. And he would provide the treasures she wanted.

He leant to kiss her, and she moved away.

'Could we—without kissing?' she asked.

'Never,' he said. 'Never,' he insisted, catching her. 'Get that thought out of your mind now. You have to believe me, and I'll show you, that your kisses are sweeter than any wine, and more potent. And if I can't prove it to you, the fault is not you, it is me.'

He took her chin and held her face close so that they stared into each other's eyes, and with all the gentleness he could summon, he brushed the barest touch across her lips. He repeated the actions several times, gently as if guarding tinder, protecting it from the gentlest breeze and letting the heat gently grow, waiting for the smallest spark to ignite.

Then he returned, letting their breaths mingle more than their bodies, gentle moist flutters of lips teasing and touching, welcoming and savouring.

Time no longer mattered, and responded only as she did.

'The true test of a good kiss…' he said, keeping her sheltered against him, holding her and then shutting his eyes to let his own body still so he would not lose control as she rested against him. 'The true test is whether you like it or not.'

'I did,' she whispered, her words against his cheek.

'So did I.'

Opening his eyes, he saw not just Guinevere, but his bride. He pulled her close with one arm, removing his waistcoat, and throwing it and the cravat to the side. Taking her in his arms, he lowered her to the bed.

Then his sight stilled, and he couldn't move his gaze from hers.

His wife lay before him.

Hopeful. Expectant.

He knelt on the floor beside the bed, his elbows propped beside her, and took her hands, their faces close. And he wanted her to know that the vows said earlier in the day were real to him. He spoke each word slowly.

'I promise to see that you are provided for. That you will never have to doubt my fidelity, and you will always have my greatest respect and honour.'

Then he sat on the bed beside her and removed his shirt and trousers and tossed them aside, feeling that he removed armour and bared more than only his body to her, but his soul.

He next clasped her slippers and let them fall aside, giving each foot a caress as he slid the stockings from her feet.

No one had ever looked at him with a glance that whispered a lullaby and woke him in a way that felt so fresh and new.

He forgot what he was going to say, but there were no words left in him. In that moment he would have taken up embroidery for her, and picking wildflowers and dancing in the rain. And in a sense he had, because he would always make certain that her life came before his own. He wanted to share with her the things which brought her joy.

He caressed her body, reassuring her with a thousand kisses, and reassuring himself that she was truly in his arms and his wife.

He traced her body, trying to imprint each curve into a place deep inside himself so that he would never forget each instance. Reaching behind her for the hooks of her dress, he then guided her nearer, letting the gown slide away, along with a corset, the scent of her soap blending with the hint of a flowery, almost strawberry-scented perfume she wore.

Guinevere savoured Reid's kisses, awed by the power of something so soft. She wrapped her arms around him, the friction of her hands against the muscles of his skin sending billowing awareness into her, causing surges of wonder, and more feelings than she'd known she could experience.

He lifted her chemise over her head, the rustling of the fabric creating a whisper that seem to augment the vows they'd made earlier.

She'd not known a man's body could feel so different than her own. A masterpiece of life and power.

Longing vibrated inside her. She had to keep touching him again and again to try and ease the growing sensations. Trying to sate her feelings by caressing him only deepened her need.

His clasp tightened at her back, and the cool locks of his hair brushed against her neck while his moist lips trailed her body. His cheek, shaved but with stubble beneath it, touched her breast, blending his rough masculinity with her skin, creating a prism of sensations in her.

He cupped her breasts, the nipples rising to peaks and weakening her, but empowering her awareness of him. Her breasts had never felt so womanly, fuller and riper, and grew a responsiveness under his touch she'd not known existed.

Her hands raced over his body, making her tense with pleasure, and the pressure of his member increased the sensations of a strength she'd never known.

He maintained control, but hers had been tossed aside with her chemise. She pulled him nearer with all her might, savouring the whisper of his breath creating a warming tingle within the path of his kisses.

His body pressed against hers, skin caressing skin, and he trailed his fingers over her. Arching against him, she tried to fill the growing need inside her.

Her gasp assured him she responded, and she arched against him again.

'Guinevere,' he whispered, and no one had ever said her name with such reverence. Then he cradled her, and touched her, causing pleasure to explode inside her, taking away all awareness of anything but the erupting vibrations that overwhelmed her body.

'Sweet Guinevere,' he said, and rose above her, his lips against her skin, and they joined, made one by the intensity of the storm created by the brush of their bodies.

He seemed to hold her aloft on a sea of pulses, and when he lost himself inside her, he finished by placing a kiss on her cheek, and settling so close that he surrounded her with his nearness.

Lying at his side, his kisses rained on her hair; he murmured to her, whispering sweet words of nothingness, but reassuring her.

She was falling asleep when she realised neither had said the word *love*.

Chapter Sixteen

Reid left his bed before dawn, careful to make no noise, and returned to the room where Guinevere lay asleep. He listened to the silence, absorbed the sight, his plan to wake her falling by the wayside.

The summit of his future lay before him.

His wife. Sleeping peacefully.

His life. Awake and shouting at him.

He could see the decisions that led up to his marriage so clearly now, and he didn't regret them. How could he? It had proceeded exactly as anticipated, more or less.

He'd almost planned a wife as a senior member of the household, although not to report to him. To have her own duties and legacy to continue.

But this was Guinevere. She was not a member of his staff.

On the carriage ride after the ceremony, he'd felt like a chessboard being appraised, each piece of him studied. The directions he could move considered. A mind rapidly moving through all his options.

The woman only knew the value of strategy. Of planning.

That night, their lovemaking had been all he'd wanted, and more, and yet the peace and fulfilment had evaporated, replaced by an awareness of how much his life had changed.

He hadn't been going back to his home after they made love. He was there. Dressing wasn't necessary because he only needed to take a few steps to go through the sitting room and be at his own bed. In fact, her bed was an exact replica of his own.

The only difference was that, instead of getting dressed, travelling back to his home and waking up in the morning as if nothing had happened the night before, his life had a new addition. And one which had as much right to be there as he did. Perhaps more.

A few short sentences had altered everything. Recording the event in a different kind of ledger. And his life had changed for ever. He was no longer alone in the world but now he was half of a whole. He knew her well.

She was his opposite. The one who might be missed at a soiree because she would be in the corner chatting with someone easily overlooked.

A woman who didn't call attention to herself. Guinevere would use her stitchery and her intellect for making something worthwhile.

Guinevere would never sew a sleeping, drunken man's coat to his chair. Never put boot blacking on the inside band of a fair-haired man's hat. So many jests and some that had almost cost Reid a tooth.

He must make sure she never became acquainted with the wives of his talkative friends. But the men usually thought the idea was their own and he had been fine with that. It would be difficult to keep her from her own brother, but still, David wouldn't want his sister to know the scrapes they'd got into or he would have already told her.

Stepping back, he took one long lingering look at her and slipped away.

He'd taken all the directions of his life away, but one. And she would far outpace him in uprightness. When she'd broken a nail, she'd said, *Blunder.* It had shocked him. Blunder? Where had she got that?

His life had changed because of a blunder, and not just the one on horseback. So many had littered the landscape of his past, and he'd been oblivious to some he should have seen. He'd never truly studied the account books until it had dawned on him that more funds were there than he'd expected.

Wondering if the man had been stealing from him, and had an attack of conscience, he'd summoned his steward with plans to question the man. But then everything had tumbled out, and the steward had procured a separate, secret ledger that he kept. Reid saw the past differently.

Travelling back to the country estate, he'd found the older ledgers and verified the steward's words. The deductions had taken place Reid's entire life, and Reid hadn't really noticed them until they'd stopped. The woman had died.

The woman not good enough to marry but too important to set free.

The hunting trip his father had taken once a year had had nothing to do with foxes. His mother had begged his father not to go once, and he'd insisted that he must. And on a separate occasion, Reid had suggested going, also, and his father had refused.

The day of the accident, Reid had been upset. He'd known all along his grandfather was flawed. The older man had boasted of his indiscretions. But Reid's own father had presented himself as devoted to his family. He was. It was just that it included the mistress.

Reid hadn't truly expected his father to be a saint—just pompously close. And he'd not planned to have the facts and figures in front of him. His father had encouraged Reid to consider marriage a sacred trust. That was what an honourable man did, he'd claimed, and Reid had expected him to have lived up to his own advice.

Reid's fury at both his father—and himself for believing an unspoken lie, and even his grandfather for keeping the secret—had enveloped him the entire night, and drinking hadn't dulled anything but his riding skills.

He'd been angry that morning when he'd saddled Hermes, refusing to wait on the stableman. Then the morning had whirled into a series of events he'd not expected.

He'd truly awoken to a stabbing pain in his shoulder and Guinevere's startled face as she jumped from his sight. That had been more unsettling than anything else. She'd appeared as if he'd stabbed her with a pin.

The once disdainful woman who'd practically dusted away any glance he gave her, assuming he would give her a true appraisal—which he did not, because she was to be respected. He would have punched one of his friends for leering at her. She was protected. By him. Her brother. Her father and even his. No one dared get close to Guinevere with anything but the best of motives.

He doubted she'd even been aware of how sheltered she was until she'd made the move away from her parents' guidance.

He'd watched her once from a balcony. Watched her. She'd strolled to some grizzled man, his eyes fogged by time, and who could pontificate for hours on whether King Alfred the Great or Queen Anne should be considered the first true monarch of England.

She'd stood talking with him while others danced. Reid could hear the man's voice rise when he'd spoken of war tactics and she'd listened with rapt attention.

When Reid had returned from a long visit to the smoking room, called back by curiosity, she still chatted with the man, his skyward pointed finger moving as if he were in the midst of some military campaign. Her lips, true jewels, pursed while she appeared to be considering every word he spoke. Even Wellington couldn't have listened to the man that long. Reid's friends barely knew who Wellington had fought.

And she wasn't sotted.

He'd considered how many wine glasses he'd held in the time he'd been gone. And Guinevere's glass was still half full. He'd not finished his last drink, satisfied by the sight of Guinevere. If she could listen to some pontificating military man discuss a battle long since forgotten by everyone else and remain rapt without numbing her senses, then he could listen to his friends. Although in all fairness, he suspected his companions were less enthralling.

Before the night ended, he'd surreptitiously searched her out one more time. Guinevere had been totally unaware of the young Viscount who'd walked near her—the same braggart Reid had once shoved and the carriage door had opened unexpectedly.

She'd not seen the Viscount, and still spoke with the military man. Reid would have wagered a horse that the younger man had wanted to dance with Guinevere but her father had stepped closer and the Viscount left.

Then the older man's dotty wife had ambled up and shaken her head.

Guinevere had patted his arm. Said something that made the man beam.

She'd chatted on, the three of them laughing until the wife guided the husband to another couple, Guinevere watching after them as if she'd been a matchmaker.

At that moment, he'd wanted nothing more

than to speak with her. To find out what the older man had said that had kept her listening so raptly. Or just hear her voice.

But her mother had called to Guinevere, and the Duke had spoken with his wife. By Guinevere's enthusiasm with her parents, he was fairly certain she was telling her father the older man's stories, and the Duke had stifled a half-yawn as he gave a few sleepy-eyed nods, and strode out the door, patting his wife's elbow as the three left.

Guinevere had been the centre of more attention than she'd ever realised.

Awakening alone, Guinevere peered around the room, momentarily jarred to see the unfamiliar surroundings. And a man's clothing strewn about with a woman's. Hers.

Instinctively, she pulled her covers up over her nakedness.

Then she remembered.

Conscious of her body in a way she'd never noticed being before, she stretched, her arms extended to their maximum length. She seemed able to absorb all the energy of the sun and stars.

Then she burrowed under the covers, aware of being surrounded by a scent that reminded her of strength, and snuggled into the previous night's memories.

Reid had left in the early morning hours to go to his room. His presence was there, but he wasn't.

She found her shift, slipped it over her head, grabbed his heavy wool garments, surprised by the size and heft of them, and peeked into the connecting sitting room, then ventured to the door across.

She swallowed, then knocked. No one answered.

She peered inside.

Nothing out of place. A servant had already tidied because Reid could not have left any area appearing so untouched.

Taking a moment, she studied the oversized, dark furniture. She could have stumbled over any piece of it, fallen and not hurt anything but herself. Little different than the area she'd just left.

The thick draperies had been opened, letting the light in, but the room still reflected a darkness due to the solidness of the furnishings.

The opposite of her surroundings at her parents' home. Different than everything she'd known.

Where she'd had delicate and flowing window

coverings to let the light in at her old room, he had heavy draperies to block the sun. Her former furniture had been smaller oak pieces painted white with floral accents.

His were sturdy, and probably could float a person across the channel.

She went through to his dressing room. His shaving kit was precisely in place, looking as if it had never been used.

She tossed his clothing over a chair and listened to her footsteps when she returned to her chamber. They even sounded louder in his room.

Thinking back to the Reid of her childhood, she recalled him dashing away. He was always moving out the door. Always had somewhere to go, a sense of purpose in his stride, a lock of hair falling against his face, and enthusiasm surrounding him. And perhaps a sense of mischief.

Even when he'd been at an event, he'd danced, or spoken briefly with someone, and then if she'd glanced around later, he would be out of view.

No one could keep up with Reid. She'd never seen him stilled until it had almost been permanent.

She wondered where he'd disappeared to. What he was doing on the day after his marriage.

She strode through to the hallway and noticed her trunk by the door, with her favourite dresses draped across it. Her mother had wasted no time having things packed and sent to her, which caused a lump in Guinevere's throat.

Well, if this was to be her home, then she would make it her own.

She studied the furniture surrounding her bed. This room matched the other too closely. She would not be comfortable in it.

She couldn't live in someone else's life.

She'd married. Her world had tilted, but she would right it.

Yes, she'd wed, and at the moment, the floor under her feet didn't feel solid, but everything else around her appeared able to withstand any tempest. She was adrift, but nothing else was.

She dressed the best she could, and then rang for a maid, and soon heard a tap from the entrance facing the hallway.

If she'd been at her childhood home, she would have called out for the person to enter, but instead she opened the door.

A woman, hardly appearing out of her teens and yet with silver streaks in her hair, stood, peering up under her lashes.

'I'm Sally. The Duchess sent a message that Maggie will be along later today, with more of your things. She said we are to tell you that your companion has been instructed it is her choice whether she stays with you or your mother, but Maggie has insisted no one else could assist you as she can, and she's packing her clothing, and would be ever so happy if you could find room for your cheval mirror.'

Then the woman smiled, and asked if she would like a tray brought to her as Lord Hartcroft preferred, or if she would prefer the dining room for breakfast, and said the servants had picked some flowers for her from the gardens.

Guinevere opted for a tray on the small table in the sitting room.

When the food was presented, she smiled, the blooms showing that she was being welcomed.

The bacon was filling, and she had more sweetbread on the tray than she'd ever before eaten in a day, so she didn't even try to finish it.

She put down the knife.

This was her home, and once she adjusted to it, the world would be brighter. She perused the furniture again, imagining it replaced with her own.

By the time she'd finished her breakfast, she'd made plans for altering what she could. She reached for the pull, deciding that she'd have her own room things exchanged for the ones around her. She might be leaving parts of her life behind, but she could have the décor she preferred close. In fact, she didn't need to devote any time to planning; she would tell the servants to arrange things just as they'd been in her old room.

All available staff was commandeered, and the room erupted into a flurry of movements, and she discovered where items could be stored, and mostly everything was removed from the bedroom, all the furniture gone except for the stripped bed which she planned to have dismantled.

Reid appeared, staring silently to study the situation of scurrying staff. 'I came to make sure you are comfortable,' he said. 'But I gathered I'm late on that.' He studied the room. 'What happened here?'

She blushed.

'I know what happened here,' he spoke, voice a low rumble, 'and I hope this is no comment on that.'

'I'm planning to select a few familiar things from my parents' house. I want to feel at home.'

'Where will you sleep tonight?'

'I'm planning to go to my old bedroom and select the furniture to be moved here.'

'That might be a thing I would like to know, on occasion. If you are abed and it's changed from the night before.'

'I was going to tell you. If it came up.'

'It would.'

He stood closer, and she remained perfectly still but her insides gasped in an awareness of the man beside her. She felt just as dismantled as the bare room, but she wouldn't let herself be diminished by his strength or his appeal.

Her mind filled in the moves for her just as it did in chess. He was used to women reacting to him. They always had, and he thought nothing of it. Something sizzled in her, and she nurtured it from awareness to a distant interest.

Now she studied him closer and saw fine lines at the edges of his eyes which made him appear stronger, and not the devil-may-care person she'd seen her whole life.

She'd expected him to stay abed half the morning, and to take his time starting a day. But she'd been wrong. He wore a cravat and coat, and his shoulders took up the width of the doorway.

'Are you going out?' she asked, after noticing his coat.

'No. My steward will be arriving here. I've not told him we are married yet. He will need to know.'

She barely glanced sideways at him. 'We do have to tell people, don't we?'

He put a hand at her waist, his voice a teasing rumble. 'Not if we don't want to.' Then he paused. 'We can see what everyone makes of it. I'll keep it a secret if you will.'

'I may have an announcement put in the newspaper. Or better yet, have my mother plan a dinner for us and invite all Father's friends. You get on well with them, don't you?'

'The ones who don't have sons or daughters near my age.'

'Then it will be an interesting experience for you. And you can show everyone how happily wed you are.'

'How I have turned over a new leaf and am immensely pleased.'

'I hope you can sway them better than you're convincing me.'

'Possibly because the happiness on your face is being reflected onto my own. And—' He gazed around. 'It appears my house is being dismantled.'

A breath. 'Our house,' he added, moving away and leaving a chilled spot where his hand had rested.

True, it had been his house, and she wasn't sure she'd not started the alterations to make it her own. And without mentioning the modifications to him—to say emphatically she had a foothold in his world. She could have spoken of it, but she'd decided so quickly and not wanted to wait a moment longer. She wanted it done—yesterday.

'I'm just concentrating on the project,' she said, not sure if she was telling the truth, but it certainly wasn't his fault they'd had to wed. True, he'd asked her first to elope to Scotland, but he could have been jesting. Then she'd made the challenge to test his mettle, which had led to a longer endeavour than he'd expected.

What if the original proposal had been little more than a silly jest and he'd had no intention of marriage? Well, she hoped never to find that out.

On second thought, why shouldn't she ask. 'That first proposal...would you have truly taken me to Scotland?'

'Dear sweet Guinevere, it's a little late for that question now.'

She made a disapproving noise.

'Because,' he continued, eyes glinting with humour, 'only a husband who wanted more dismantled than his wife's room would say no.'

She crossed her arms. 'I don't know what to believe.'

'Believe your mind.' All the lightness evaporated. 'Your instincts will lead you better than any words anyone else might speak.'

'My mind is telling me—' Her mind was warning her she'd made a terrible error. She should have fought back when her father said she must wed Reid, and yet she didn't dare voice the words. On the surface, he was accepting of the marriage. But she could feel the upheaval inside him.

'My mind is saying that I cannot bear this room to look as it did. I have a table set and dressing mirror that I've had for years. And if my mother doesn't mind, and I'm sure she won't, I'll just bring everything here. I plan to get the room measurements today, and perhaps a few of the other rooms.'

'You should make it your own.'

'Do you mind if I alter a few items in the connecting sitting room?'

He considered it, and strode to the area. 'Make it as you wish. I don't care a mite about any fixtures in the house except the chairs my grandfather had had made to fit him, and we're the same height. Plus, I'd like my bedroom and the library to stay the same.'

'Your domain,' she said.

'Yes. It was yesterday. Now it's ours.'

'Do you mind if I have the chairs you prefer reupholstered?' She indicated, and picked at, the nap. 'I'll match the fabric as closely as possible. It appears overdue.' She tapped the worn spot, and true it wasn't bad, but she doubted anyone had truly examined the upholstery for years.

The thought of his chair being changed caused a tightening of his jaw.

'I'm sure it will be an improvement. Tell them to be quick about it.'

'I will.'

She touched a picture frame, straightening it, frowned and then removed it from the wall, pointing out the brighter paint under the artwork, and returned it to the hanger.

'Since the place will be out of sorts while the chairs are gone, I'll have the painting done at the same time, and perhaps a shade less likely to show discolour,' she added, knowing several staff members could complete that quickly. 'The pictures can stay, for now, and the rug is also a fine quality.'

'The paint smell could take months to evaporate.'

'Yes. But we could just avoid this room until then. Open the windows.' She organised the project in her mind, wanting to minimise the servants' movements. The staff wouldn't dare express any displeasure, but she didn't want to stress them.

'Well, I don't think this area has been used

much since my father was alive, and it's good to know it will be utilised again.'

'And there is a painting of three dancing ladies in your room. Wouldn't…perhaps, a landscape be more befitting a marquess?'

He stilled. 'I didn't know you'd been in my room.'

'When I woke. It's well-appointed.'

'Just like this one was. The furniture was all replicas.'

'And quite sturdy.'

'You can remove the picture of the women,' he said. 'If it's replaced with something I dislike, I will let you know.'

'If the adjustments bother you, I'll wait.'

'It's time. The rooms are overdue for an update, I suppose. I can't remember the last time anything's been altered. I didn't think about it.' His nod was more for himself. 'I appreciate the time you're taking to make the changes.' He glanced around the room. 'All the changes.'

'There won't be many.'

He smiled, met her eyes, may have looked upward when he turned away, and his chuckle lingered as he left the room.

Chapter Seventeen

The fireplace warmed the room, and Reid opened the window, and sat at his desk. He turned ledger pages, letting the figures nudge his recollections. It wasn't his father's life in review, but his own.

No surprises, but many things he didn't relish sharing with Guinevere.

Everything had seemed like a good idea at the time. But not now. He shut his eyes, running fingertips over the closed lids, memories stirring. He would be incensed with a child of his if it acted so rash. No wonder his father had been so infuriated at times.

He would have advised Guinevere not to wed this man. He would have told her to run while she had the chance. And she had. To her aunt's. But she'd invited him along, and at first he'd been unable to refuse. Perhaps he'd expected them to be discovered, but after a few days, he'd left, seeing the error of the charade.

She was too innocent. Protected.

And he would have taken her to Scotland.

A tap on the door.

'Come in,' he said, standing. It could only be one person, and he was suddenly flooded with the realisation he'd been away from her too long.

His breath caught at the sight of her, and he drank in her grace. She carried folded papers in her hand, and left the door open behind her.

'You don't have to knock,' he said. 'I truly don't care at all. In fact, I would prefer it if you didn't.'

He stared at his ledgers. 'We shouldn't have secrets between us.'

'I agree.'

He realised what he'd said. That they shouldn't have secrets between them. But it didn't mean they wouldn't.

She didn't need to know about his father's life. He didn't want to disparage the man in her eyes. After all, she'd looked up to him.

Another part of him did want the Duke to know. The Marquess would have kept that private. But Reid wasn't certain he truly did know his father. Perhaps no one did. And if that was the case, then the Duke would have been kept in the dark.

Anger flashed at his father, and all the admonitions he'd given Reid. The man couldn't follow his own advice.

Except—he studied Guinevere. Reid would now do as his father had suggested. He would not let it be a pretence. He would remain a true husband. If, at some point, Guinevere wanted to leave him, he would accept that, and they could part. He would have one life. One wife. One family. One Guinevere.

That would be no different. He had always had one life and lived it to the full. The sums definitely proved he'd engaged in the world around him.

'You're staring at me,' Guinevere said.

'I thought I had changed completely from my old life. But I realised I hadn't. I altered direction, but in the past when something intrigued me, I pursued it.'

'That can be disconcerting to hear.'

'I suggested Scotland. The commitment. That is the difference. I won't be like—' He'd almost said that he wouldn't be like his father, but she would misunderstand that. She perceived his father a moral man. 'I will be a husband.'

His features masked something she couldn't

truly comprehend. She believed him when he said he wanted to be a husband. At least he did for the moment, and her mind could not help running through the different possible moves in front of them. But for now, he definitely needed her. She was a necessary addition to continue his lineage. The Marchioness he'd wanted to go along with the rest of the staff. But she didn't believe he truly envisaged her to be agreeable always.

'Reid, I want to make certain that you are accepting of something I've written.'

He raised a brow.

She thought of her own friends, and how she'd embellished the truth. She held the letters in her hand, where she'd written them of her marriage, given her new location and invited them to visit. Her fingers had almost cramped from the writing.

'I told my friends that you'd had an accident and…' She put her head down. 'I may have left out a few events. I did awaken you. I mentioned a kiss goodbye and how your eyes opened with amazement. And you have not truly seen another woman since that moment. One thing quickly led to another and a wedding. We could not help ourselves.'

'No one had to teach you embroidery, did they?'

'Well, my friends are all married and have tried to encourage me to follow suit. They are hopeless romantics. They will be so happy for me.'

'Not chess players?'

'No. We have an embroidery club and I used to meet with them at Jennie's home on Tuesdays until I went to my aunt's. I'm hoping to continue to meet with them.'

'An embroidery organisation. Chess. It sounds as if you have the exciting events all sewn up.'

'Right there along with a husband who has been distracted today.'

He gave a one-sided shrug. 'Guilty.'

She lifted the pen from his desk, inked it and touched the tip of it to her palm, leaving a dot. 'So, if the subject is mentioned, how will you describe awakening?'

'I opened my eyes and saw an angel.'

She didn't move, but the truth he put into the words hit her with the same awareness she'd felt when she'd thrust the pin at him and his eyes had opened.

'You're better than I at embroidery,' she said, returning the pen to him. 'But you wouldn't swear at an angel.'

He challenged her with a grin that could have fluttered any wings or halo. 'You don't know me very well. If she'd stabbed me with a sharp object, I would have.'

'I believe you. And you could have charmed that halo right off afterwards.'

'I would have tried if she looked like you.'

'You're good at this.'

'It's easy with you.'

It was meant as a compliment, and she understood it, but it didn't make her feel better.

Her body reacted to him but that discomfited her; she felt betrayed by it. He had not lied to her. He wanted a bride who fit well into his life. And she did.

She thought back to the conversations they'd had, and how little time they'd actually spent together before his accident. Almost none as adults.

She'd not expected a marriage to make her feel more alone than she ever had.

He studied her as closely as she studied a chessboard with a stellar opponent on the other side.

Footsteps in the hallway announced an arrival and the butler appeared. 'Your Lordship. The steward is here.'

'Yes.' One word, delivered without emotion.

Guinevere paused, but she didn't leave.

* * *

Reid listened to the footsteps of the servant retreating. A small clunk as something burned away in the fireplace and the other pieces fell into the vacant space.

The fire had been readied to burn his father's past.

'You don't have to stay for talk of business,' Reid said.

'I don't mind waiting.' Guinevere watched the fire. 'It's lovely. And I was getting chilled in my room.'

A rotund man stepped inside, a satchel clasped close to his chest.

'Marchioness.' Reid indicated her with a nod. 'Meet Mr Shepherd, my man-of-affairs.'

'Most pleased to meet you, my lady. Much pleased.' He bowed, appearing more shocked than pleased, his bag gripped even closer against his chest. His robust frame appeared to be guarding it.

Reid held out his hand, and the man hesitated before opening the satchel and giving Reid a grey volume.

'Thank you,' Reid said, standing to take it. Then he asked his man-of-affairs, 'Is this the only one?'

The man nodded.

He'd planned to ask for the ledger to be burned in front of him because he would not trust anyone to do that out of his sight.

'We won't need a second set of books in the future,' Reid said.

'Of course.' The man tipped his head.

'Thank you for bringing it. I'll take care of this one from now on. And you can take the black ones to bring them up to date.'

Reid indicated the black ledgers. 'The most recent one has a brief letter tucked in it announcing my marriage. I want you to make a copy specific to individual tenants in the countryside, and I will sign them and we will work out delivery details. Most people are to be given a reduction in rent this year as celebration of my marriage. You'll see the figures. And I have already written two letters and will see that they are taken care of.'

Those two men were to be given an entire year of freedom from rent. As a youth, he'd galloped his horse through one man's crop and trampled some of the grain. With the other, he'd been too arrogant.

'Let me know when it is done,' Reid said.

'Certainly.' The steward grasped he was being dismissed, took the black ledgers and left.

Reid ran his fingers over the leather, opened it to the beginning and looked at the dates on the pages, then closed it.

'What is it?' Guinevere asked.

'Financial matters.'

'Can I see it?' she asked. 'I'm fair with mathematicals.'

Reid thought about the earlier dates. Around the time of his birth. 'They have the family secrets in them,' Reid said. 'I'd rather you didn't.'

'I thought you wanted no secrets between us.'

'I don't think you'll like seeing the book any more than I will.' He lifted a pen. 'Dwelling on the flaws of the past doesn't make them go away.'

She moved closer.

'You heard me tell him not to keep a second set of books in the future.' He walked to the fire, and opened the book, gripping the pages in his fist to rip them out.

'No.' She held out her hand. 'Don't burn it.'

'Why shouldn't I?'

'You're afraid I'll read it.'

'I don't want anyone seeing them.'

'Is it truly that bad?'

He stopped, closed the book over the crumpled pages. 'Some things only cause pain and have no good left in them. Although I suppose the documentation helped Shepherd keep his job.'

He sighed. 'If I burn it, you'll always think the worst of me. But that's fair. I'm prepared for that.'

Chapter Eighteen

Reid followed her, and she strode into the room that now had had the bed removed.

She reached the pull and tugged on it.

'I don't want secrets between us, Guinevere, but the truth of the past will do neither of us any good,' he said behind her, voice softened to a calming timbre. 'And the more people who know a thing, the more likely it is to be bandied about.'

'If everyone knows, it doesn't hurt anyone anew. I saw you dancing with women. I heard the tales. It is no surprise to me. It wasn't at the time.'

'Then why do you want to see documentation of anything?'

'Because it feels like a secret. If it hurts me, I have no one to blame but myself. I asked to read the ledger.'

She wouldn't believe there was any truth in

him if even his upstanding father had a secret life. And what would she think of his mother for shutting her eyes to it?

His attention snapped to the ceiling. 'I can't adjust my past. I can't change anyone's past.' His voice hardened. 'The true fault is my own. The person I'm angriest at is myself. I should have travelled to Shepherd's. Or insisted he burn the records. Then we would not be having this conversation.'

The room where he now stood had become silent. The master chess player watched him. No emotion on her face.

Something inside him churned. The ledger he held exonerated him more than anything. But still, his family would suffer.

The ones Shepherd had taken were the current ones.

The ones that detailed the expenses he'd spent on the women of his past. Shepherd had put names and descriptions. The man should be commended, but Reid had no wish to thank him. The jewellery he truly didn't remember until he'd read about the pieces again. They'd not been inexpensive.

He told himself it was in Guinevere's best interest. He didn't want her meeting a former sweetheart of his at a soiree and feeling jealousy.

Or seeing a jewel on a woman's wrist and knowing it had been purchased by him.

He'd made his own brilliant chess move. He held a ledger that told of his father's infidelity. A man she liked and trusted. And Shepherd had walked out with the ones detailing Reid's excesses.

'I want a fresh start. With our marriage. I do. And if the past is rising up to me, I won't be able to start anew. Perhaps in part I wanted to wed to make sure I never lapsed back into the life I'd left,' he said.

'If you can't do it on your own, don't expect a few sentences in front of a cleric to make a difference.'

'Don't forget, you were there, also. At my side. Together with me.'

'But were we together, or merely married at the same time?'

He didn't like hearing those words from her. 'My past is no secret. I don't want to dwell on it. I had time to think about it after my accident. I almost lost everything. I want to leave a better legacy than what has gone before me.'

With a feeling of finality and an awareness of his resolve, he summed up why Guinevere had been the woman he wanted to take to Scotland.

He'd not really considered she'd want to

spend anywhere with him but being partnered at events, or in the bedroom creating the children she would nurture. But then he'd spent a few days with her, and his views had altered. He'd discovered that to be with her would be to love her, and she might not be capable of the same feelings.

'Do you want a true marriage?' he asked. 'Is it important to you?'

'We have a true marriage. It may not feel like it, but I have moved into your life. I'm in your house, under your roof.'

'This is not how I wish. And you are not here to follow my whims, and if you tell yourself you believe that, it is not the truth. You began rearranging the surroundings as you wanted. As you should. But it was your decision, and yours alone. You began to change things to suit your needs, not questioning anything else. Not mentioning it to me until afterwards.'

He told himself he should be thrilled. She was more concerned about the changes in the house. About stepping into her role as marchioness and her own duties. He got exactly what he'd wished for—at first.

'Guinevere, you know it is not my belief that softening words makes them easier.'

He saw her body tense. Perhaps he should gentle his speech with one person. Guinevere.

She reached up and touched her ear, seeming to move a wisp of hair away. 'Well, I am pleased we cleared that up. It is nice to know where you stand and how the marriage will progress. I'm enlightened now.'

Then she put a lone finger over her lips. 'I wonder if my eldest brother believes the same thing and has told his wife. Now I understand our marriage so much better. You decided on quality, not quantity, and I am the peer's daughter that fulfilled that order.'

'At the time I travelled to the country, I needed a wife. I had half-heartedly courted others in London. I didn't stay here to look for a wife because you weren't here. I followed you to your aunt's. But when I arrived there, I saw your happiness. I didn't want the pretence any more. Any charade. In my life. And I don't want it now.'

'Any time promises are made with paperwork involved, it is not make-believe.'

'But is it a façade of a marriage?' He felt the weight of his next words.

He held out the ledger, but not within her reach. 'This needs to remain in the past.'

'It's not a secret, you say, but you don't want me to see the ledger.'

'The fire was for me to burn this. You will have to trust me. Trust is like honesty. You either have it or you don't.'

'I don't know what we have. Burn the ledger if you must.'

Chapter Nineteen

Reid decided he would give her anger time to subside, and she would understand. After all, she had grown up among the peerage. She'd seen the leaders of the country. Been at soirees with them. She knew how society conducted itself. Besides, she was a strategist. She would not let her emotions rule her.

Later, he heard more bustling outside his door.

More alterations to his house, and his life. He would keep his silence and let her get over her anger. Perhaps once the house was ordered the way she wanted it, she would become aware of him. Truly aware. Not see him as only a husband, but as Reid.

Then he reconsidered. She had known him her whole life, and they'd not got on well when he'd been Reid. Perhaps she had to see him as the man he now was.

He had to return to her bedroom. Striding inside, he wondered why he'd bothered. The bare room echoed the feeling of the rest of the house. Silent. Deserted, yet with only one person missing.

He'd wed his marchioness, but in truth, he didn't have her. And he wondered, if this was a strategy. A part of the game to keep him at arm's length… If she even had a heart, or if she'd been born to approach others from a distance and could never alter… If she'd kept the smile on her face and the pleasantry in her words because it achieved her goals best.

His country estate had felt more like a home when she was there.

Now, at his town house, four bare walls mocked him. Then he went into his room. The same painting was on the wall. Three dancing ladies.

He rang for a servant.

When a maid arrived, he reached up, took the picture and handed it to her. 'Put this away, and replace it with…' He thought of the insipid artwork that had been in the other room. 'That… other one.' He paused. If Guinevere returned, the floral one would please her. He pushed his cravat back into the neck of his waistcoat. 'The one which was in Lady Hartcroft's room.'

'The *flowers*?' the maid with the grey streak in her hair questioned, her brows rising.

He examined the empty spot on the wall. 'Her Ladyship prefers it. Over the dancing women, anyway.'

'Yes, Your Lordship.' The maid agreed, nodding, and he saw the approval in her eyes as she scurried away.

Guinevere sat watching the game pieces in an extra room at her parents' house where she'd had her childhood chess set relocated—because her own furnishings were being packed and readied to transport.

Her mother had tried to coerce Guinevere to explain why she'd returned, but she said it was only for one night, and because she needed her mother to assist her with the ideas she'd imagined for her new residence.

Her mother's voice had squeaked when she'd asked, 'Does Reid know?'

And her father had fumed, telling Guin marriage was not a game and he was certain that it would not be played best from different boards.

She'd brushed away their concern, reminding them that she and Reid hadn't been in love when they married, and that she'd merely wanted to make sure all the objects she wanted to take were gathered correctly, and admitting that she'd had all the articles removed from her room at his house to be replaced with familiar ones.

Her mother commented it was indeed a shame that Reid had not had extra space for her to spend the night in the town house. 'Guinevere. He's your husband now,' she'd muttered, leaving her daughter alone.

Guinevere stared at the game, sitting as she'd arranged it. The singular item she'd insisted she pack herself, and she stood, perusing it.

In a flash, she had moved one piece, then reached across the board and played for her imagined opponent.

At first, Reid was the imagined challenger, and then she changed strategies. In the second game, she was the adversary.

This time, she chose more slowly, and walked around the table, looking at the pieces from different angles. She didn't know which side would win. It didn't matter. Only her strengths concerned her.

She lost herself in the game, but didn't linger over it.

When she finished, she readied the board again.

But she grasped that she was playing against herself.

She didn't want to do that in life. Nor did she want Reid as an opponent, and she didn't see any other games on the board.

She dressed for bed, went to the mirror and glanced at herself while she brushed her hair.

She would always be her biggest adversary, and her own colleague, and if she were giving herself advice, it would be not to play against Reid, because one of them would always have to lose, if not both.

The marriage, life—everything was fluid. The pieces changed spaces, and she could control only a single player, but the best outcome she could hope for was one in which she'd considered the strategies and adopted her best tactics.

She ran the soft bristles of the brush over her hand, longing for Reid. The comfort of being in his arms. Missing him.

Hurt because he'd ignored her all day, even though he was in the residence. That had been like a pinprick in her own arm, and she'd awakened to the loneliness of her surroundings.

In his life, she was truly an outsider. She wasn't even sure he wasn't an outsider, also.

She was aware he'd sent a message to his mother to tell her of the marriage. He'd had his man-of-affairs in the house. The only other person he appeared truly aware of was his valet,

Beckham. His cousin had lived with him—that merest segment of a worm, Stephen—and Reid justifiably wasn't close to him.

She'd refused to let her parents push her towards Stephen. That had been unthinkable. She'd needed no help in that decision or in speaking her mind.

Yet, she'd been afraid to commit to Reid.

He'd been right.

She'd not approached him wholeheartedly.

She'd not made the decision firmly and for all to hear.

Chess was strategies. Imagined armies, controlling the area.

But marriage. That was a concept where the adjustments were not so precise. Each player could progress any way they wished, and to be removed from the board didn't usually lead to another match with the same person. Even if it did, there would be scars from being placed in the discard heap.

Returning her attention to the chessboard, she lifted the king and examined it.

The rules in chess were finite. Easily understandable, and it was her game.

To her the queen was the strongest piece, and she wondered if that was part of the appeal. The game was lost when the king was captured so his value was great, but the queen was his main protector. As it should be.

True, she wanted Reid, but did she want marriage? Was he just a figure in her life, carved and nearby?

They could touch, have children, attend events, and then both be put back on their respective boards to do as they wished. And maybe it would be the best marriage of all. Tidy. Ordered. Polite. Each would be the centre of a world of their own making. A wooden figure to dust off.

She slid into the chair, and played again, against herself, at the quickest pace possible, reassured by the click, click, click of pieces landing on the board.

Marriage. Two people. One game with different rules. The couples around her seemed to have strategies all their own.

She thought of her brother and his wife, alike in so many ways and in the beginning deeply in love. One could hardly breathe without asking if it would please the other one. Until suddenly they'd had a flare-up, and now never visited at the same time. No one seemed to know what the disagreement had been about.

From the start, she'd considered her sister's marriage deplorable. But her sister's husband had dissimilar rules for the union. He wanted to do as he wished, and had his wife agreed, he could have considered his wife a gem. Or he might have considered her worthless, and been even more demanding. Her sister couldn't win but could only hope for less of a defeat.

Her parents had a loving marriage, but her father mostly did as he wished, and so did her mother. They were faithful, and united, but not always on the same path, and yet truly happy with each other.

Her parents preferred not 'tripping over each other,' as her mother had once explained.

Marriage needed fixed rules, or at least the couples needed to understand them. They were going to be playing the same game, on possibly the same board, and the winning favour was contentment. Or happiness. She wanted both.

She wanted to love Reid, and to be his friend, and to be a part of him. She wanted him at her side, on her team, playing to win together, and to have long talks in the late hours, sharing feelings and hopes and dreams.

But he had made a point. And she understood it. Reid had spoken directly, just as he tended to, and she preferred his honesty and straightforwardness, even if it might mean hearing something she did not want to be told.

She'd wavered. She'd made the vows just as he had, but she'd not taken them to heart. She'd moved locations and acquired a husband and the items with him. But she'd not moved to his side.

If he'd wanted to make a statement, he had, by leaving her alone all day.

She stared at the king. But no matter how much she wished it, you could not put life into wood. That king would never come alive.

She held the queen again, and dropped it aside.

She didn't want a life of wooden figures. She trudged to the attic and found the old container that the set had once arrived in, and carefully placed each piece inside, and then she took the box back to where it had been stored and left it.

The game hadn't really meant that much to her. It had been easy to grasp. The act of winning had been the true joy. But that got old when there was no challenge.

She didn't want to spend her life considering strategy for painted wood with nothing inside it. With marriage, there was a chance of two people working as one. Of perhaps even love.

Reid had had little sleep, lying in bed, thinking. His bed seemed to have grown two sizes, and he'd always slept in it alone. The night darkened and lengthened.

He put his trust in Guinevere's words. In time, she would perceive that he had done what was right for the family and for them. He assumed the Duke and Duchess would be fuming at him because Guinevere had spent the night away, but if so, he would handle that as it appeared.

A winter chill enveloped his home, and the night was unseasonably warm.

He understood how he could miss someone after only one day of marriage because it was Guinevere. A rare person. A gem.

He dozed, but early in the morning, the sound of footsteps in the hallway woke him. He waited, hoping she might find her way to him.

The door remained closed, which erased all the goodwill in his heart. He felt the end of the pin again.

Reid would continue on his path, and not even mention their disagreement.

But he was pleased she'd returned. He'd been almost afraid she would change her mind in the night, vowing never to return.

Then he grimaced. Likely the Duke would send her back to him. The man was eternally irritating and should mind his own affairs, but Reid was happy to have her under his roof.

Thankful she'd arrived home, he decided to force himself to continue about his day as usual.

He rang for Beckham, and dressed, wanting the cook alerted that he would be needing breakfast soon.

Beckham arrived, took the request, left the tray with the chocolate and added, 'Your cousin has arrived, and is in his usual room.'

'Stephen?' He'd dared return. 'It wasn't—'

'Your cousin.' Beckham acted as if the question were a normal one.

'Stephen? Is here?' The brashness surprised him.

'Yes. Apparently, his latest sweetheart has grown tired of him and told him to leave.'

'Send him to the library. Now.'

Reid slammed from the room and waited.

'Hullo,' Stephen called out after a good half hour, strolling in, his cravat off. His hair fresh from a windstorm and the smell of drink preceding him. 'I was asleep and your valet didn't even knock. He demanded I see you. You should sack him. I don't think he likes me. What is he so insistent about? Something happen?'

'Did you know I'm wed?'

'You?' Stephen drawled out the word. 'Who did you— Oh. Guin.'

'Yes.'

'Well, you can't win them all—all the ladies anyway. At least I can't. Just most.'

'And you tried to blackmail her. Guinevere. And you dared show up here?'

'It was just a jest.' He shrugged. 'You know I'd never do that.'

'No. Because I'd bury you in the middle of the street and people would be driving out of their way to run their carriages over you. Unless you tell me a different location, your things will be sent to the Albany. You can no longer stay here.'

'Just because you married?'

'No, because you were unkind to Guinevere. That will never be tolerated.'

'She's a duke's daughter so you have to act all sweet about her.'

'I am not acting all sweet about her.'

'You'll grow tired of it soon. Trust me. I know. We're cousins. Cut from the same cloth. Two of a kind.'

'I am not.'

Stephen's lips fluttered. 'You lie to yourself.'

'You're drunken. I'm not.'

'Today. How many times have I stopped drinking to excess?' He chuckled. 'You are just like me, only I see that I'm not perfect. How many women have fallen at my feet, and I just walked right by? We all have to marry some day, and I would have wed Guinevere if she'd had me. And we would have lived happily ever after, and I would have said all the sweet things to her and begged her forgiveness when she caught me. She would have been happy as long as she didn't watch me too closely. It would have been her choice.'

Stephen glanced around. 'She must be a late sleeper or I'm sure she would be here giving me an earful.' He went to the pull. 'I'll have someone summon her so I can give her my condolences. Er, uh, apology.'

'You pull that cord and you'll have broken fingers.'

His cousin coughed, but didn't touch it. 'I would have thought Lady Guinevere would have put you in a better mood. Trouble already brewing?' he asked. 'Or is it that you've realised that you've someone to answer to now?'

'Get. Out.'

'Oh,' he grumbled, striding to the door. 'Very well. Do you have some money for a hackney?' He paused at the exit. 'I've had a run of bad luck. Didn't get to marry a duke's daughter and that should be worth something for me to have pointed her your way.'

Reid glared, and Stephen sauntered out. 'Fine.

Have it your way. Was going to use some of the money to buy you a wedding gift.'

Reid let Stephen leave, and he returned to his room and gathered his hat.

He could not be like Stephen. He could not. He could not. He would not.

He wondered if he should let Stephen return. It would be a constant reminder of what not to do.

He went to the sitting room, and then her chamber and knocked on her door. No answer. Next, he stepped inside, just to make sure she'd not arrived without him noticing it.

He gazed around. Emptied. Bare. Just like the rest of his home without Guinevere.

He heard a clatter, and stepped aside as one of his footmen, and a servant he didn't know, brought in two delicate chairs and a spindly table.

The other person with them, whom he recognised from the golf game as Maggie, started directing all the furnishings that followed, insisting the table and one chair went by the windows, and the embroidery stand went on the other side.

'Her Ladyship's request,' Maggie said. 'I know just how she wants the room.'

'Is the Marchioness with you?'

The woman shook her head. 'No. She's consulting with her mother about some measurements she collected of the other spaces. Her Grace is an exemplary artist, and she's likely sketching magnificent ideas.' The woman spoke ever so subserviently but her eyes twinkled smugness. 'The Marchioness also knows just how she likes things.'

'Exactly as I'd hoped,' Reid said.

Chapter Twenty

Reid had given up on all attempts of thinking about anything but Guinevere. He needed to make sure his marchioness had not forgotten her new location.

He found his satchel, added the balls, and one other item, and collected two of his remaining golf clubs, after having the butler summon a hackney. Reid gripped the clubs in one hand with the satchel under his arm and jumped inside the coach when it appeared.

Arriving at the Duke's estate, he asked the butler, 'Is Lady Hartcroft here? I would like to see her.'

'I will see if she is in.' The bushy eyebrows didn't flicker and Reid didn't think the man meant any slight from it, but spoke from years of habit.

'I will wait,' Reid said. The man turned to the

stairs. 'No. I won't,' Reid added. 'It's my wife. I will see her in the sitting room. And this is my family now.'

He heard a familiar ducal snort and saw her father at the top of the stairs. Grimacing.

He stood firm. Used one of the clubs to tap his chest. 'Husband. Marquess of Hartcroft. And son-in-law. In that order. I'm sure that is what you were thinking when you urged Guinevere to marry me. You wanted to be with me every holiday, every family celebration. Sundays. Weekdays…'

'Pshut,' the Duke said, but before he left, he turned back. He gave a victory wave. 'And I will be your children's grandfather.' He shut his eyes and shivered in mock happiness. 'A ducal grandfather outranks a marquess father on each of those days you mentioned. Raise them right, Hartcroft, I want to be there to give them treats.'

Reid glanced at the butler. 'After the children arrive, we may be spending a lot of time at my country estate.'

The servant bowed deeply, taking Reid's clubs. 'I am proud you are a part of the Duke of Glouston's family, my lord. They are all gentle, compassionate souls and you will fit in well with them. I will keep these clubs for the time being until we see how you adjust to a morning with His Grace.'

'I know how gentle they are,' Reid spoke softly when he strode by the man. 'Because we are all family now. And I want them all on my side in any disagreement.'

'I agree, Your Lordship. If you will go to the harp room, a maid will fetch Lady Guinevere.'

'I would appreciate it,' Reid added.

Guinevere finally arrived with what appeared to be a filled sketchpad under her arm, and it didn't have artwork on it, but lines. He assumed it the measurements of the rooms in his house.

He suspected he would have got a pleasanter greeting if he'd been the lowliest servant. He received what he considered must have been the errant husband welcome. He imagined he should get used to it.

'When are you returning?' he asked.

'The servants are still packing a few things for me, and when the wagon returns to be filled, I think that will take care of everything. I want to be comfortable, and if I move my room exactly as it was, I'll feel at home more quickly. I don't want to feel I'm on an island I've never seen before.'

'You plan ahead.'

'Without even meaning to,' she said, musing. 'Most times.'

'What about when you agreed to wed? Those moments? Was it truly what you wanted?'

'I only deliberated on keeping everyone at peace. And you do intrigue me. I didn't— The event— I'm not sure what I was thinking.'

She studied the sketchpad, but he knew she considered her words. 'It was as if I woke up the next morning after we wed and wondered if it had truly happened.' She shook her head. 'A few words. A signature. And *voilà*.' She made a fist and then extended all her fingers. 'A wife. I would have thought it couldn't have been done so simply.'

'I offered to take you to Scotland.'

'That would likely have made it more memorable, but I believe, in good time, it will become noteworthy on its own. For good or ill.'

'Good would be best.'

'True. But we both tend to have opinions.'

'I have big homes, though. I wouldn't think you'd have had to leave last night. We could rarely be in the same room if you prefer a distant marriage.'

'I needed to think. To say goodbye to my old life. To pack it up—so to speak. It's easier to leave when the past isn't there any more. My room here is almost empty now and the draperies have been changed. A few furnishings in the attic will be transferred to it today. It's behind me now—my life here. Maggie should be making sure all is in order at your house, so I can walk into my bedroom and have familiar items near.'

He paused. 'I told Stephen what happened. He visited my home.'

She shuddered. 'He's your cousin, and I once liked him, but I detest him now.'

'When I saw him, it made me realise I could never be him. Never. Whether you are in my life or not. The life I want is not of a vacant house. The house was empty when he and I were there. Always. But now I would like it filled. With you and me. Not alone. But together.'

He indicated the walls. 'I did change the painting of the women, but I want to keep the chairs. Still in the same upholstery. Wear and all. My grandfather was by no means perfect, but he put those worn spots on the arms.'

'Of course. I understand and will leave them alone.' She stepped closer. 'You changed the picture?'

'Yes. To that hideous one with flowers in it. And the house still felt just as empty. It needs you.'

'Do you believe that?'

'Have I ever said anything I don't mean?'

'Well, you did compare me to an angel.'

'Again. You are. My angel. The one who woke me.'

'But I don't want to kiss you back to sleep,' she said.

'And I won't be a chess piece for you.'

'How can you think that?'

'I am the king to complete your game pieces. Your parents are the bishops. Your siblings and everyone else make up the rest of the set.'

She studied him, unwavering. 'You were the one man I couldn't strategize about. The one who did what he wanted, took the parts of society he liked, ignored the others and—' She hesitated. 'Perhaps I did the same as you.'

'Is it truly how you see things? You are skilled at playing both sides of the board. A game against yourself. Are you doing the same now?'

'No,' she admitted. 'When you left me in the country, the enjoyment I'd had from arranging the servants and furnishings disappeared, though I am so fond of my great-aunt. I was at a loss. Nothing meant so much to me at that point.'

She spoke with her eyes closed. 'I grasped that I did not know you.' Then she shook her head minutely and looked at him. 'But I didn't fully understand it until I became your wife. Before, I saw reckless Reid, the boy, and the rake. And then to be at your home, and be *ignored*, by a rake?'

'It may have seemed I was ignoring you. I wasn't.'

'You were so quiet.'

'What you saw of me when I was at events was only a part of me. The social world. Perhaps I exaggerated it when I was among others. As a youth, it was true exuberance. It wore thin, and thinner, and then I was angry at myself for taking everything as a jest. I'm not perfect and will still make errors. And if you can help me see where I'm making others, I will adjust to make our lives better.'

'I would like it to be our life—not our lives. Perhaps I need you and honesty more than anything else.'

He reached in his satchel, leaving it on the table but taking out the book. 'I would like this burned,' he said, holding the grey ledger and placing it in her hands. 'You may read it. But first I must tell you what's in it.'

He moved to the unlit fireplace, lifting the iron scoop, and it clinked when he arranged it in the stand. 'I discovered something was amiss in Shepherd's accounting books before the accident and it puzzled me. More funds. Not a lot, but there was an expense that I'd not considered before, and it was gone. An expense for a hunting steward. Plus, repair expenses he always seemed to be needing. And that caused me to go over Shepherd's numbers carefully and study them.'

He pointed to the ledger. 'This was the detailed account. The one Shepherd kept secretly. For my father.

'Shepherd said the woman had had no children, and that she died a few years ago.' Reid shook his head. 'I'd meant to go to my father's hunting box after he passed, but never got around to it. And I just forgot about it.

'I'll trust you to burn it and keep quiet about it. It won't do anyone any good to bring up the past and Father isn't here to defend himself. And I would like it if the Duke doesn't know. Besides, I don't think he'd believe it anyway, and that would be for the best.'

'Your father wed your mother late in life. Perhaps it was simply an old romance and he still wanted to take care of her.'

'Possibly.'

She pursed her lips. 'But I don't think so. I think you should mention it to my father.'

'No.' The word was short and clipped. 'I do not want him to know my father's shortcomings. My grandfather was open about his life.

But I don't want any mud splashed on my father's memory.'

'Well, if you are comfortable knowing about your grandfather's past, then perhaps my father could explain. If the woman was named Maria, then perhaps your father was visiting his half-sister. He didn't find out about her until he was older, and some felt she was taking advantage of your grandfather's status, but your father wanted to give her the benefit of the doubt, and he visited her once a year. He had to keep it a secret from your grandfather while he was alive.'

'How do you know?'

'My mother and yours discussed it one day. Your mother definitely felt your family was being used, and your grandfather didn't know that funds were being diverted to Maria. He'd claimed it an untruth, and would have been livid. Your mother feared he would have taken it out on your father. So, your father had to send the funds quietly. I thought you knew, but it was all very surreptitious. And after your grandfather passed away, they kept things the same, not wanting to take any risk with change.'

'I didn't know.'

She touched his cheek. 'We've not had much time to talk.'

'Well,' he said, pulling her close. 'It may be

a while before we have a lot of time to talk. But I look forward to it, and we need to start now. I can't be the perfect chess piece, but I'd like to be the mate you want. Let's start the marriage over, Guin. It's Tuesday. A safe day when things hardly ever go wrong. A good day for a beginning.'

He spoke, choosing words carefully. 'I don't want to live in a marriage alone, for even an hour. And if here is where it's to be, I'm prepared. I'll wait,' he said. 'I brought my clubs.'

And he knew he would wait, even if she lingered all day, or the rest of the week, or the rest of his life. She was his wife. A few moments had changed that for ever, but all in all, he'd had the luckiest month he'd ever had.

'Perhaps we will have another competition then,' she said, 'while the last things are being moved.'

'I agree. Let's go to the gardens,' he said, retrieving the balls from the satchel. 'But the things you said about my father seeing his half-sister. It could simply be a lie he told to cover his tracks.'

'Well, your best chance of discovering the truth would be to discuss it with my father. He would likely know.'

'True,' he said. 'But he and I can discuss it

later. Right now, I want to be with you. I'm challenging you to another game. I don't really play the sport, but it's how I like to relax. I hope it doesn't bother you if I don't let you win.'

'It doesn't bother me to lose,' she said. 'It does bother me to have victory *all* the time, as I tend to do with chess. It takes the fun out of it.'

'Perhaps you'll like marriage then. I've heard you can't win all the time.'

'I was hoping to win most of the time,' she said.

'I hope we both do,' he answered.

They secured an empty bottle and moved to the gardens. 'These aren't my favourite clubs,' he said. 'I'm going to have to retrieve them from your aunt's.'

'Oh, I didn't know they meant so much to you.' Her eyes widened, and she put her hand over her mouth.

'They do. I can't believe I left them behind.'

'I expected you didn't want them. I gave them to the servants.'

'Well,' he said, then chuckled. 'I hope they like them as much as I did.'

He put the bottle at the edge of the gardens, far from the bush that had bothered him in the night.

She surveyed the distance.

He put the club in her hands, dropped the ball at her feet and said, 'You go first. Make your foundation strong,' he said. 'Plant your feet.'

'You're so much better at this than I. You won't let me win?'

'No. That's the only way we can gauge how quickly you're progressing, and when you win, you'll feel even better than all the times earlier put together. You'll know you did it.'

'Let's try,' she said.

He didn't let her win, but it was difficult to put his whole spirit into the game. Watching her study the grass, estimate the swing, give a little feminine wiggle and do her best intrigued him more than anything else, besides helping her with her swing.

They played several matches, and he noticed she really played against herself. In fact, it seemed to him that she hardly watched his own attempts, always thinking of her next steps. This was his wife, and he liked watching her concentrate.

'I'm ready to stop,' she said. 'But it has been fun. Will you learn to play chess with me?'

'And how do you think that will turn out?'

'Brief.'

'You're much more capable of learning golf than I am of chess.'

He propped their clubs against the bench and tucked her hand around his arm.

'I want everyone to see you at my side when we go in,' he said. 'The only marchioness for me.'

'You are trying to sweet-talk me.'

'Very much so. But it's true. I did mention eloping several times to you. You weren't a gamble. When I truly saw you, when I opened my eyes, I knew you were the jewel in anyone's crown.'

'I may have been afraid to accept your proposal once, but I wouldn't be now.'

'That's fortunate,' he said, gently tugging her close.

He peered into the distance. 'Staring at your empty room this morning, I decided I received what I needed most, a strong woman who had her own opinions. I saw you hush your father the Duke. You never snapped your fingers and gave instruction, but you expected, even without knowing it, for your wishes to be carried out. I'd never seen anyone so determined, except myself. You are not just the daughter of a duke, but you are instilled with the ducal spirit, perhaps even more so than your father.'

'I don't know if that is a compliment.'

'It is. The highest. You are a leader, Guin,

and you do so with kindness. I thought of when I stood on a beach in Cornwall once and how the wind whipped around, and it was good to have my feet planted and feel the power of being able to withstand the currents. Ships are the same. Even the smaller vessels must be strong enough to sail the same oceans as the larger ones. And a wife needs a foundation of strength. At least, my wife does. I knew it wouldn't be easy to live with me. No one's ever suggested that. An oversight, I'm sure.'

'But have they ever dared tell you that you're difficult to live with?'

'I've only lived with family.' He smiled. 'I've heard that many times.'

'I would tell you.'

'I know.'

And if he told her she had strength, he had to trust her to have the power to withstand the truth of his past.

'What I didn't tell you, Guinevere, is that the steward has the true financial ledgers for my expenses. If you want to see them, you can. They detail my life. I saw it spelled out in front of me. The billing for liquor. Every jewel I purchased is listed in the accounts, and a detailed description, and the name of the woman who received the item. I promise I will purchase more expensive gems for you.'

She waved away his words. 'No need to select anything costly for me. I only wear a few sentimental pieces. And the brooch is my favourite. It has memories of both you and my mother.'

'But what if you are at an event, and a woman greets you, and you notice she is wearing something I purchased?'

She laughed. 'Then I will be certain to admire it and tell her that whoever gave it to her has exquisite taste.'

Stopping, she faced him, and met his gaze while clasping both his hands. 'I was at the soirees and heard the talk. I don't have to read the ledgers. I saw your romances flame and flicker away, and how you were more entranced with life's adventures than anything else. Then when we married, I was surprised when you rose early and went to work. I did not expect that.'

He tugged her against his side, hugging her close, the connection between them removing all the ragged edges from his life, and giving him the first true feeling of being a husband. 'You may not love me now, Guin, but if you give us a chance, I believe your fondness will turn into something much deeper. I want you to care for me as much as I love you.'

Then he couldn't help himself, and twirled her around in his arms. He wanted them seen as a couple. To everyone, and particularly himself and Guinevere. 'I love you,' he whispered. 'Today and for ever.'

That night, after making love, he kissed her, slipped on his trousers, took a lamp and went to his library.

After he sat studying, he peered up to see her propped against the door frame, wearing his dressing gown.

'You will have to have one made just like that for you.'

She held the wrist to her nose. 'Yours smells so good. Makes me feel powerful. Your shaving soap.'

He laughed. 'That's why I use it.'

She walked to stand beside him, peering over his shoulder. 'If you can teach me golf, you can teach me about your properties. The risks you took that failed and the ones that succeeded. The mistakes you look for.'

'I don't want you to have to spend your time doing something mundane like this. Before long we could have children. You'll want to make more changes in the house. Not that I can see any left to make.'

She waved his words away. 'The house managed before I got here, and I've directed almost everything altered that I want. And Maggie will assist with the children.'

She ran her hand over his shoulder and put her face near his cheek. 'I can help, or you can tell me not to.' Her breath heated his ear.

'You would?'

'Absolutely. I adore studying strategies. Finance sounds like a game to me. Like moving funds from place to place, capturing some and sometimes leaving some behind in order to get more. An adventure on paper.'

'It can be extremely tedious.'

'It sounds not unlike a certain game I find enthralling.'

'True. I can see you becoming proficient at increasing holdings.'

'That would be thrilling. And what I would like. It would be wonderful to ride a carriage past a property that I had nurtured and seen flourish into something thriving.'

'I don't know if having you at my elbow will be favourable to my concentration.'

'I hope it isn't. I would not feel a success if I couldn't disrupt your thoughts.'

Chapter Twenty-One

They left the next morning to visit the Dowager Marchioness, with Reid taking along his ledgers so he and Guinevere could study them. But first they went by the Duke's house to let her parents know they would be gone for a few weeks, and to give Reid a chance to talk with her father about the hunting lodge.

He'd had plenty to say about Reid's grandfather, but only praise for Reid's father, who'd helped Maria after she'd fallen on difficult times.

That had caused them to get a much later start than expected to Reid's country estate. Guinevere had wanted to let the woman who'd opened the portrait gallery to two little girls for playtime, and been such a friend, know that she was happy to be a part of the family, and hoping they could spend even more time together in the future.

Her new mother-in-law cried tears of happiness. Reid reintroduced himself to his mother, and she patted his arm and gave her attention to her new daughter, Guinevere, and claimed herself the best matchmaker ever, and not at all surprised they'd married.

Then Reid had insisted Guinevere go with him to meet two different tenants. Reid had greeted the reserved, wary-eyed men, and begged their pardon for his wrongdoings of the past. Then he and Guinevere spoke with them a bit before he gave them a sealed letter, wished them well and left.

The following day, in the carriage on the way to her aunt's, Reid laughed, telling Guinevere he'd never felt so successful as when he'd seen her with his mother, planning the celebration dinner they would be having in honour of the marriage.

Then he clasped her hand and rested his head against the seat. She noticed the tiredness under his eyes, and kept quiet, happy to have him sitting at her side.

In moments, he appeared to fall asleep.

The trip seemed different with him near her, even with him dozing. More of an adventure. A feeling of completeness, of being alone together with someone who understood her.

She gouged him with her elbow. He jumped awake, and she raised her brows. 'I thought you were pretending. To be asleep. Besides, I could not help myself. I had to wake you.'

'I was sleeping, but being awake with you is so much better.' He yawned. Then he put his arm around her.

He pulled her close and she wouldn't have thought anyone his size could have nestled against her so completely, but he did.

When they arrived at her aunt's, they stepped out of the carriage and he suggested they stay in the stableman's quarters. Then he paused. 'I'm not superstitious, but you should know there is a mirror cracked in there. I had nothing to do with it.'

She directed the driver to take their things to the cottage.

Then she reached in her reticule and took out a small cosmetics jar, opened it, dipped her finger in it and smeared a bit of it on the doorway.

'What is that?' he asked.

'The Romans believed a bit of lard could ward off bad fortune. I put some on the doorway to your town house, also. If nothing else, it will give the insects a meal. I'm not superstitious either. But I like fattening the bugs, I suppose, and increasing all the odds in my favour.'

The butler greeted them, staring at Reid when they walked into the house, Guinevere on his arm.

'I'll be staying in the cottage,' Guinevere told the butler, 'with my husband.'

'You wed the stablemaster?' The manservant gasped.

'Well, he was only a stablemaster for a short while,' Guinevere said. 'And I promoted him.'

'Marquess of Hartcroft,' Reid said. 'Lady Guinevere is Lady Hartcroft now. We had met earlier and I had tried to talk her into going to Scotland to wed. She didn't want to, but finally we agreed on a Special License.'

'Well, in that case, I will confess,' the butler whispered to Guinevere. 'Your aunt and I have been secretly in love for years.'

Her mouth dropped.

'Yes. Your great-grandfather once sent her here to think about her future. And we fell in love, but we didn't want to marry until the time seemed right.'

He tugged at his cravat, loosening it, and pulled out a chain with a small ring on it. 'Her wedding ring,' he said. 'I have it so if she ever says the time is right, I'll be prepared.'

'Does anyone else know?' Guinevere asked after admiring the gold band.

'Possibly everyone under the roof, but she refuses to let me leave my post. I like to know what goes on here, and she says a worthy butler is harder to find than a decent husband.'

'Have you enjoyed my clubs?' Reid asked, interrupting.

'Why, yes. We have.' He gazed at the wall. 'Not a bad sport you've taught us. I fear we've let our duties slide a bit, but it's been great fun.' He gave a bow. 'Would you like another tournament? We'd be pleased and honoured.'

'Well, I'm keeping the ones I brought this time. But I would like to have a tournament later.'

'We've changed the playing field.' The man's head rose. 'And you might find some competition.'

'I will look forward to it.'

After they greeted her aunt and ate, the older woman clutched Reid's arm and sat outside in a place of honour to watch the tournament, clapping her gnarled hands together each time the game became tense and got spirited.

With Guinevere at his side, and the game in front of them, everyone accepted him, and even cheered him on as they did their utmost to best him. A spirit of camaraderie flourished.

As the sun set, the servants called it a night and scurried inside to prepare the last meal of the day.

Guinevere expected a wait, but discovered the meat had been started earlier. Pies had been cooked at breakfast time, and the cook had slipped inside before the end of the game so she could have everything ready.

Reid appeared to genuinely enjoy the meal with her aunt, accusing her of applauding loudly for everyone who won a game but him, and she admitted it was true.

They lingered and when they finally retired to the cottage, Reid opened the door to find lamps burning low, and that the servants had been in straightening things and adding little flourishes. He saw the table they'd added in the middle of the room, extra pieces of pie, and noted the scarf covering the large mound in the centre.

He took a piece of the apple pie. For a woman who couldn't cook porridge, the cook was a master at everything else.

'That was a good match. The staff certainly enjoyed it.' He paused. 'I almost didn't win.' He frowned. 'You don't think they were letting me, do you?'

'I saw the footman's face. He was not playing

lightly. And you did insist on playing with your favourite club.'

'I like that club. And I've missed it.'

'The activity with the servants was fun. And I enjoyed it, but I can't see your town house staff being comfortable in this countryside. They're used to a different structure, and they were hired for it, and trained. The people here are more relaxed, and this suited them better.'

'Perhaps that's why they've stayed. I agree that Beckham would have felt instructed to enjoy himself, and would have played the game but it would have been another chore on his list.'

It would have been similar to how she felt when she had to dance with someone she preferred not to be near. She always was polite, pretending happiness and kindness, but not wanting to give them the impression that they would be stealing away for a deep conversation.

'Perhaps both staffs are right for their homes. Like us.'

'When you moved into our house, you wasted no time creating the little nest of your things around you.'

'I needed to be secure.'

'I want you to be sheltered with me.' Then he added, 'And while we were playing, I had the driver put out a gift.' He waved to the table.

She stepped forward, lifted the edge of the scarf, her mouth opened wide, and she shouted in delight. Instantly, she pulled the covering away.

Then she looked at the queen and gasped. 'They're beautiful. It's the loveliest gift I've ever received,' she said, and then lifted the king and held it clasped in her hand, resting it against her chest while she gazed at him. 'The queen's job is always to protect him.'

'And she is judged the most important on the board, but even if she weren't, she is the most important in my life.'

'I saw this in the shop once, and wanted it, but Mother said I had enough chessboards and couldn't have any more.'

'I thought about having special pieces made for you, but didn't. It would have taken a while, and I wasn't sure about it, after I thought it through.' He'd really not wanted their likenesses on the wood.

'I'm so glad you changed your mind,' she said. 'This one is perfect. I will cherish it because you understand me. It's not another jewel that you had someone else select. You chose it with me in mind, no one else. And I know you'll always remember giving it to me. You won't forget.'

'No. I won't.'

She slid into his arms, and he kissed her, confection sweet.

'My only regret is that the accident didn't happen sooner. That you couldn't wake me earlier,' he said.

'I think you're giving the accident credit for your change, and it may have had something to do with it, but I believe you were already on a search for a new direction when you left London.'

He held her close. 'The accident woke me, but you changed me. You made me see what was important to me. When I was recovering, and you were trying to find things to talk about, I was aware you were going to go away from me, then I knew my path wasn't the path I would continue. It's true, I'd already begun the changes before the accident, but one phrase you said made me realise I truly had the chance to change.'

'I thought you jested away everything I said.'

'You said I'd be going back to my old habits. The thought made me sicker than anything else that had happened. And in your trajectory, I saw a chance for a new pursuit. Life with a woman who would spend her evenings by the fireside, sewing. Something I thought tedium, you made sound like the most priceless gift of all—contentment.'

He took her lips for the lightest kiss imaginable.

'That was to be my quest, but on the way to search for it, I saw I could have even more than that with you in my life. I will love you for ever, Lady Guinevere, and I will be so thankful you took the stone from my heart and replaced it with love.'

She hugged him close, all the love for him she had inside bursting out, and bringing tears of happiness to her eyes.

'I will love you always and for ever. My husband. My heart.'

* * * * *

COMING SOON!

We really hope you enjoyed reading this book.
If you're looking for more romance, be sure to
head to the shops when new books are
available on

Thursday 18th August

To see which titles are coming soon, please visit

millsandboon.co.uk/nextmonth

MILLS & BOON ®

Coming next month

HOW TO WOO A WALLFLOWER
Virginia Heath

Hattie shook her head in exasperation. 'The last few weeks have been a never-ending maelstrom of nonsense. It is a relief to have an excuse to escape for the afternoon—although I have been deliberating whether or not I should walk to the hospital.'

Jasper wanted to ask if she was capable of a five-minute walk, but didn't, respecting her pride. 'As I have abandoned my own conveyance in favour of Shanks's pony, I would be delighted to escort you. That is if you do not fear what being seen with a scandalous reprobate like me will do to your reputation?'

She laughed and allowed him to help her out of her carriage. Because it felt appropriate given her injuries, he offered her his arm and pretended not to notice how heavily Hattie leaned on it. The first few steps were obviously difficult for her, but she covered her pain with breezy small talk about her dreaded debut, making his heart simultaneously bleed for all she had lost and swell with pride at her resilience and tenacity.

'You never know, you might enjoy it all once it starts.'

She blinked at him as if he were mad. 'It is difficult to feel enthused about taking up my place among the wallflowers.' Her expression was wistful. Accepting, and that bothered him.

'You shan't be a wallflower, Hattie.' The mere thought

was inconceivable. 'Your dance card will be so full I doubt there would be space for me to scratch my name on it. In fact, I shall insist you reserve me a waltz in advance.' An impertinent request which tumbled out before he could stop it.

'That is very decent of you to offer—even if it was done out of obligation—but I am afraid I shall have to politely decline.'

'It wasn't done out of obligation.' The truth, although he couldn't even explain to himself why. 'I would be honoured.'

Her smile this time did not touch her eyes. 'And yet still I must politely decline.'

The disappointment was instant. 'Because you *do* fear for your reputation after all or because you have already promised the waltz to someone else?' The flash of jealousy came out of nowhere, but he managed to cover it with a conspiratorial wink.

'Because I can't, Jasper.'

For the briefest moment, her light seemed to dull, before she banished it with a matter-of-fact shrug.

'I physically can't.'

Continue reading
HOW TO WOO A WALLFLOWER
Virginia Heath

Available next month
www.millsandboon.co.uk

Special thanks and acknowledgement are given to Virginia Heath for her contribution to the Society's Most Scandalous miniseries.

MILLS & BOON

THE HEART OF ROMANCE

A ROMANCE FOR EVERY READER

MODERN

Prepare to be swept off your feet by sophisticated, sexy and seductive heroes, in some of the world's most glamourous and romantic locations, where power and passion collide.

HISTORICAL

Escape with historical heroes from time gone by. Whether your passion is for wicked Regency Rakes, muscled Vikings or rugged Highlanders, awaken the romance of the past.

MEDICAL

Set your pulse racing with dedicated, delectable doctors in the high-pressure world of medicine, where emotions run high and passion, comfort and love are the best medicine.

True Love

Celebrate true love with tender stories of heartfelt romance, from the rush of falling in love to the joy a new baby can bring, and a focus on the emotional heart of a relationship.

Desire

Indulge in secrets and scandal, intense drama and plenty of sizzling hot action with powerful and passionate heroes who have it all: wealth, status, good looks…everything but the right woman.

HEROES

Experience all the excitement of a gripping thriller, with an intense romance at its heart. Resourceful, true-to-life women and strong, fearless men face danger and desire - a killer combination!

To see which titles are coming soon, please visit

millsandboon.co.uk/nextmonth

JOIN THE
MILLS & BOON
BOOKCLUB

* **FREE** delivery direct to your door

* **EXCLUSIVE** offers every month

* **EXCITING** rewards programme

50% OFF
YOUR FIRST
PARCEL

Join today at
millsandboon.co.uk/subscribe